"We're going to hit the FBI."

"What do you need me to do?" Mack Bolan asked.

"You're an experienced combat veteran, and I want you on one of my assault teams. We're going to use the RPGs to take out the building, the motor pool and the helipad. We should be able to blow up enough vehicles to prevent pursuit."

"When's it going down?"

"Tomorrow night," Grey replied. "We'll drive over in the morning, recon the area, finalize the plan and hit them at midnight. We'll be back here by dawn with no one the wiser."

Bolan had needed to accelerate the investigation of the militia, and this was his in. So far the Brotherhood hadn't crossed the line into overt criminal activity. If this hit went as planned, the militia situation was about to become a crisis.

*Other titles available in
this series:*

DON PENDLETON's
MACK BOLAN.®

REBELS
—AND—
HOSTILES

A GOLD EAGLE BOOK FROM
WORLDWIDE.®

TORONTO • NEW YORK • LONDON
AMSTERDAM • PARIS • SYDNEY • HAMBURG
STOCKHOLM • ATHENS • TOKYO • MILAN
MADRID • WARSAW • BUDAPEST • AUCKLAND

First edition April 1998

ISBN 0-373-61459-4

Special thanks and acknowledgment to
Michael Kasner for his contribution to this work.

REBELS AND HOSTILES

Printed in U.S.A.

A well-regulated militia, being necessary to the security of a free State, the right of the people to keep and bear arms, shall not be infringed.

—United States Constitution
Second Amendment 1791

No great improvements in the lot of mankind are possible until great change takes place in the fundamental constitution of their modes of thought.

—John Stuart Mill

Violence isn't the way to effect political change in this country. Innocents always get caught in the cross fire. It's the government of the people, by the people, for the people, and until that changes, I'll do what it takes to prevent the spilling of innocent blood.

—Mack Bolan

CHAPTER ONE

Dilbert, Idaho

Mack Bolan stepped inside the door of Mac's Grill and Tavern, pausing to let his eyes adjust to the dim light inside the bar. The early-afternoon streets of the small northwestern Idaho town were almost deserted, so the three battered pickup trucks parked in front of the place had to make it the civic center. And a bar was always a good place to start taking care of business in a small town.

When he could see, Bolan headed for the bar at the side of the room. Other than the female bartender, the only people in the room were three men sitting at a table in the back. Bolan assumed they were the owners of the three pickups parked in front, and from the looks of them, they weren't the town's best or brightest citizens. Nor, from the number of empty glasses on the table, were they men who had daytime jobs.

SAMANTHA WHITING WATCHED the big man walk into the bar and shivered, but not from fear. Rightly or wrongly, she had always prided herself on being able to peg a man with a single glance. When she was honest with herself, though, she had to admit that her instant assessments had been wrong as often as they had been right. For instance, they had been dead wrong about both of her ex-husbands.

Nonetheless, she was getting a strong first impression from this guy, and it had been a long time since she'd felt the particular combination of excitement and danger that the man carried with him like a cloud. Though she knew better, she was anxious for him to sit down at the bar so she could get a better look.

"What can I get you?" she asked, trying not to sound too eager. Her better judgment told her that if this guy was in this bar, it could only mean that he was a loser, a drunk, a deadbeat or an ex-con merely passing through the town. But the hope hadn't yet died that some day someone would walk through the door and take her away from Dilbert.

When the big man locked his blue eyes on hers, Whiting had to look away for a moment. Damn, she hated it when that happened, but she hadn't been able to help it.

"A draft is fine," Bolan told her, smiling.

"You're new in town," she said as a statement rather than a question as she reached down for a glass.

He nodded and took the opening. "Sure am. I've always wanted to see this part of the country and had time on my hands, so here I am."

Whiting sighed as she pulled the tap to draw his

beer. Just her luck, another bullshit artist. No one in his or her right mind ever came to Dilbert, Idaho, by choice. The usual way a person washed up here was blind drunk and staggering off the weekly Greyhound bus. The running dog was the usual way you got to town and the usual way the lucky ones left. The unlucky ones, like her, were still here.

"You're either on the run or just out of jail, aren't you?" she asked as she placed the beer in front of him.

Bolan raised one eyebrow as he took a long drink.

"And," she continued, "you don't have what anyone might call a profession or a trade. And since this isn't Saturday, you drove into town instead of taking the bus. You're probably driving a clapped-out old van that's about to puke oil all over the curb—if we had any curbs, that is. And you're sleeping on a lumpy mattress in the back with all of your clothes stuffed into a duffel bag until you can find a coin laundry where you can jimmy the machines so you can get cleaned up."

She paused and eyed him severely. "How am I doing so far?"

"I think you've been working here too long. You've started to get cynical."

"Spend as much time behind this damned bar as I have, mister, and see how much you laugh."

"My name's Jack," Bolan said, offering his hand. "Jack Vance."

"Sam," she said, ignoring the hand. "Short for Samantha."

"Nice name."

"Bullshit."

Bolan dropped the smile. "No, I mean it. I've always liked the name Samantha."

"And I remind you of—" her eyes swept him up and down "—your second—or is it third?—wife? She was named Samantha, right?"

Bolan shook his head. "Nope, I've never been involved with a woman named Samantha."

"Probably a good thing." She nodded at his empty glass. "You want another one?"

"Sure."

As she turned aside to draw him another beer, Bolan glanced at the mirror behind the bar and saw that the three locals at the back table were eyeballing him. That was always the problem in small towns. The locals in a bar at this time of day could almost always be counted on to be hostile to any stranger who walked in. From the look of the redhead, that hostility was going to turn into combat before too long.

He would rather not have to start out that way; he had wanted to keep a low profile for a week or so before he made a name for himself. But the Executioner was prepared to go for it now if he had to.

"Here you go," Whiting said, handing him his beer.

"Thanks."

"Hey, Sam!" the redhead called out. "How about

a little service here. If, that is, you're not too busy trying to get laid." His cackling laugh drowned out the country tune playing on the jukebox.

"Screw you, Red," the woman said without a great deal of emotion. "You know the house rules. You want another beer, you come up here to get it."

"I'm coming to get it, all right," he said, sneering as he pushed back his chair.

"Friend of yours?" Bolan asked. Since it was going down, he wanted to get a handle on the local relationships before he committed himself.

Whiting shot him a glance that would have peeled an inch of solid granite off the Rocky Mountains. "I may be on the wrong side of forty, mister, and I may be stuck in the armpit of the lower forty-eight, but I'd gladly stick a gun in my mouth and pull the trigger before I'd let that idiot touch me."

"I heard that, Sam," Red said as he walked up. "And if you want a gun to put in your mouth—" he grabbed his crotch "—I've got it right here."

"You've got a nasty mouth, mister," Bolan said casually.

Red spun on him. "Just who the hell do you think you're talking to, pal?"

Bolan cleared for action and looked the guy up and down. "I know I'm talking to a drunk who's forgotten his manners. You shouldn't talk to women that way."

Red smiled. "Well, how about that? It's been a long time since we've had a Boy Scout in here.

Where do you come from, faggot, San Francisco? Maybe you'd like a little of what I'm carrying, too."

By the unwritten rules of manly conduct that seemed to apply in every small-town bar in the United States, Bolan knew that he had just been challenged. He also knew that it would be better for him to let this loudmouth take the first swing before he played this out.

It would be best, though, if he could avoid this confrontation until he had a better idea of the local situation. For all he knew, Red could be the mayor or the sheriff's best poker-playing buddy; his type often was. The problem was how to back off without looking like a complete wimp and blowing his chances to establish himself in town. He was framing a reply when the bartender took the situation out of his hands.

"I've had about enough of your crap, Red," the woman said as she brought a 12-gauge double-barreled shotgun out from under the bar. "I don't have to take that from you or anyone else in town. Just get out of here. You've had enough today."

Eyeing the twin muzzles of the scattergun, Red backed off three full steps. "Come on, Sam. You know me. I was just kidding. I didn't mean it."

"I do mean it," she said, the muzzles of the shotgun steady as she tracked her target. "Get your sorry ass out of here now. You come one step closer, and I'll blow you in half."

"Okay," Red said, keeping his hands at his side.

"Okay, I'll leave. I don't like to drink where I'm not wanted.

"But you, faggot," he added, turning to Bolan. "I'll catch up with you later."

Bolan locked a hard stare on the man. "Any time."

As Whiting put the shotgun back under the bar, Bolan said, "Nice customer. Do you have to do that often?"

"Someday I'm going to blow him away. It'll be worth going to jail to see him bleeding all over the floor."

"Remind me never to make you mad."

The woman didn't smile.

"Anyway," he said as he drained the last of his beer, "can you tell me where I can find that laundry you were talking about, so I can wash that duffel bag of dirty clothes? I promise not to jimmy the machines."

That brought a smile to her face. "It's down at the end of the block on the other side of the street. You can't miss it."

"And," he asked as he reached into his pocket to get out his wallet to pay for his beer, "is there someplace around here that a man can park a van overnight without getting busted for vagrancy?"

"You want the state park by the bridge on the west side of town. It's open to overnighters."

"Thanks."

"Don't mention it. I'm used to being the town's welcoming committee."

BOLAN WALKED OUT to his van, relieved to see that Red and his two drinking buddies were nowhere in sight. That suited him at this point of the game. He spotted the laundry across the street and drove over so he could keep an eye on the van while he washed a few already clean clothes to make it look good.

He had the place to himself, so while his shirts and a pair of worn jeans ran through the long cycle, he had time to plan his next move. His mission in northern Idaho was simple. His old friend at the Justice Department, Hal Brognola, had asked him if he would look into rumors of foreign involvement in the American militia movement. A couple of weeks earlier, the big Fed had contacted him and had asked to meet him at the entrance to the Vietnam War Memorial in Washington, D.C.

When Brognola appeared, he immediately launched into the problem. "I don't know if you've been in touch lately, but it looks like we have foreign military advisers working with some of the more serious militia groups. They're supplying heavy weapons and training them in tactics. We've already had a couple of scattered incidents that show the marks of professionals being involved, and we've been able to interdict a couple of weapons shipments coming in. But so far the agencies haven't been able to make much headway with this, and the President asked if I could get you to look into it."

Bolan didn't bother to mention that the problem was that the federal agencies weren't very good at infiltrating this kind of organization. There were so many leaks in their operations that the word was bound to get out. As he well knew, though, one man alone had a chance of getting inside.

"I don't have anything else going right now," Bolan said. "I'll give you a hand with it."

"Thanks," Brognola stated, sounding relieved. "I'll pass it on to the President this afternoon."

"One thing, though," Bolan said.

"What's that?"

"When I go undercover on this one, I'm going all the way under, so don't expect to hear a word from me until it's over. I won't be contacting anyone until I'm ready to come in from the cold."

"The President isn't going to like it going down that way. He said that he wants to be kept informed of your progress."

"He knows that I work best alone. Tell him that if he wants daily updates, he can send in the FBI or the ATF. But if this could be handled by them, you wouldn't be talking to me today, and he knows it."

Brognola had worked with Bolan long enough to know when he had reached the crunch point. When the soldier said that he would go no further, he wouldn't. Trying to get him to change his mind was a complete waste of time and breath.

"Okay." The big Fed sighed. "We'll do the lone-wolf thing again...."

"I've coordinated this one with the Stony Man team," Brognola went on, referring to the nation's ultrasecret counterterrorist organization. "And we've worked up a rock-hard cover for you and have a complete background in place."

Bolan had worked with hundreds of cover stories over the years, and the one thing he had learned was that they were never as solid as their makers claimed. He had to admit, though, that Aaron Kurtzman and the Stony Man team created the best covers he had ever used.

The Bear could dig into cyberspace and create a persona that was a virtual reality. Everything from first grade report cards to dental records and an employment history was a snap to him as long as it was electronically recorded. Creating the hard copies took a little more work, but with the help of Brognola's office, he could do that, as well.

Brognola opened his briefcase and took out a thick packet. "It's all in here—the background legend, a billfold with the proper documentation and background items, a letter from your brother in Alaska and the keys to your new wheels. You'll find your clothes in the back of the van."

"I take it that you're in a hurry on this?"

Brognola nodded. "The latest situation updates are in there, as well, but I can tell you that we're worried. We've got to get a handle on this before it blows up in our faces."

"I'll go over this and get back to you before I move out."

"Good luck."

"Right."

CHAPTER TWO

As confident as Bolan had been when he talked to Hal Brognola in Washington, D.C., he now had a greater appreciation of the problem the federal agencies were facing as they tried to get a handle on the militia situation. He had gone deep into militia country, the rural areas that politicians and the media liked to call Middle America, but he had little to show for the two weeks he had spent searching. He knew the militias were there, but everywhere he went he was a stranger, and strangers didn't get invited to join a conspiracy against the government.

There had always been militias in America. In fact the first shots in the war that would create the United States had been fired by American militiamen. State militias had played a prominent role in the wars that followed, as well. With the formation of the Army National Guard at the turn of the century, most of the organized state militias were brought under the control of the federal government, and the movement died for a while.

The Vietnam War and its aftermath brought the

birth of a new militia movement that was decidedly different from the earlier ones. The new militias were an offshoot of white-supremacist and survivalist reaction to the social changes of the sixties and seventies. Unlike the militias of earlier times, they weren't formal, state-sponsored organizations. They were simply men who armed themselves and banded together for a common cause.

Before the bombing of the Alfred Murrah Federal Building in Oklahoma City, the new militia movement hadn't been a problem to national security. For the most part, the militias and the other white-supremacist groups had kept to themselves and bothered no one except, perhaps, their immediate neighbors.

That tragic bombing brought the militia movement into the forefront of the evening news. Most of the media coverage in the aftermath of the bombing, however, had been, according to some, liberal hysteria designed to create a public backlash that would make it easier for Congress to impose more gun-control laws. Guns had played no part in the Oklahoma City tragedy. Those people had been blown up by a bomb, not shot.

That didn't mean that all the high-profile coverage had generated much hard-core information on the movement. It had given some people an exaggerated sense of their own importance, however. When commanders of so-called militia units started to hold press conferences, it was theater of the absurd on a grand scale. The gun-toting, camouflaged, militia wanna-bes weren't the problem. And anyone who posed for the news cameras instantly became a name on an FBI list of "persons of interest."

Feeling the pressure of unwanted publicity, some militia groups faded from sight completely. They disbanded, fearing that they would be next to face the guns of federal agencies out of control. They didn't change their beliefs; they simply feared for their lives. Other groups, however, took the Ruby Ridge and Waco incidents as a warning, a call to battle, and dug in even deeper.

Then there were the groups like the one Bolan was trying to track in this small town. They had recently formed, born out of the ashes of Ruby Ridge and Waco, and there were many similar organizations throughout the nation. These new groups were made up of men who had left most of the radical right-wing, white-supremacist, anti-Semitic rhetoric behind and didn't seek publicity of any kind. But they truly believed that the end of American civilization was close at hand, and they were as serious as death.

In the strictest sense of the word, they were patriots and they saw themselves as acting as the nation's founders had when they revolted against the king of England. They saw the federal government as being completely out of control and felt that it was the worst enemy the American people had ever faced. For the most part, their intentions were good. They sincerely wanted to save the nation from what they saw as federal tyranny. The way they had chosen to do it, however, was the problem.

Where the average citizen fought for his rights at the ballot box, these men had lost faith in the power of the vote. All too often they had seen the federal government run roughshod over their votes. They had seen their communities dictated to by an imperial Washington. They had seen their children bused to schools far from their homes and indoctrinated on orders from Congress and the Supreme Court. They had seen local control of their lives and communities swept away in a sea of federal regulations and mandates.

The last straw had been when they saw federal agencies go to war against people whose only crime had been that they had wanted to be left alone. Randy Weaver's stand and the death of eighty-five men, women and children at the Koresh compound sent a chill through these men. If the federal government could kill these people at a whim, no one was safe. An FBI sniper killing a mother with an infant in her arms was the symbol of all that was wrong with the federal government, and they wanted no part of it.

Unlike the earlier militia and antigovernment movements, the new organizations knew enough about the real world to know that if they stuck their heads out and sought publicity, they would lose them. Taking a page from the successful insurgencies of the twentieth century, they went deep underground.

They didn't design identifying insignia and wear

them proudly. They didn't put up signs and posters denouncing the government. They didn't carve compounds out of the wilderness or build churches and hold public meetings. They did none of that because they had learned the lessons taught by the ATF and FBI well. They saw themselves at war with a government all too ready to kill them. They knew that for them to survive until the time came to strike a blow for freedom, they had to be invisible like Chairman Mao's proverbial fish in water. And that was why Bolan had had such a difficult time getting a lead.

He had been about to report failure when a chance comment he had overheard in a Spokane, Washington, gun show had sent him to Dilbert, Idaho. This was his last chance, and he had to make good on it.

WHEN BOLAN WALKED into Mac's Grill and Tavern the next morning, he was surprised to see that Samantha Whiting wasn't behind the bar. "Where's Sam?" he asked the new woman after he ordered his coffee and breakfast.

"She had a small accident last night," the woman answered, glancing around to make sure that no one could overhear her. "She ran into a fist."

"What happened?" Bolan asked, his voice cold.

"Are you the guy who talked to her yesterday afternoon?" the woman asked. "The new guy in town?"

"Yeah. I'm Jack Vance."

"Sam asked me to tell you to look out for Red Gillum. He's gunning for you."

"Did he assault her?"

The woman snorted. "I guess you could call it that. He tried to rape her, but she fought him off."

"How is she?"

"She's fine, but she's taking the day off."

"When does Red come in?" Bolan asked.

"Sam said you'd ask that, and she wanted me to tell you to watch out for him."

"I can handle myself. When does he usually come in?"

"Right about now," she replied after glancing up at the clock over the bar.

"Can I get a refill on the coffee while I'm waiting?"

The woman smiled. "Sure thing, mister."

BOLAN WAITED until Gillum and two of his drinking buddies got settled down before making his move. "I understand that you like to beat up on women," he said as he approached Gillum's table.

"Oh, you mean your new girlfriend. That was just foreplay. She likes it rough."

He laughed and turned to make sure that his drinking buddies appreciated his wit.

Not wanting to continue the verbal chest thumping any longer, Bolan reached down with his left hand and jerked Gillum to his feet. His other hand snapped out and hammered the man across the side of the face before letting him go and stepping back to give the other man room.

"You son of a bitch!" Gillum bellowed, and charged.

Bolan blocked his wild swing and hit him again. The object of the game was to hurt the man, but not to hurt him too much, too quickly. For this object lesson to sink in, it had to be done professionally.

But a bare-knuckle fight has its uncertainties. Gillum snuck one past Bolan's defense and hammered him. There was power behind the blow, and the Executioner realized that he had to ratchet up the intensity several notches if he didn't want to get hurt in return.

Slamming a fist deep into Gillum's solar plexus, Bolan followed it up with a flurry of stunning blows to the face. Like a bare-knuckle prizefighter, he concentrated on his opponent's eyes and mouth, his most vulnerable and painful areas. When Bolan stepped back, Gillum was a mess. Both of his eyes were swollen shut by the blows hammered into his eyebrows. His lips looked like he had kissed a blender set on puree, and one of his cheeks was laid open to the bone. He had slumped to the floor, unconscious.

"That's enough, mister," a commanding voice said behind Bolan.

Stepping back, the Executioner turned to see a tall man in his late forties or early fifties who carried himself as if he expected his words to be obeyed. He was dressed in cargo pants, boots, an open-necked shirt and a sports coat. In a town like Dilbert, that was considered a businessman's suit.

"Fred," the man said to one of the onlookers, "get Red out of here. Take him to the clinic."

"Sure thing, Mr. Grey."

Bolan caught the honorific and knew that he was about to be judged by the powers-that-be in Dilbert, and the success of his mission would depend on the outcome of the trial. If he screwed up, he'd end up in jail for sure.

"Red's got a bad mouth on him," Bolan said to set the tone for his defense.

"He's an asshole," the man acknowledged, "but he's also the sheriff's brother-in-law."

"Give the sheriff my condolences. And you might recommend that he keep Red away from women and children. He slapped Samantha Whiting around last night."

The man looked at Bolan for a long moment. "He won't give Sam any more trouble."

Bolan met his look. "Good. Women weren't put on this earth to be punching bags for drunks."

When the man stuck out his hand, Bolan knew that he had passed the test. "The name's Bolton Grey."

Bolan took his hand. "I'm Jack Vance."

"Where you from, Vance?"

"California, originally. Since then, I've been all over."

"What do you do?"

Bolan shrugged. "Just about anything that needs done. I'm pretty flexible."

"Are you planning to stay in town?"

That was the question Bolan had been working up to all day. "I'd like to," he said honestly, and glanced at the door Gillum had been dragged through on his way to whatever medical facility the town offered. "If I can find a job."

"You can work for me if you want. I can always use another good man."

Not wanting to appear overanxious, Bolan hesitated. "What did you have in mind?"

"I have a fuel-supply yard, and I need someone to run it for me. There's a room behind the office you could use until you get settled down and find a place to live. I'll start you off at eight bucks an hour and won't charge you for the room."

"That sounds fair," Bolan said. "When do you want me to start?"

"I'd like you to start this afternoon. I've got some farmers who're going to need fuel this week, and Red's in no condition to work for a while."

Bolan wisely didn't comment on the reason that the job opening had occurred. If Grey was willing to drop it, so was he. "If you want to show me the job, I can get started right now."

"Good," Grey said approvingly. "I've got my rig outside, and you can follow me."

BOLTON GREY'S RIG turned out to be a brand-new Dodge Ram V-10 pickup. Bolan made a bet with himself that Grey's other car was a new Cadillac. Nothing else would do for a man like him in a place like Dilbert.

When Grey pulled out of the parking lot, he headed east out of town, keeping his speed down so Bolan wouldn't have a difficult time keeping up in his battered old van. Bolan held back a little instead of simply hammering it and letting the big Chevy V-8 under the hood give the shiny new Dodge a run for its money. His van looked like it was overdue for a slot in a junkyard, but that was only external. The dirt, faded paint and the rust were all too real, but he wasn't going to risk not being able to make his escape if he had to.

The engine and running gear had all been recently gone over and, within the aerodynamic limits imposed by the boxy van body, he could run with the best of them, and the suspension was up to the power the engine put out. He wasn't in a hurry, however, to have anyone see what the van could do.

A little less than five miles out of town, Grey turned off into a cyclone-fenced fuel yard. The neatly painted sign outside the enclosure simply read Grey Fuel and Oil, and after listing the hours of operation, it gave a contact phone number for emergencies. Both the tanks and the office building by the pumps were freshly painted, and the yard looked well kept. Whatever else he was, Bolton Grey ran a tight ship.

"Think you can handle something like this?" Grey asked.

"I've pumped a little gas in my day," Bolan admitted, letting his eyes take in the facility. "And this looks a lot like the fuel dump at Kadena on Okinawa."

"You were in the service?"

"Yeah," Bolan said casually. "I did a hitch in the Marines."

He had an answer prepared if Grey asked why he got out, but most men considered that an impolite question.

"What was your MOS?"

"I was a grunt."

"Did you get over to Vietnam?"

Bolan nodded. "Yeah. Right at the end of it."

Grey absorbed the information and changed the subject. "Let me get you to fill out some employment forms, and then I'll show you the pump controls and the ledgers. Like I said, I'm expecting some customers this afternoon."

After running Bolan through the procedures and controls for the fuel pumps, Grey handed him a key ring and got back in his truck. "It's all yours, Vance. If you need me—" he reached into his pocket and pulled out a card "—this is my number. My secretary will know how to get in touch with me."

"I think I have it," Bolan replied. "But I'll call if anything comes up."

CHAPTER THREE

Bolan wasn't surprised to see Bolton Grey pull up in his pickup as he was locking up for the night. The businessman had hired a complete unknown and had put him in charge of a very expensive operation. It was natural that he would want to see if he had made an error in judgment. All Grey really knew about Bolan was that he could hold his own in a bar fight.

"How'd it go today?" Grey asked as he stepped down from his truck.

"No problems," Bolan replied, and consulted the invoices on his clipboard. "And it was kind of quiet. I only had seven rigs come in. Five for gas and two for diesel. If it doesn't get any busier than that, you're paying me too much."

"Business will pick up real soon," Grey promised. "The farmers are starting to put their spring crops down. In a couple more days, you'll have them lined up along the side of the road for half a mile."

"That's better than sitting on my ass," Bolan said, smiling.

Grey glanced at his watch. "Why don't you go on

into town, Vance, get some dinner and have a couple of drinks? I need to use the office for a couple of hours tonight, and I work best when I'm by myself."

"I don't drink much when I'm working, Mr. Grey," Bolan said. "But now that I *am* working, I can afford a good meal. How long do you need the office?"

"We'll…I'll be done by ten."

"I think I can keep busy till then. I'll get some dinner at Mac's Grill."

When Grey went into the office to go over the books, Bolan went around back to his room, cleaned up and changed clothes for his trip into town.

BOLAN DIDN'T SEE Red Gillum or any of his drinking buddies when he walked into Mac's Grill and Tavern, and that was just as well. Now that he was getting established he didn't need to draw any more attention to himself, but he did need to keep going to this particular bar. Men like Jack Vance tended to be territorial, and it would look odd if he changed watering holes now. Particularly after he had made such an impression on the barmaid.

Samantha Whiting was on duty when he walked in and she greeted him professionally, but with a bit more warmth than the day before. "Draft?" she asked, remembering his order.

He shook his head. "Coffee right now, and I'd like to take a look at the dinner menu."

After she took his order for a chicken-fried steak

and baked potato, she leaned closer. "Jack, I want to thank you for what you did for me this morning," she said softly.

"It wasn't much, Sam." He shrugged. "I just don't like to see anyone beating up on a woman."

"It meant a lot to me," she continued. "And I'm not going to forget it. Your dinner's on me tonight."

"Better than that," Bolan replied with a smile, "why don't you let me buy you dinner this weekend? Somewhere other than this place."

She backed off and looked at him.

"Just dinner," he said, holding both of his hands up in a disarming gesture. "You don't owe me anything."

She flashed a smile. "Okay. Let's see..." She glanced at the Grey Fuel and Oil calendar on the wall above the cash register.

When she turned back, the smile was gone. "I forgot, I can't do it this weekend. We're going to be real busy here, and Mr. Grey will need me."

"He owns this place?"

She snorted. "He owns damned near everything in this town worth owning."

"I didn't know."

"I know you didn't, and I think that's why he hired you. Every other competent man is town is already working for him one way or the other."

Bolan ran that idea through the mental computer, and it came out both positive and negative. Working for Grey meant that he could be easily watched. And since he was a complete outsider, he was an easily expendable fall guy if one was needed. If he should suddenly stop breathing, no one in Dilbert would really care.

"Do you work here every night?" he asked.

"I have tomorrow night off," she said hesitantly. "We could have dinner then."

"I'll put that on my calendar."

The cook dinged the bell, and she turned to get his order. The plate Whiting brought was loaded with food as only a restaurant in a farm town could be. Along with the sixteen-ounce steak and the baked potato piled high with real butter and sour cream, there were two large dinner rolls and what looked like fresh peas and steamed carrots.

"You want catsup or horse radish with that?"

"No, thanks. I'll take it as it is. I could use a refill on the coffee, though."

She got the coffee refill and left him alone to eat his meal.

After dinner, Bolan ordered a beer and slowly sipped it. Beyond a couple at one of the tables and two guys down at the end of the bar, the place was deserted.

"When does the crowd come in?" he asked Sam.

"Crowd? You must be thinking of someplace else, Jack. This is the Thursday-night crowd at Dilbert. It's also the Monday, Tuesday, Wed—"

"I get the picture. How about on the weekends?"

"We'll get a dozen more, maybe."

"And this weekend?"

"That's different," she said without stating why. "Once a month, we get a crowd."

After finishing his beer, Bolan made his excuses and left the bar early.

RAMON DE SILVA HATED Idaho, and he particularly hated Dilbert, Idaho. What the Cuban hated most about Idaho were the ignorant people who lived in the state and the way they treated him. It wasn't like he was a black or a half-breed Mexican. Despite his use of a cover name, he prided himself on being a pure-blooded Spaniard who could trace his ancestors all the way back to the Spanish army that had conquered Cuba in the early 1500s.

That Bolton Grey wouldn't meet him except at night and even then only in the office of his gas station added to the insult. The American businessman's patronizing explanation that the people of his town didn't like Hispanics did nothing to wipe away the stain. If anything, it only made it worse.

Were it not for the fact that the board of directors of the Cali cartel had ordered him to carry out this mission, Silva would have happily killed Bolton Grey. But were he to fail to carry out the orders he had been given, he would be the one who would be killed. As an ex-officer of the DGI, the Cuban Intelligence service he had a name for following orders and he would follow them this time, as well.

When this was over, however, he had vowed that

he would return to Dilbert, Idaho. And when he did, this nowhere town was going to need a new patron.

That was, of course, only if his partner on this mission, Hassan Rahman, didn't get to him first. The Libyan mercenary was more incensed about the way the Americans were treating him than Silva was. At least the Cuban had been in the United States before and knew how all too many Yankees treated his people.

This was Rahman's first trip to the United States, though. And as a strict Muslim, he was having difficulties living in the Christian country. But as a Catholic, Silva knew that he would have some of the same problems if he were ordered to work in a Muslim nation. The difference was that he wasn't a Catholic in the same way that Rahman was a Muslim. The Cuban was able to put his religion aside to take care of business where Rahman had difficulty doing that. If the Libyan didn't adjust his thinking before much longer, Silva would have to talk to the Cali board about having him replaced.

Silva still wasn't sure of the wisdom of the board having invited the Islamic Jihad to join the cartel in this venture. The plan to destabilize the United States using American dissidents to conduct terrorist operations had been Silva's idea, and he had spent a long time putting it together. It had been the board, however, who had decided to invite the Muslim fundamentalists in on it. Though the two groups were as different as night and day, their goals in this enterprise were the same—the complete and fatal disruption of American society from within.

The cartel wanted to see the destruction of American society because it would open up new markets for its primary export, cocaine. Cops who were busy looking for domestic terrorists wouldn't have much time to hunt down drug dealers. Plus the social disruption would cause stress and make people anxious for anything that would take their minds off their problems even for a little while. As the cartel knew, cocaine was good for that.

The Islamic Jihad leaders, however, saw anything that hurt America as being to their advantage in their holy war against the Great Satan and their Jewish puppet state. They believed that American society was so corrupt that it would fall apart if it was stressed just a little further. And with the United States' strength diminished and focused inward, they would have a freer hand to advance their cause in the Middle East and Africa. When the cartel offered them a chance to send weapons and military advisers to the United States, they jumped at it.

With the collapse of the Soviet Union in 1989, the Islamic fundamentalists had been cut off from the seemingly never ending flow of weapons and ammunition they had come to expect since the beginning of the Cold War. But while the Russians were out of the business of freely giving weapons to anyone who wanted them, that didn't mean that the weapons weren't still out there.

Now, however, it took more than a vow to fight against decadent capitalism to get the Russian weapons. With the fall of communism, capitalism reigned supreme in Russia, which meant that the weapons and ammunition had to be paid for.

Fortunately for the Islamic radicals, the geological crap shoot that had given a nonindustrial people the control of most of the industrial world's oil reserves, money wasn't a problem. It was true that after the end of the Gulf War of 1991, money from the oil-rich Arab states had almost dried up, as those who had sided with Iraq against Kuwait and Saudi Arabia were punished. That had been a time for the settlement of old ethnic scores more than political ones.

Once the point had been made, however, the money started flowing again. Syria had been the first to re-open her purse strings again to the jihad movement, and the other countries soon followed. To keep the fundamentalist wolves from their doors, the oil-producing states from Saudi Arabia to Oman and the small emirates all paid a percentage of their oil revenues to Islamic Jihad. These ongoing bribes didn't ensure that there would be no trouble in the countries that paid, just that the trouble would be controllable.

To the Western mind, it was ironic that until the last oil well in the Middle East had been pumped dry, a percentage of every petrodollar would go to men who wanted nothing more than to burn the very oil fields that supported them. To a Middle Easterner, however, this wasn't a contradiction. God had willed it that this was the way things were and how they always would be.

The men who would come with the weapons had been more difficult to find. Every fighter in the jihad movement was ready to die for Islam, and the chance to take a few Americans with them was more than welcome. The problem was to sort through the hundreds of volunteers to find those few men who spoke fluent English. The arrogant Americans couldn't be expected to speak foreign languages, even Spanish, and there were few jihad freedom fighters who spoke English. But enough had been found, such as Silva's partner, Hassan Rahman, to fulfill their commitment to the cartel.

Rahman was one soldier of Islamic Jihad who spoke very good English. He hadn't particularly wanted to come to America, but he had long-since dedicated his life to Jihad, and if his masters wanted him to martyr himself in the land of the Great Satan, he would do it. While this meant that he was forced into almost intimate contact with infidels, at least he wasn't being defiled by contact with filthy Jews. These Christians in Idaho hated Jews almost as much as a true follower of the Prophet.

He couldn't understand how the American Christians had allowed the Jews to take control of their country. But when the mission was over, the Jews would be gone from the government of what would be left of the United States, and that was reason enough for him to be here. If he lived or died, the cause of jihad would triumph.

BOLTON GREY CHECKED for the third time to see that the snub-nosed .357 Magnum pistol riding in the concealed carry holster in the small of his back was secure. The weapon wasn't there because he didn't trust the two men who were meeting with him this night. He trusted them, all right, but he trusted them to do exactly what they wanted to do, whenever they wanted to do it. They owed him no loyalty, and he expected none from them. Were it not for the fact that Ramon de Silva had access to weapons and equipment he desperately needed and couldn't get anywhere else, he wouldn't have a damned thing to do with him or the Arab.

Grey saw himself as a patriot and a loyal American. He didn't advocate the overthrow of the American government, either from without or from within. He saw, however, that the government of the people, by the people and for the people was under serious siege from the New World Order mentality of the government. Every day the sacred rights of Americans were being eroded, and the nation was far along the road to becoming a completely totalitarian state.

It was ironic that now that the Soviet Union was no more, the American government had taken its place as the chief enemy of freedom around the world. Grey saw himself and the others in the Brotherhood of Patriots as being the American people's first line of defense against a government that was totally out of control on many fronts.

He knew that if the existence of his unit was discovered, he would face the awesome power of the federal government the same as Randy Weaver had faced it in his home on Ruby Ridge. He only hoped that if it came down to that, he would have the courage that Weaver and his wife had shown. That was why his meeting with Silva tonight was so important. If it came to a showdown against the Feds, he wanted to have enough firepower to make an impression on them.

He might not be able to win, but at least he wouldn't die trapped in a burning building like those poor bastards in Waco. When he died, he would die fighting the enemies of liberty, and he wouldn't die alone. The weapons he had ordered from Silva would see to that.

CHAPTER FOUR

Bolton Grey went to the door of his fuel-yard office when he heard a car drive into the parking lot. "Gentlemen," he said as his visitors got out of the vehicle, "please come in."

The two men walked past him with hardly as much as a glance and waited in the middle of the room for him to close the door behind them. As always, the Arab looked like he had been sucking on a lemon for the past hour, and the Cuban looked like a Miami used-car salesman who had just lost out on a big sale.

Grey didn't have to be a mind reader to know that they were both angry at having to meet him at night at the fuel yard, but they were going to have to live with it. He had tried to explain to Silva several times why it wasn't wise for either one of them to be seen in town and that it would be dangerous for Grey to be seen with either one of them anywhere. But instead of even trying to understand, the Cuban had taken offense. The misunderstanding was getting in the way of their doing business, and Grey didn't like anything that got in the way of doing that.

First, last and always, Bolton Grey considered himself to be a businessman, and to him, that meant more
than simply making money. Doing business meant
trusting, setting priorities and getting the job done on
time. This went with the actual business ventures he
ran, as well as his unit of the Brotherhood of Patriots.
Anything that prevented his getting the job done was
a waste of time and was to be avoided. It was too bad
that Silva and Rahman didn't see it that way.

"Gentlemen," Grey said, "please have a seat. Can
I get you anything? A drink? Coffee?"

"When do we get to start training your people, Mr.
Grey?" Silva got right to the point. "I have men waiting on you."

"As I have said before, gentlemen," Grey explained patiently, "I really don't need you to do anything more than supply me with the weapons, ammunition and equipment I need. Our training needs
are already being taken care of."

"Others of your compatriots are using us to train
their units," Silva reminded him. "Why not you?"

"I know that several of the other units are using
your services," Grey said politely, "but as I explained before, each unit of the Brotherhood is an
entity unto itself until the general call to arms is
sounded. Until then, I and I alone run my unit."

He leaned forward and tried again to make the Cuban understand the situation he had to work with in
Dilbert. "I've lived with the men in my unit all of
my life," he said sincerely, "and I know how they

think. This is a small town, and we have small-town ways here. My people aren't used to being around foreigners and, I'm sorry, but they wouldn't trust you the way they trust their friends and neighbors. If I bring in outsiders to train them, I'll start having trouble with them. For my unit to function well, it has to be done my way. Can't you see that?"

There was a strained silence until Silva reached into his briefcase and took out a manila envelope. "The weapons you ordered have arrived in Seattle," the Cuban announced as he handed Grey the envelope. "The information and shipping forms are here. All you need to do is go pick them up."

"Good," Grey said quickly, looking through the forms. "There'll be no problem making the payments on the schedule we agreed to. Please tell your principals that I appreciate their efforts, and I look forward to doing more business with them."

"I will tell them what you have said," Silva replied, "but I cannot guarantee that they will be happy with what I have to tell them."

"Why is it so important that we use your trainers?" Grey asked intently. "That is what I don't understand."

"My principals are concerned about putting such powerful weapons in the hands of—" the Cuban spread his hands "—may I say it without offense?—amateurs. If they were to be misused, it might cause problems for them later on."

"If they are worried about our security," Grey

said, "you can assure them that our security is as tight as we can make it. Only the top officers in the Cadre have any idea who is supplying us. As for our using the weapons properly, I can assure you we know what we're doing."

BOLAN KNEW that he was taking a chance by returning to the fuel yard before Grey wanted him to. But it was a chance that he couldn't pass up. Grey's behavior had aroused his curiosity, and he had to see if he could find out what was going on that required him to keep away.

After leaving the bar, he drove back toward the fuel yard and parked his van in a clump of trees half a mile away. After making sure that the vehicle couldn't be seen from the road, he carefully made his way to the fenced compound.

The same fence and security lights that gave him such good security at his temporary quarters now made it difficult for him to get as close as he wanted to the office building. At this stage of the game, it wasn't worth risking too much, so he would have to be content to see what he could from the outside of the enclosure. But that wasn't much. Grey had closed the blinds on the front windows of the office, but had left the one window at the end of the building uncovered.

While still staying outside of the lighted areas, Bolan could see only the backs of the two men who were talking to Grey. The businessman seemed to be trying to convince his visitors of something important. He was leaning toward them, his hands gesturing as he spoke. Bolan couldn't read lips, but he could read facial expressions. Whatever Grey was selling, they weren't buying it.

The meeting didn't last long, and Bolan ducked back into the darkness when he saw the visitors stand up. With the night security light in front of the office turned off, he couldn't make out the faces of the two men when they got into their car and drove off. He did, however, note the color, make and model of the rental car, as well as the plate number. But since he was working alone this time, the information would stay with him until he finally broke cover. Then the FBI could track the guys down and learn their story.

As soon as the car was gone, Bolan saw Grey come out, get into his Dodge pickup and drive toward Dilbert. Waiting until the pickup was out of sight, Bolan walked back to retrieve his van. Though he had gotten little information for the risk he had taken, it hadn't been a complete waste of time. The men Grey had been talking to had come in a rental car, so they weren't locals.

While not much to go on, it was a start to putting the pieces together.

"WHY DO WE CONTINUE to deal with that imbecile?" Hassan Rahman asked as Silva drove back to their motel. "If he was dead, someone more reasonable might take over and we could deal with him instead."

Ramon de Silva had gone over his point with the Libyan many times, but the Arab seemed to have trouble grasping the realities of the middle-class American mentality. Any local who replaced Grey would have his same prejudices and, more than likely, they would have the same problems with him.

In fact, even though he had told Grey that other Brotherhood units were using his men for trainers, the program of using the cartel and jihad military advisers wasn't going all that well. And for the same reasons that Grey had so well outlined, they simply weren't trusted.

The Americans welcomed the weapons, particularly at the prices the cartel was charging. But when it came time to teach them the insurgent tactics they would need to be effective, too many of them simply didn't want to listen to outsiders. There were too many Army veterans of Vietnam and the other American imperialistic wars who thought that they knew everything there was to know about guerrilla warfare. They would have to be proved wrong before they could overcome their smugness and admit that "greasers" and "ragheads" could teach them anything.

But that shouldn't be too difficult to arrange, particularly since he knew more about the Brotherhood's operations than Grey thought he did.

"It might be better," Silva said, "if Mr. Grey suffers a setback and loses some of his most experienced men. He will have to turn to us to take their places."

"How can this be done?"

"I know an FBI informer who can pass on information for me. Grey's men intend to rob a bank in Lewiston tomorrow morning. And, if they are to be stopped, it will put pressure on him because he needs the money to pay for the shipment that is coming in. It might even put enough pressure on him to change his mind about using our services."

"He had better," Rahman said. "I have a dozen men wasting time waiting to go into action. My superiors in Tripoli are not happy with how this operation is going. So far, even though we have delivered thousands of weapons, no blows have been struck at the government."

"It will happen soon enough," Silva stated. "I can promise you that. But in the meantime, I have word that a group in Montana is ready to start using our services. Why don't you take your men there and get a training program started?"

"How many men are involved?"

"I am told two dozen," the Cuban answered, fudging the numbers a bit to get the Arab's interest. He wanted Rahman kept busy before he did something stupid.

"Maybe that is better than trying to work with Grey."

"I think so."

Lewiston, Idaho

THE MAN WHO CHECKED into the Lewiston, Idaho, Motel Six as Buck Jackson the next evening had been known by another name when he had been court-martialed in 1991 at Fort Bragg, North Carolina, for dealing cocaine. He had been a company supply sergeant in an Airborne unit back then and, as the supply sergeant, he'd had the perfect job for a military drug dealer. No one had ever questioned his frequent trips into town during duty hours or the troops who had stopped by his office at all hours. In fact he had been considered to be one of his battalion's best supply sergeants before the CID bust that had almost put him behind bars.

Back then, he had been SSG James B. Billings and, after being found guilty in the military court, he had been headed for the Army penitentiary at Fort Leavenworth. The MP who was driving the van that was taking him to the airport, however, had been one of his old customers. There had been an accident on the highway. He had been slipped handcuff keys and had managed to escape in the confusion. Figuring to put as much distance as he could between himself and Fort Bragg, he hitchhiked to the West Coast.

It had been easy enough for him to change his identity and start a new life in Idaho, where people minded their own business. Do-it-yourself manuals on the topic were advertised in almost every men's magazine published in the United States and were best-sellers at gun shows. Knowing that his fingerprints were on file with the FBI, he had been forced to go completely legit and become a law-abiding citizen. He knew that getting stopped for a traffic violation that merited a trip downtown and the taking of his prints would send him to Leavenworth in a flash. He was such a model citizen, in fact, that he had been invited to become one of the Brotherhood of Patriots.

Since his new name wasn't on anyone's Most Wanted list, he had passed the militia's security checks. Even though he had been a supply sergeant in the Army, he had been a fully trained infantryman. Regardless of assignment, every paratrooper was expected to be a grunt first and last. Because of his training, Jackson had risen fast in the ranks of the Brotherhood. He went from training recruits in small arms and basic tactics to having been chosen to join the inner circle and to lead one of the unit's hand-picked assault teams.

The Brotherhood had two levels of membership. Most people who were asked to join became first-level Patriots and were the grunts in the battle to save the United States from her many domestic enemies. From the general ranks were chosen the select few who called themselves the Cadre, and they were the brains behind the organization. They were the movers and shakers who intended to dismantle a corrupt government and replace it with an enlightened leadership that would make the United States the great nation it had once been.

Unlike the liberal pundits and naysayers of the media, the Cadre didn't believe that the United States was a failed dream. Its members saw America as a dream that had just been sent off track by socialists, liberals, Jews, homosexuals, minorities and others who wanted to render the country into factions so they could rule the pieces. The Brotherhood of Patriots existed to prevent that from happening, and prevent it the Patriots would.

That wasn't to say that even the Cadre believed that it would be an easy job. Of all of the Brotherhood, the Cadre knew better. It would be a tough fight as every federal agency was arrayed against the militiamen. The ever growing ranks of the faceless, heartless alphabet soup of arrogant bureaucracies that existed only to suck the life out of the small communities of America were relentless in their campaign to destroy the freedom and liberties of Americans. From the ATF and the EPA to the IRS, they were the enemy and the nation wouldn't be free again until they had all been put down. The Brotherhood knew that wouldn't be an easy task.

But the Brotherhood also knew that its enemies weren't found in the armed forces of the United States. Many of the men in uniform, both officers and enlisted, were secret Patriots and had taken the Patriots' vow to preserve the country at all costs. When the final battle came, the Patriots were confident that the majority of the armed forces would stand beside them.

Even so, they were well aware that the federal agencies were rapidly becoming small private armies.

Both the FBI and the ATF were well-known for their firepower. Even the Bureau of Land Management had obtained combat-capable aircraft and had equipped its men with up-to-date small arms and tactical vehicles. The Brotherhood would have to have equal or better weapons and equipment to just defend itself, much less defeat its enemies. And doing that, though, required a great deal of money.

Napoleon had once said that an army moved on its stomach, but were he alive today, he would change that dictum to read that a modern army moved on money. Training and outfitting an army, even a small one like the Brotherhood, took a great deal of money, and most of the nation's money was in its federally insured banks.

Back in the 1930s, when the notorious bank robber, Willie Sutton, had been asked why he robbed banks, he replied, "Because that's where the money is."

Sixty years later, that was still where the money was, and that was why the Brotherhood had taken up robbing banks as its primary means of fund-raising.

In the morning, Jackson and two other Cadre members would hit the Wells Fargo Bank in Lewiston. It was coming up on the first of the month, and the money to cash local paychecks would be in the vaults. If their information was correct—and it was, because they had a man on the inside—they could net over a million dollars in small bills from this one bank. That would cover the Brotherhood's operating expenses for some time and would ensure that the weapons shipment could be paid for.

Buck Jackson was a man known to take a drink now and then, but he made a point of never drinking on the job. So, after checking into his motel room, he didn't go to the lounge for his usual couple of evening brews. Instead, he clicked on the cable TV and searched for the Playboy channel. After watching the girls shake for half an hour, he'd get a good night's rest.

It was going to be a big day tomorrow, and he wanted to be at the top of his form.

CHAPTER FIVE

Buck Jackson woke early in his motel room the next morning. After grabbing a quick shower, he dressed in the nondescript clothing of a typical Idaho working man: jeans, boots, a khaki shirt and a dark windbreaker.

As he dressed, he thought about the job ahead. Once more the federal government was supplying the money for the Brotherhood to work for its downfall, in effect, financing its own ruin. Best of all, the bank's depositors, their own friends and neighbors, wouldn't suffer one bit because the Feds would make good the losses. It was a wonderful concept, and it worked like a charm.

Robbing banks in the nineties wasn't at all like it had been back in the Bonnie and Clyde days, when bank jobs had often turned into bloody shoot-outs. Nowadays bank tellers and armored-car crews were taught to let the money go without a struggle rather than risk their lives. Basically all they had to do was show up at the right time, flash a piece and the money was theirs to load into the van. It was easier than taking candy from a baby.

This was Jackson's third bank raid, and it was beginning to be old hat for him. The other men on his assault team were also military veterans, men who could be counted on to keep their heads under fire. Not that they had been fired on yet, but if it came to that, the Brotherhood didn't want them killing innocent bystanders. The people of Idaho weren't their enemies, only the federal government was, and to keep the people on their side, they couldn't make mistakes. Also bloodless robberies didn't incite the kind of local police response that would work against them.

For the most part, the Brotherhood considered the local police forces to be its allies. So far, the response to the bank jobs had been lukewarm at best. Part of that was simply because so many key local law-enforcement officers were either secret militia members or at least sympathizers and supporters. The militia also had many friends in the ranks of the Idaho State Police. As long as the Brotherhood didn't target state and local police officers, it wouldn't be investigated too vigorously.

The so-called federal police agencies, however, from the FBI all the way down, weren't friends of the Brotherhood. The Feds were the enemy and if they got in the road, they would pay the price for being on the wrong side of the battle for the nation's soul and its future.

As of yet, none of the Brotherhood had had to bust caps on the Feds during the bank jobs. But when it came to that—and Jackson knew that it would be when, not if—he still didn't have a problem with it. He didn't owe the federal government a damned thing, and if it wanted to play John Wayne, he'd show them that he was still Airborne all the way.

As soon as he was ready, he got into his car and drove to the nearby Rig and Pancake for an early breakfast and to meet with the rest of the team. The thought of hot coffee with eggs over-easy, pork links and a short stack made him drive faster. He always got ravenous before he went to work.

FBI SPECIAL AGENT Tom McCarthy was cruising at five thousand feet over western Idaho on the bank-robbery aerial-search detail. The flat-black-painted North American OV-10D Bronco turboprop surveillance plane he was piloting was more of a fighter than it was an observation plane.

This Bronco was no classic bird dog armed with nothing more than the pilot's guts and a lightweight flying suit. This thing was as fast and as maneuverable as a WWII fighter plane, and it carried more armament and was better armored. The speedy twin turboprop had been designed for battlefield surveillance during the Vietnam War, and after an outstanding career as a FAC plane, a Forward Air Controller for artillery, gunships and jet fighters, it had been converted into a light-attack fighter itself.

Armed with machine guns, rocket pylons and a 20 mm cannon turret in the belly, the D model Broncos had been used as night-interdiction fighters over the Ho Chi Minh Trail during the closing months of the war. After brief service again in the Gulf War of 1991, they'd been phased out of service and put into long-term storage in the desert of Arizona in case they were ever needed again.

The Bureau of Alcohol, Tobacco and Firearms, the now well-known ATF, had secretly been given two dozen of the mothballed Bronco D turboprops. The Broncos had been taken out of the storage facility at Davis-Monthan Air Force Base outside of Tucson, Arizona, refurbished and flown to a secret airfield in Georgia. There the ATF pilots had been trained by Air Force instructors, including a full onboard weapons-training program.

Though all of this training had been conducted in the greatest secrecy, somehow the word got out. Right-wing media pundits everywhere immediately asked angry questions when they learned that the ATF had acquired its own air force of armed combat planes. The most significant question that they asked was what did a domestic federal agency working for the Treasury Department need with combat aircraft? Whom did they expect to kill with them?

The ATF responded by citing terrorist incidents and attacks by the drug cartels, but the question was never really answered. The public, with its notoriously short attention span, didn't seem to mind that the question remained. So, even with the uproar from the conservatives, the ATF managed to hang on to its own private air force.

What wasn't as well-known, however, was that the FBI had "borrowed" six of the ATF's armed Broncos and was using three of them to try to stop the wave of bank robberies that had been sweeping through the Pacific Northwest. The Coeur d'Alene office of the FBI had the planes at its disposal, and one of them was on ramp alert at all times. This day, however, all three Broncos were in the air waiting for the robbery attempt the Feds had been tipped off to. Supposedly the elusive gang was going to hit the Wells Fargo Bank branch in Lewiston.

McCarthy had a full ordnance load on his matt black ship—both the machine guns in the sponsons and rocket pods on the underwing pylons were fully loaded—and he wanted nothing more than a chance to shoot at something, anything. This was always the problem with giving men guns, particularly big guns; the urge to use them always kept cropping up.

The military dealt with this urge by letting its people shoot their guns on a regular basis. Military fighter pilots trained with their missiles and onboard cannons all the time. They got to shoot up target drones, drop bombs at ground targets and launch missiles from time to time. Even some of the DEA gunship pilots got to swap rounds with Colombian drug runners. FBI and ATF pilots, however, didn't get much chance to play with their weapons, and McCarthy was eager to fire his first shots in anger.

He was so eager, in fact, that his weapons were "hot" even though the rules of engagement he had been given forbid him going to "weapons hot" until he had been fired at or faced a situation where someone's life was in danger. McCarthy didn't really care about the rules of engagement, though. He was a hot-rock pilot, and he could handle the plane's fire-control system no sweat.

McCarthy's rear-seat observer in the Bronco, Russ Warner, wasn't as confident as the pilot. Warner didn't like flying with the underwing pylons loaded down with rockets and ammunition belts in the sponson machine guns. He saw himself as a law-enforcement officer, a federal cop, not a fighter jock. When he got back on the ground, he was going to talk to the agent in charge of this detail and insist that he be given another assignment.

He didn't want to end up on the short end of the stick. All it would take was for McCarthy to squeeze the wrong button at the wrong time and they'd find themselves in front of a Senate committee frantically trying to keep themselves out of jail.

But for now, though, he was stuck riding the back seat while McCarthy and the other two Bronco pilots were orbiting on station outside of Lewiston, waiting to see if the tip they had received was going to pan out. If it went down as they had been told it would, their job would be to try to spot the getaway vehicle in traffic and follow it to its destination. Then they would direct the tactical teams in and provide aerial fire support as necessary.

BUCK JACKSON HAD STARTED the day confident that this bank heist would be like all the others had been—quick in, make the snatch and quick out. He almost had second thoughts, however, when he noticed that the shopping-mall parking lot on the northern side of Lewiston was only sparsely populated. The target bank wasn't open yet, but the stores in the mall should have been and there should have been more cars parked there. He was about to say something to the driver when he saw the black-and-white armored car parked at the back of the bank and the guards wheeling the bags of currency inside.

Seeing all of those bags of money made Jackson forget his concerns about the empty parking lot. There was work to do, and he was eager to get at it. The fact that a few large-denomination bills always seemed to stick to his fingers after one of these jobs had a lot to do with his anticipation. He pulled back on the charging handle of his M-16 to chamber a round and got ready to rock and roll.

The driver, Dwight Mulligan, was also an ex-GI, and he knew the drill. Without being told, he turned the van into the empty parking lot and headed for the rear of the bank, slamming to a halt a dozen yards from the armored car. Mulligan and Doug Cheevers were the first out of the van, with Jackson following hard on their heels.

All three of the militiamen were wearing Army-issue flak vests over their field jackets. They hadn't been shot at yet, but only a fool doesn't take precautions. Combat boots, ski masks and thin leather gloves completed their work uniform. They were armed with black-market, Army-issue, full-auto M-16s because the Army assault rifles were readily available and they knew how to use them.

The trio was ten yards from the armored car when Cheevers raised his M-16 and shouted to the guards, "This is a stickup! On the ground and no one will get hurt!"

No sooner were the words out of his mouth than the FBI agents hiding out of sight opened fire. All three militiamen went to ground at the first shot, but Cheevers hit the pavement harder than the other two.

When the first shot rang out, Jackson instinctively went into counterambush mode. Dropping to the pavement, he triggered off half a magazine on full-auto before he checked on his two cohorts.

One look was all it took to see that Cheevers was dead. He had been wearing the same type of flak vest Jackson and Mulligan were, but the vest didn't cover his head. The two 9 mm holes in his neck and face had already stopped bleeding, which meant that his heart had stopped beating. He was dead.

"Leave him," Jackson snapped at Mulligan as he laid down on the trigger of his M-16, sending another long burst of 5.56 mm bullets at their adversaries. None of them was carrying identification, and while he hated to leave his buddy behind, he knew Cheevers would have done the same thing had their situations been reversed.

"Cover me," he shouted to Mulligan as he reached into the pocket on the front of the flak vest and pulled out an M-26 hand grenade, "and get ready to pull back!"

Rising to one knee, Mulligan flicked his M-16's selector switch to 3-shot-burst mode and cut loose. Swinging the muzzle in an arc, he placed bursts on all of the Fed positions.

With the suppressive fire ringing in his ears, Jackson pulled the pin on the grenade and tossed the bomb underhand at the armored car. He was pleased to see it roll under the rear wheels before it detonated.

Unlike in the movies, the explosion of the grenade didn't lift the vehicle off the ground. It did, however, send red-hot shrapnel into the unarmored fuel tank. The detonation of twenty gallons of gasoline provided the movie-style special effect.

The roar, heat and blast of the fireball momentarily stunned the FBI agents and gave the two would-be bank robbers the chance they needed to sprint back to their getaway vehicle. Jackson laid down a base of fire from the side door of the van as Mulligan hit the ignition, slammed the gearshift into First and floored it.

Tires squealing, the van leaped out of the killing

zone and, beyond a few holes in the bodywork, it wasn't damaged. It was stolen anyway, and as soon as they cleared town, they'd dump it and come back for their own cars.

The militiamen's swift, military-trained reaction to the ambush had taken the Feds completely by surprise. Being used to dealing with disorganized criminals, they hadn't expected that violent a reaction and didn't have their chase cars in place to follow them immediately. The van was completely out of sight by the time the cars arrived.

Once Mulligan was on the street, he was in the clear. After running south for four blocks, he hooked a hard right into an alley and drove down to the next street. After making sure that the road was clear of cop cars, he turned north and headed for the freeway entrance to U.S. 95 two blocks away. Another thing they had prepared for in military fashion was their escape route.

Minutes after the first shot had been fired, they were just another vehicle in the stream of midmorning traffic heading north.

"Goddammit!" Mulligan snapped. "We were set up!"

"I know we were." Jackson grabbed two M-16 magazines from the duffel bag in the back of the van. "And it ain't over yet. Keep a good eye out for chase cars."

"Someone's going to hear about this."

"Right," Jackson said. "But we have to get the hell out of here first."

"IT'S GOING DOWN!" Russ Warner, the observer in Tom McCarthy's Bronco, yelled over the intercom.

"What're they saying?" the pilot asked Warner, who was monitoring the tac-team channel while he monitored the command-and-control frequency.

"Damn," Warner said. "They got one of them, but the other two escaped. It looks like they're heading south."

"I'm on them."

The pilot jerked the Bronco up onto one wing and snapped the plane's nose around to head back toward Lewiston. Since he could make over 350 miles per hour, he could fly there before the van had a chance to get out on the freeways. Holding the stick between his knees, McCarthy took his hands off of the controls and tightened his flying gloves over his fingers. He didn't want anything to prevent him from having complete control of his aircraft on the greatest day of his career.

"Do they have a description of the vehicle yet?" he asked his back-seater.

"Yeah," Warner replied. "It's a ten-year-old Chevy van, light blue with blacked-out side windows. The last three on the plate are six, nine, two."

Dropping to less than a thousand feet, McCarthy intently scanned the roads and highways below. He had been given a target, and he was going to find it.

CHAPTER SIX

By the time Tom McCarthy reached the southern approaches to Lewiston, he found that he was sharing the airspace with the other two FBI Broncos. The agent on the ground in charge of the operation had vectored all of them in to the same area, thinking that the robbers had continued fleeing south. It didn't take much time, however, for the agent to realize that it was self-defeating to have all three of his spotter planes checking out the same small area.

On the orders to split up, one of the Broncos headed northwest, following U.S. 195 in case the bank robbers were trying to escape to Spokane while one of them continued searching the state roads to the south. McCarthy, however, followed a hunch and headed due north on U.S. 95 toward Moscow. Thanks to the initial screwup, the would-be bank robbers had now been on the road for almost half an hour, but he was confident that he could catch up with them.

Twenty miles north of Lewiston, the traffic thinned out enough that Russ Warner had no trouble checking individual vehicles from the back seat of the Bronco. "I think I've got him!" he called out.

"Where?" McCarthy asked, his finger hovering over his fire controls.

"We're coming up on him in the middle lane. He's passing that eighteen-wheeler with the white trailer."

The light blue Chevy van with the blacked-out windows was moving fast, but not much faster than the rest of the traffic so as not to draw attention from any state troopers that might be lurking under the overpasses. Now that the fifty-five-mile-per-hour speed limit had been done away with, a vehicle could do almost ninety on an interstate without drawing undue attention to itself.

"They sent a partial plate number. Drop back so I can check the plate on him."

McCarthy dropped his flaps partway and chopped his throttle, causing the Bronco to dramatically lose speed. Banking to the left, he went into an orbit to let the van pull ahead of him before coming up on it from behind again.

"That's it!" Warner said excitedly. "The last three they sent match."

"Call it in," McCarthy yelled back to his observer as he pulled his flaps back up. "Tell them that we've got them."

The pilot went into an orbit off to the left of the freeway again to keep pace with the speeding van.

FROM THE BACK of the van, Buck Jackson kept a sharp eye out the rear window for any sign that they were being pursued. So far they were clean, and he was just about to relax when Mulligan shouted, "Buck! I think we've got a plane tracking us!"

"Where?" Jackson asked as he squeezed back into the passenger's seat.

The driver pointed over his left shoulder. "I caught a flash of it in the side mirror."

Peering through the side window, Jackson saw a dark-painted twin-engined aircraft orbiting off to their left at about a thousand feet.

"Shit, that's a fucking Bronco," he said, recognizing the aircraft from his days with the Army. "It's got to be the Feds. No one else flies those things."

Mulligan stepped on the gas, and the van shot forward. When they stole a van for their bank jobs, they always made sure that they got one with a V-8 engine that looked to be in good running condition. This one was, and he ran it all the way up past the ton mark and to hell with the State troopers. Their only chance was to get to the next freeway exit.

Jackson had no illusions about their being able to outrun a plane and he had long ago decided that he wasn't going to let the Feds get their hands on him alive. He knew what life in a maximum-security federal prison would be like, and he wasn't going to end his life that way. If he was going to die, he was going to do it like a man, on his feet. He'd show the bastards how a paratrooper died.

But before he died, he was going to take a couple

of Feds with him, namely the two in that Bronco. Even after having been ambushed and losing Doug at the bank, they'd have gotten away clean if it hadn't been for that plane up there. But Jackson had a way to deal with it.

Reaching into the footlocker in the back of the van, he brought out his ace in the hole. The four-foot-long, olive-drab fiberglass tube bore yellow markings identifying it as an M-41 EZ Redeye antiaircraft missile.

With all the attention the more-advanced Stinger missiles had gotten in the press, its predecessor, the humble Redeye missile, had been all but forgotten. The Army had more or less forgotten them, as well. Several crates of Redeyes hadn't been missed when they disappeared from a Fort Lewis, Washington, ordnance depot and reappeared on the weapons black market. Since they weren't as well-known to customers as the Stingers, they also hadn't been as expensive, and the Brotherhood had acquired a few of them for its arsenals.

The Redeye wasn't as "smart" as a Stinger. In fact it was a pretty simpleminded missile that was easy to decoy with a flare or an IR interrupter beacon. But Jackson was betting that the Feds hadn't bothered to equip that Bronco with decoy flares. They never would have figured that they would be going up against someone armed with a ground-to-air missile. They expected to kill unarmed women and kids with it. The last thing the bastards would expect was to have to face someone who could fight back against a combat aircraft.

Maybe they'd learn something from this before the morning was over.

IN THE BACK SEAT of the Bronco, Russ Warner saw that the subject vehicle had speeded up and was traveling at well over a hundred miles per hour. Before he could say anything to McCarthy, the pilot had pulled out of his orbit and was closing in on the van.

"Tom," he called up on the intercom, "they told us just to hang back and keep it under surveillance."

"He's endangering the other vehicles," the pilot replied. "I'm going to take them out before they kill someone."

"Tom! Don't do this!"

"Just shut up and observe like you're supposed to," McCarthy barked.

The pilot was so intent on fixing the hood of the van in the center of his gun sight that he didn't see Jackson open the sliding side door and lean out with a missile's launch tube on his shoulder. A horrified Warner saw it, though, and yelled a warning just as McCarthy triggered his port-side under-wing rocket pod. "Tom! They've got a missile!"

A 2.75-inch rocket left the Bronco's pod with a whoosh and streaked toward the freeway.

Jackson fired his missile at the same time, and it streaked skyward on a column of dirty white smoke at several times the speed of the rocket from the Bronco.

The missile had been designed as a weapon to be used against low-flying aircraft, and the FBI plane was well within the range of its IR-seeker guidance system. From where Jackson watched, it looked as if the missile instantly appeared in front of the plane's left-hand engine and was followed by a flaming explosion.

"I got the bastard!" Jackson yelled triumphantly as the starboard turboprop on the Bronco ripped away from the boom and plummeted to earth. The low-flying plane instantly went over on her port-side wing and followed it into the ground.

Just then, the Bronco's rocket streaked over the top of the blue van and slammed into the center of the roof of another van in front of the fleeing militiamen. The vehicle flew apart as the four-pound HE warhead penetrated the roof before detonating. Sheet metal peeled back like tissue paper, and a ball of fire erupted as red-hot shrapnel from the explosion ripped into the gas tank.

Distracted by the destruction of the Bronco, the driver of the blue van slammed into the burning wreckage in front of him at slightly under a hundred miles per hour. For a split second, the blue van tore through the rear of the burning vehicle like a movie stunt car. Then its full fuel tank exploded, as well.

By some quirk of fate, the wreck was situated in one of those empty spaces in traffic that occur on even heavily traveled freeways. The vehicles following the two vans slammed on their brakes and tried their best to keep clear of the disaster in front of them. Many of them got off the road in time, but others rear-ended the vehicles in front of them. Well to the rear, a semi driver jackknifed his rig and put the trailer crossways in the road, which ended the carnage.

When the dust cleared, a lot of bodywork would need to be unbent and a few necks would be stiff the next the morning, but the only casualties were in the downed plane and the two vans. By ones and twos, the stunned drivers and passengers got out of the other vehicles and stared at the wreckage laid out in front of them.

The column of thick smoke rising from the site of the crashed Bronco was matched by the inferno consuming the wreckage of the two vans.

DAN BUTTERFIELD, agent in charge of the Boise regional office of the FBI, surveyed the wreckage of the Bronco along the side of U.S. Highway 95 with disgust. But his disgust wasn't because of the bodies of the two FBI flyers that were trapped in the tangled wreckage, nor because of the waste of an expensive aircraft that he was ultimately responsible for. He was disgusted because he saw his career with the Bureau going down the toilet. Twenty-six years of honest and faithful service was going to be wiped out because one cowboy had to disobey his specific orders.

He had seen what had happened to the senior

agents who had been in charge of the Ruby Ridge fiasco and the siege at Waco. Sure, they had gotten away with it for a while. But the long arm of Congress had finally reached out and dragged them in front of a Senate committee hearing where they had been slaughtered like lambs for the congressmen preening in front of the TV cameras.

But as bad as his congressional enemies were, the media vultures were even worse. He had been able to keep the TV reporters and their cameras on the ground far enough away that they couldn't get any detailed shots of the wreckage. But there was nothing he could do about the ones in the air. His call to the FAA to try to get a restricted-airspace designation for the area had been met with a laugh. He had four local TV station choppers up there right now, and another one was closing in fast. If there was a midair collision, he was going to fry the simpleminded FAA flunkie who had denied his request to clear the airspace.

"I think we're done here," reported the agent making the preliminary investigation of the wreckage of the two vans and the Bronco.

Butterfield nodded. "Get the bodies under cover, then."

"It's already being taken care of."

"And where's that meat wagon I requested?"

"It's coming from Lewiston."

"Right," Butterfield muttered.

The FBI man hated this part of the country. He had spent most of his career working organized crime in

the northeastern states and saw his recent assignment
to the Northwest as a hardship tour. He hated the
climate and he hated the countryside, but the worst
part of it, though, was the attitude of the local citizens
toward the Bureau.

On the East Coast, he had been feared but still re-
spected for being an FBI man. Here, outside of the
few major cities, the citizens saw him and his agents
as the enemy, pure and simple. And the reception he
got from the local police forces wasn't much better.
There was none of the respect, even though driven by
fear, that he had known for most of his career as an
FBI agent. Here he was simply seen as a blood-suck-
ing Fed, another waste of their hard-earned tax dollars
who was sticking his nose into local affairs. But he
wouldn't have to worry about taking that kind of
abuse much longer.

When the investigating team arrived from Washington, he expected to be relieved on the spot and
ordered to report to D.C. for the start of a long congressional inquisition. At least he had his twenty-five
years in and could retire with his pension intact—as
long as he wasn't held personally responsible for this
and thrown in prison.

At least, though, he had learned one lesson from
other people's mistakes and had signed hard copy
backups of the orders he had given to the Bronco
pilots. No one would be able to accuse him of order-
ing his men to fire rockets at fleeing bank robbers.
Every man on this detail had signed a statement that

he had read and understood the rules of engagement. That was supposed to cover his butt, but he knew that this was going to go down in the public eye as another "shoot first, ask questions later" situation perpetuated by a federal agency.

Dammit, it wasn't his fault that a van driven by a traveling salesman had entered a combat zone and had been fired on by two hot-dog agents in a borrowed fighter plane. At least it hadn't been a van full of Sunday-school kids, a family on vacation or something like that.

The worst part was that the two Feds in the Bronco were dead, as well. Had they survived, Butterfield would have thrown them to the wolves without thinking twice. Hell, he'd be willing to personally execute them on national TV if it would help. With them dead, however, he was the one who was going to be drawn and quartered for the public's pleasure.

As Butterfield mentally prepared for his public hanging, the agent whose job it was to try to identify the still smoldering bodies walked up to him. "We have confirmation on the body of the driver of the first van," he said, "but we're not sure about the body in the back because—"

"I know, dammit!" Butterfield snapped. He didn't want to hear again that the body in the back of the van over the fuel tank was so badly burned that it couldn't be identified as being human, much less what sex it was or who it might have been. According to the company the driver worked for, he should have been alone. That made it likely that the second body was a hitchhiker who would never be identified.

"What do you have on the two in the second van, the bank robbers?" he asked.

"Nothing yet."

"Get something now!"

"Yes, sir."

The bearer of bad news walked away only to be replaced by yet another agent with even more of the same. "The deputy director's office called to notify you that he's left Washington and will be here as soon as possible. They want you to have all of the preliminary reports ready for him to look at as soon as he lands."

"I'm on it," Butterfield muttered. "I'm on it."

An Idaho State Police officer walked up to him next. "If your men are through here," he said, "we want to get the highway reopened."

"Yeah, we're done."

The state cop walked away without a word.

CHAPTER SEVEN

When Samantha Whiting accepted Bolan's invitation for dinner, she'd said that she didn't care where they ate just as long as it wasn't in Dilbert. Bolan could understand that. Small towns weren't a good place to be if you wanted to keep your life a private affair. There was already talk around town that the reason Vance had kicked Red Gillum's ass was that he was putting a move on her, and neither one of them wanted to fuel that rumor.

In an earlier day, the Crossroads Restaurant would have been called a roadhouse, a home away from home where people could gather for good food and companionship. It was fifteen miles out of Dilbert where the east-west state highway crossed the north-south route and, except for the house where the restaurant owner and his family lived, it was completely surrounded by farm fields. Idaho might have been famous for potatoes like the motto on the license plate read, but in the northern part of the state, the primary crops were wheat and green peas.

The parking lot in front of the Crossroads was populated with farm rigs, mostly pickups and station wagons. Inside, the decor was what Bolan had expected, bulls' horns and pictures of horses on the walls. The diners were mostly in work clothes, and baseball caps with John Deere and beer logos appeared to be mandatory.

"What's good here?" Bolan asked, not bothering to open the menu that stuck out between the salt-and-pepper shakers on the red-and-white-checked tablecloth.

"All of it," Whiting replied. "But I'd recommend the trout. There's a fish farm not too far from here, so they're really fresh."

"That sounds good to me. I haven't had a fish in quite a while."

Keeping in persona, Bolan ordered a beer with his trout while she had a glass of white wine.

"So, how'd you end up in Dilbert, Idaho?" he asked over the salad course.

"It's a long story," she replied. "I came from around there originally, but moved out to the coast when I got out of high school and ended up in Seattle. After I got divorced, my dad died and I came back to help Mom. One thing led to another," she said, shrugging. "And I'm still here."

Bolan knew that was the short version of the story, but it would do for now. At this stage, he really didn't need to know much more about her other than the fact that she was a good source of information about the local situation. At this point of his investigation, he needed all the inside information he could get.

"How about you?" she asked in return. "What brought you to this part of the country?"

"My story's a little more complicated than yours," he said.

"I'd love to hear it."

Even though he knew that a lot of women loved long, detailed life histories, Bolan knew that his Jack Vance persona wouldn't be spilling his guts on a first date. A man like him would only reluctantly reveal anything more than the most-superficial details of his life. And since he still didn't know where she fit into the situation he was investigating, he would only skim the surface of the legend Hal Brognola and Stony Man Farm had prepared for him.

"I was raised in California," he started, "and I went into the Marines right out of high school. I stayed in for a couple of years, then made the mistake of getting out. Since then, I've kind of been a wanderer. I just never found anyplace I wanted to stay for more than just a couple of years. And like I told you that first day, I'd never been to this part of the country, so here I am."

"Did you ever get married?"

He nodded. "I was married once, but it didn't work out."

That answer, however short, satisfied her completely. Like most women her age, she knew enough not to even think of getting involved with a man his age who had never been married. That was always a danger signal. A man who had been divorced, however, could be brought back into the state of husbandhood easily enough. He might have bad habits, he might not smell too good and he might be gunshy around women, but if he had been married once, he was salvageable.

Their main courses came, and for a few minutes they took care of the business at hand. When they had finished their meal, they both ordered a dessert and coffee to go with more conversation. Now that the initial phase of the "getting to know you" game had been concluded, Bolan could get down to business.

Even though he had figured out that Bolton Grey was the power in Dilbert and the surrounding area, he needed an insider's view of the man. "Mr. Grey seems like a pretty square guy," he offered. "He's sure treated me well for being an outsider and all."

"He is that," she replied, "but you don't want to cross him. His family's been running this part of Idaho for so long they think it's their private kingdom."

"What's the story on that?" he asked.

Whiting launched into a long and detailed history that started with a pioneer named Dilbert Grey who moved into Idaho and built the first general store in what would later become a town bearing his name. The narrative was full of names and local references that Bolan didn't understand, but he didn't need to.

He only needed to get a feel for how the man operated.

"It sounds like he takes pretty good care of 'his' town, though," he said when she paused.

"He does," she agreed. "But you might have noticed that there aren't any what you might call 'people of color' in Dilbert."

"Not even Mexican farm workers?" Bolan was surprised to hear that, because Mexican laborers, both undocumented and legal, were the backbone of the agricultural business in the Northwest. Even with modern farm machinery, there was still a great deal of hand work involved in getting the crops in and to market.

"Nope. Not a one. Never have been, and as long as Bolton's running the show, there never will be, either. All the farm work around here is done by white men either from the farm families or by guys like you who drift into town at the right time."

She looked at him as if for the first time. "And drifters don't always stick around very long, either. If they don't like to work, they get moved on. The fact that Bolton hired you means that you'll be here as long as you want to be. But you may find that he's not an easy man to work for."

"But how about you?" he asked. "You work for him, don't you?"

"That's a little different," she said. "He used to date my older sister, Kate, before she went away to college in Boise, so I'm almost family. I can get away with things no one else in town can."

Catching a tone in her voice that hadn't been there before, Bolan zeroed in. "Your sister didn't come back to Dilbert, I take it."

"No, and she didn't want to. She met a foreign student at college and was going to marry him before she was killed."

"What happened?"

"No one seems to know," she replied, her voice strained. "She was found dead on campus, strangled, but no one was ever charged with her murder."

"What happened to her boyfriend?"

She took a deep breath. "He disappeared at the same time and most people think that he killed her and ran away."

"But you don't, I take it."

She shook her head.

"He was a foreigner, you said?"

She nodded. "A Mexican exchange student."

"I take it that Grey never married."

She frowned. "How do you know that?"

"Just call it a good guess," Bolan said. And a good place to look for the start of a life history that went a long way to explain what was going on in the sleepy little agricultural town of Dilbert, Idaho. More than one man had gone wrong over a failed romance. If Grey blamed the Mexican student for his ex-girl-friend's death, it could follow that he wouldn't want Mexican workers in his town. It could also mean that he might be inclined to join a movement that, for the most part, wanted to keep the country free of non-whites.

It wasn't much to work on, speculation wasn't enough to call in the cops. But it was a start, and it gave him a working theory.

"Shall we go?" he offered when his companion seemed lost in thought.

"Sure," she said.

Whiting was quiet on the trip back to Dilbert, and Bolan didn't try to engage her in conversation. When he pulled up in front of her small frame house, he stepped out and, going around to the other side of the van, opened the door for her.

"Thanks for dinner," she said as she stepped out. "I haven't had a night like that in a long time. One of the problems with living in a place like this is that after a while, you know what everyone's going to say before they say it. A new face and new conversation are hard to come by."

"I'm glad you enjoyed it," he said. "Maybe we can do it again."

"Maybe," she replied cautiously.

Even though he was in the heartland of America, Bolan waited until she reached her door before starting his engine and driving off.

WHITING PAUSED at her door and turned to watch her dinner companion drive away. Part of her was a little annoyed that he hadn't made at least a tentative pass at her or had tried to invite himself in. But the other part of her was glad that he hadn't. She knew herself well enough to know that she might have taken him up on it, and she didn't need the distraction of a handsome, interesting stranger right now.

There was a lot about her life that she hadn't told Vance in the restaurant. More than her father's death had brought her back to Dilbert, much more. She had made a vow at her sister's grave that she would find her killer, and that was what had brought her back to Dilbert. Kate had lived almost all of her life in Dilbert, and Sam had always felt that the answers she sought were there, as well.

She had never bought into the theory that Kate's fiancée, Juan Carlos, had killed her in a lovers' fight and then fled. Sam had seen the two of them together and knew that he would have died before he would have hurt Kate. He worshiped her, and they were to be married as soon as he could get his family's permission.

She also believed that whoever killed Kate had killed Juan Carlos and disposed of his body, as well. No one, not even his family, had heard from him since that sad day, and he had been devoted to his family even more than he had been to Kate. Had he lived, even running for his life, he would have contacted them so they wouldn't have worried.

Entering her house, Whiting went into her kitchen, took a bottle of whiskey from the back of her cupboard and poured herself a tall drink. Telling Vance about Kate's death had bothered her more than she had thought it would. But it had been a long time since she had gone over it, and the retelling made the old wounds bleed again.

She would mourn her older sister again tonight. But in the morning, she would be ready to continue her long quest to find her killer.

BOLTON GREY DIDN'T have time to mourn the loss of the man he had known as Buck Jackson. Fortunately for the Brotherhood, the Feds were handling the bank jobs as simple criminal activity, and now that they had three dead bank robbers, they were satisfied. The loss of the aircraft and the two civilians on the freeway was causing them some trouble with the media. But so far, no one had even mentioned the word *militia.*

Nonetheless, he needed to find another experienced ex-soldier and bring him into the Cadre to take Jackson's place in the bank team for future operations. He had enough funds on hand to finance the arms and ammunition he had ordered from the Cuban so far. But the time would come when the Brotherhood would have to go to the bank again. The problem was that Grey didn't have anyone in the unit he felt was ready to advance to a higher position.

The new man, Jack Vance, however, was looking better and better every day. Grey had secured a copy of his service record and had found it interesting reading. He had learned that in Vietnam, Vance had been disciplined for refusing to risk the lives of the men in his rifle squad to rescue endangered South Vietnamese troops. At his court-martial, he had said that not one American life was worth the entire nation of Vietnam. He said that he would gladly kill the North Vietnamese when and wherever he could, but that he would never risk an American life for any number of Vietnamese, North or South.

The military court had found him guilty of failure to obey orders and had fined him, and had reduced him in rank. But because of the Silver Star he had been awarded for heroism on the battlefield, they hadn't sent him to prison. After finishing his enlistment as a private, he had gotten out of the service and had hit the road. Apparently he had been there ever since.

That was the kind of man Grey was looking for, a man of principle who wouldn't back down in the face of popular opinion. He had also been impressed by the beating Vance had given that white-trash loudmouth, Red Gillum. From what Grey had seen of the fight, it had been a very professional job and Vance had fought cold, which was another good sign.

Grey didn't need men who lost their tempers in the Brotherhood of Patriots. To do the job that had to be done to save the country, the men in his unit had to be determined, clear-thinking men who acted from calm calculation, not emotion. There was no place for hotheads in the Brotherhood. Too much was at stake.

And speaking of loudmouthed hotheads, Vance had

done Grey a big favor when he had hammered Red Gillum into the hardwood floor of the bar. Gillum had been Dilbert's resident asshole for a long time now, and Grey had had about all of him that he wanted to put up with. But his connection to Sheriff Frank Banner had always protected him, just like he protected Sam Whiting. Gillum hadn't been invited to join the Brotherhood, but he knew entirely too much about it for Grey's comfort. The real possibility of his shooting off his drunken mouth to the wrong person had troubled Grey for a long time. It wouldn't trouble him again, however. Neither would Sam ever be bothered by him again.

Red Gillum had finally reaped the reward of a life of slothful, bullying drunkenness. His beat-up old pickup had been found off the side of a road in the mountains to the north. The investigating officers chalked the accident up to drunken driving, and that ended it.

Before Grey made a decision about Vance, though, he would send him to the training camp in Washington. Even though he liked what he had seen so far, he wanted another opinion before he brought Vance inside the unit, much less into the Cadre. With the increased federal interest in the militia movement, there was always the possibility that Vance was a plant.   His gut, though, told him that Vance wasn't a Fed. The way he had dealt with Gillum was proof of that. No Fed in his right mind, even one posing as a redneck, would have taken the chance of getting in trouble in a strange town that way. Vance's reaction to Gillum had been straight from the heart, the act of a natural gentleman.

His gut also told him, however, that there was more to Vance than was on the surface. The man was hiding something, but that wasn't necessarily a crime. His record was clean, and it could be that he was just running from a woman. The number of men who were on the run from vengeful women or the courts was on the rise.

He trusted his instincts enough to send Vance to the training camp, and he would make a decision about the rest after Vance returned.

CHAPTER EIGHT

Bolan had been a little surprised when Bolton Grey invited him to his house for dinner that Saturday evening. It had been only a little over a week since he had started working for him, and it was a bit too soon for a social invitation to the boss's house. But if Grey was running a militia as Bolan thought he was, it could be a recruiting call.

Bolan arrived right on time and Grey led him directly into the dining room. Dinner was served by Grey's housekeeper-cook and, while plentiful, it was plain, down-home cooking like you only get in a farming community. After the plates were cleared away, Grey invited Bolan into his study for a drink.

"What can I get you?" Grey asked as he stepped up to an antique sideboard doing service now as a bar.

"Whiskey on the rocks?"

"Coming up."

"I did a little background check on you, Vance," Grey said as he handed over the drink. "And I'm pleased with what I found."

"How's that?" Bolan asked with exactly the right amount of suspicion. To have one's new boss checking you out could be either good or bad. And a man like Jack Vance was not going to like having anyone checking in on him no matter what the result was.

"You've led a somewhat unsettled life, but apparently you've been an honest man. People speak highly of you."

Bolan wondered exactly whom Grey or his employees had spoken to. Hal Brognola had to have gone the extra mile on this one to prepare a watertight "legend" for him by planting key people to talk about him if anyone inquired. And it seemed to be working.

"I'm glad to hear that," Bolan answered modestly.

"Tell me a little about your service in the Marines."

Bolan shrugged. "There's not much to tell. I did a four-year hitch and got out."

"There was a little more to it than that, wasn't there?"

"Yes, there was," Bolan said with the right amount of in-your-face honesty. "I was court-martialed for disobeying an order I didn't like."

"An order to do something that would have unnecessarily risked the lives of your squad mates."

"That's right," Bolan replied. "And I don't regret doing it. I'd do it again under the same circumstances."

"I'd be disappointed if you said that you

wouldn't,'' Grey said. "It would mean that I have been wrong about you, and I don't like being wrong about people. In my business, I can't afford to make bad judgments.''

Grey took a seat behind a huge oak desk and motioned for Bolan to take a seat in one of the upholstered chairs in front of it.

"As you've probably figured out by now," Grey said, "I pretty much run the town here. It's not something that I set out to do. It just ended up that way. I've always been pretty good with money and was able to take over things when others went broke. Anyway, I also have interests outside of Dilbert, and I don't mean financial. I'm concerned about the road America has taken recently.''

Bingo! Bolan thought as he leaned back to hear what Grey had to say. It was recruitment time.

Grey lurched into a typical militia lecture about the sorry state of individual liberty in the United States, the federal government's ever increasing encroachment on civil liberties, excessive taxation and the threat to individual freedoms that it represented. Bolan had heard it all before in many guises, but was still very attentive. He needed to know what kind of rebel Grey represented.

"In short," Grey concluded, "there's a group of us in the Northwest who have banded together to do what we can to prepare for the major social changes that we think are coming. We call ourselves the Brotherhood of Patriots, and when the crisis hits, we want to be ready to deal with it. America is a great country that has fallen on evil times. We aren't willing to stand by and see her destroyed without even trying to defend her.''

Grey locked eyes with Bolan. ''I think that you're the kind of man we want to have at our side, a proved patriot and a man of honor. I'm offering you a chance to join something that will make a difference in shaping the future of our country. Not many men get a chance to take part in history, but if things keep going the way they are, some of us will get that chance and I'd like you to be with us when we do it.''

Bolan couldn't appear to be too eager. That was the sign of a plant. Grey was much too smart to get sucked in that way. Bolan knew that it would be best if he had to be convinced to get involved, not ask to join.

''Let me think about it, Mr. Grey,'' Bolan said. ''This is obviously a serious undertaking, and I'm not sure where I would fit in.''

''Let me put it to you this way, Vance.'' Grey leaned forward. ''Dilbert sure as hell isn't the big city, and we can thank God for that. But life is good here. We look out for each other like neighbors and we live the way men should live. It's a small town, granted, but there's always a place for a good man like you in Dilbert. I, for one, hope that you'll put down roots and stay with us. We can use you, and maybe it's time that you found yourself a home.''

He smiled. "There's sure as hell worse places to call home."

This was the emotional side of the recruitment spiel and was designed to strike a chord with the loner, the man like Jack Vance, who had never found the right place to stay long enough to feel that he belonged. It was ironic that Bolton Grey had no idea that the man he was talking to was even more of a loner than he appeared to be.

Mack Bolan, the Executioner, had no home, nor would he ever have one. He was the ever wandering warrior, a man who called few other men friend. He was a man of a hundred faces, and most of them weren't even his. There had been those times in the past when he would have welcomed settling in a quiet little place like Dilbert. But those times were long gone, and they would never return.

What Jack Vance wanted, however, was another question. He was at that point in his life when a smart man quit chasing shadows or dreams, and settled in to live his life with some amount of certainty. But Vance would be cautious because he was also old enough to know that there was no such thing as a free lunch. Grey had something in mind other than charity, and Vance would know that.

"Like I said, Mr. Grey, I'll sleep on it and let you know what I come up with."

"Call me Bolton. All my friends do, and I'm hoping you'll become a friend."

Bolan stuck out his hand. "I really appreciate the meal, Bolton."

"We'll do it again," Grey said as he shook his hand.

"I hope so."

WHEN BOLTON GREY went by the fuel yard the next morning, Bolan had his answer ready for him. "I gave some thought to what you said last night," he told him. "And if you can find a place to use me, I'd like to stick around. Like you said, maybe it's time that I found a place to call home."

"Great. I was hoping that you'd say that. You've been doing a good job here, and I need someone I can depend on. And," Grey went on, "since you're not settled down here yet, I'd like to ask you to go over to Washington for a couple of days on Patriot business. With the FBI swarming all over the place right now, we don't hold any of our training here. The Brotherhood has a camp in the mountains set up to train our recruits and issue their equipment. And you can probably use a refresher course on the weapons and equipment we're using. They're more up-to-date than what you were trained to use in Vietnam."

"But what about the job?" Bolan asked, looking out at the fuel tanks in the yard.

"The job will be here when you come back," Grey promised. "As much as I need you here, I need you brought up to speed in the Brotherhood even more."

"When do you want me to leave?"

"Tomorrow morning," Grey said. "I'll make a few calls today, and they'll be expecting you. Get your things together tonight, and I'll have someone take over for you in the morning."

"Sounds good."

"I'M GOING TO BE AWAY for a week or so," Bolan told Sam Whiting at the bar that night. "Mr. Grey wants me to take care of some business in Washington for him."

The woman looked at him like he hadn't cleaned his boots before he came in. "I thought you were smarter than that, Jack." She sighed. "But I should have known that you'd get caught up in that shit, as well."

"What do you mean?"

"You know damned good and well what I mean. You've joined Bolton Grey's little soldier-boy club. You're going to wear a camouflage uniform, carry a gun and run around in the woods pretending that you're saving the country from the Commies or whatever. All you're going to do is get your damned-fool head blown off by the FBI like those damned fools who robbed that bank."

"I don't rob banks, Sam." Bolan tried to sound offended. "I'm not a thief. I just think that Bolton's right about a lot of what's going on in the country right now, and I want to help him if I can."

She sighed the sigh of a woman who has heard it

all many times before. "I know, I know. You sure as hell don't owe me a damned thing. As a matter of fact, I still owe you for taking Red off of my back."

"You don't owe me anything, either, Sam. I was more than happy to take Red out."

"I understand that you did a real professional job of it, too." She stared at him, a serious look in her eye. "The way I hear it, you hurt him about as much as a man can be hurt without doing any serious damage. But you were careful not to use any of those fancy martial-arts moves. That was smart because these good ol' boys see that shit as being the mark of a Fed."

Bolan went on alert. Leave it to a woman to get right to the meat of the matter. "You don't think I'm a federal agent, do you?"

"Are you?" She raised her eyebrows.

"No," he said honestly. Working free-lance for his old friend Hal Brognola didn't make him a federal agent.

She looked at him for a long time. "I believe you," she said. "But some of the boys around here have their doubts, so you'd better watch your ass over there in those Washington hills. They carry live ammunition when they play soldier over there. It'd be too easy for them to miss a target and shoot you instead if they had a mind to."

"I'll keep that in mind."

"You'd better."

"What else are they saying about me?" Bolan

asked. As long as she was on the subject, he could use an update.

Now Whiting smiled. "Well, you got your two camps on that subject. Some of them are pissed off that you seem to be scoring big time with me."

"Am I?"

"Let me finish. Those are the ones who think you also might be a Fed. Then there are those who wish that they'd had the balls to kick Red's ass the way you did, because he had it coming for a long time. They're on your side even if you are new in town."

"What's the split?"

"About thirty-seventy."

"Which way?"

"You have the majority with you."

"And you?"

"You're okay, Jack," she said, smiling. "Just don't get your head blown off by any of Red's friends."

"How's Red doing, anyway?" Bolan asked. "I haven't seen him lately."

She looked surprised. "You don't know?"

He shook his head. "Know what?"

"Mr. Grey invited him to leave town permanently."

"And he did?"

Whiting nodded. "Like I told you, that's the way things work around here. Bolton'd had about enough of him anyway, and you just made his mind up for him. Plus, like I said, Bolton and I are old friends, and he didn't know that I'd been having trouble with Red. When you pointed that out to him, he took immediate action like he always does.''

"He sounds like a bad man to cross.''

"You don't know the half of it.'' Seeing that she was getting into dangerous waters, she quickly switched subjects. "Can I get you another beer?''

"Sure,'' Bolan said. "But that'll have to be the last one. I've got a long drive ahead of me in the morning.

"I'll check in with you when I get back,'' he added when she didn't respond.

"I'm not planning on going anywhere,'' she said.

"Good. I'll be back, then.''

A few minutes later, Samantha Whiting watched him walk out of the bar. Not for the first time, she almost wished that he hadn't come to Dilbert. There was something about him that she couldn't put her finger on, but she knew that his coming to town would have lasting effects. Not only on herself, but on the way of life she had grown accustomed to.

But maybe he was the way for her to finally get out of town, so it wouldn't be all bad.

CHAPTER NINE

In the Cascade Mountains

After turning off Interstate 90, Bolan drove up into the foothills of the Cascade Mountains to the small town of Bender, Washington. He went into the Twelve Point Café and ordered coffee and a maple bar. When he paid on the way out, he asked the man behind the cash register if he knew of a good place to hunt jackrabbits.

The man looked him up and down before replying. "We don't get many jackrabbits around here, Mister."

"Thanks, anyway."

"Don't mention it."

Outside, Bolan got back into his van, but didn't start the engine. A few minutes later, the passenger's-side door opened and a man slid into the seat. "Head west out of town" was all he said.

Bolan fired up the engine and pulled back out onto the state highway. He kept within the speed limit and asked no questions. His passenger remained silent until they were a dozen miles out of Bender.

"There's a turnoff five hundred yards ahead on the right," the man said. "Take it."

"Got it."

A hundred yards after turning off, the pavement ended and they were on a gravel road running through a thick fir forest. As they rounded the first bend, the passenger said, "Stop here for a minute."

The man got out and disappeared into the woods. Through the trees, Bolan caught a brief glimpse of two men in woodlands-pattern camouflage fatigues with M-16s slung over their shoulders talking to his passenger.

The man returned in less than a minute. "Grab your gear and follow me," he said.

"What about the van?"

"You leave your keys with me. I'll take care of it for you."

There was nothing incriminating in the van, and Bolan didn't want to give up his mobility, but he had no choice except to play it the way they wanted.

His escort didn't speak as he led Bolan deeper into the thick old-growth forest. After half a mile, he stopped in a small clearing. "Wait here," he told Bolan. "Someone will come and get you."

With that, the man turned and started back the way they had come.

It was evident to Bolan that whoever had set up this training camp was a real pro. What he had seen so far of the security here was straight out of a guerrilla-warfare handbook written by a master. There was no way that anyone was going to blunder into this camp without being picked up by the security outposts.

How the camp had escaped detection by the Forest Service, however, was another question. The most likely answer was that they had a man inside who made sure that the federal agency conveniently overlooked this particular corner of the Wenatchee National Forest. It wouldn't be the first time that something like that had happened, and it only underscored one of the reasons the FBI and ATF had had such a difficult time pinning these people down.

In Bolan's opinion, the government had drastically underestimated the level of public support for the militia movement, as it was being called. Mistrust and fear of the federal government was perhaps at an all-time high in Middle America. But while many Americans felt that way, they also saw little they could do about it. No one in his or her right mind went head to head with the federal government, not unless he or she had a death wish. But there were always small things, the safe things, they could do to help those few who were taking the big risks. The people who did those small things were called sympathizers, and every successful insurgent movement in history owed most of its success to its sympathizers.

One of the things Bolan needed to find out was just

how widespread the sympathy for the militia movement was. It was a key element in getting it under control, perhaps the key. First, though, he had to go back to boot camp. And he had to graduate as a full-fledged Patriot before he could continue his investigation.

BOLAN HAD BEEN SITTING on the log for less than half an hour when he heard the sound of a well-muffled engine approaching. A camouflage-painted Hummer tactical vehicle pulled into the clearing and headed toward him. He got to his feet and stood still as it stopped in front of him and a man in camouflage stepped out of the driver's side.

"Jack Vance?"

"That's me."

"Throw your gear in the back."

After doing as he had been told, Bolan climbed into the passenger's seat and the man drove off north down a barely perceptible path through the towering trees. Fifteen minutes later, the Hummer pulled into a tent city completely hidden under the forest canopy. The underbrush had been carefully thinned to provide room for the camouflaged tents, but enough of it had been left intact so it would pass a casual inspection. The place looked very much like most of the Vietcong jungle camps Bolan had seen in Vietnam. Even from the air, it would take an infrared device or radar to spot it.

The man who stepped out of the main tent to meet

the Hummer looked as if he were in his early forties and had to have seen active service. His carriage and bearing were that of an experienced officer, either infantry or Marine Corps; it was a look that couldn't be faked. More and more, this was looking like a professional operation.

"I'm John Williams, the camp commandant," the man said as he extended his hand.

Bolan took his hand. "Jack Vance. Glad to meet you, sir."

"Bolton Grey's said some good things about you, and we're glad to have you on board. Come on inside, and we'll get a cup of coffee."

Williams's tent was set up like an infantry-company command post. He had the radio gear, field desk, wall charts and paraphernalia that went with running a military operation. He also had a well-used Army-surplus thirty-cup coffeemaker that was plugged into the power cord from the well-muffled generator outside.

"Our program here is simple," Williams said after pouring two cups of coffee and inviting Bolan to take a seat. "You'll find it a lot like the boot camp you went through in the Corps except that it's minus all the extraneous military bullshit. We're training for war here, not to march in parades. You'll get a weapons orientation and refresher course, marksmanship training, demolition work and small-unit tactics. Our goal is to turn out a well-trained soldier who is able to operate effectively in a small team."

Bolan nodded his understanding.

"The rules around here are simple," Williams continued. "But if you violate them, you're in deep shit."

Again Bolan nodded his understanding. Whoever this guy was, he acted like he was commanding his own private army instead of a militia.

"First off," Williams said, counting off a finger, "no alcohol, even beer, is allowed unless it is issued to you. Secondly drug use will not be tolerated, period. Orders are to be obeyed without question. Fatigue details are shared by both the officers and trainees, and they, too, are to be done without bitching. Lastly there will be no personal conflicts or hassles. We're all in this together.

"Do you have any questions at this point?" the commandant asked.

"No, sir."

"Good. Cadreman Jenner will issue your uniforms and equipment and show you to your quarters. Dinner is 1800 hours, and there'll be a training session in night movement after dark."

Williams stuck his hand out again. "Good luck."

"Thanks."

AFTER BEING ISSUED two sets of camouflage fatigues and cold-weather gear, boots, bedroll, his tactical equipment and an AK-47 assault rifle, Bolan was shown to an Army-surplus medium-sized tent. The tent was erected over a built-up wooden floor, and there was no heating stove inside. But Bolan knew from experience that with the wide flaps tied down, the tent would stay fairly warm from body heat alone. Eight Army-surplus folding cots were lined up on each side of the tent, and most of them were occupied.

Picking the empty bunk by the door, he laid out his sleeping bag and started putting his gear away in the footlocker underneath the bunk. He was fitting his ammo pouches to his assault harness when he heard voices at the tent's door. The troops were returning.

"Look at this, boys, fresh meat!"

Bolan looked up to see a smiling man, wearing mud-covered camouflage fatigues and carrying an AK, walk in followed by a dozen others.

"I'm Jack Vance," Bolan introduced himself.

"Bud Tilton from Spokane," the man said, sticking out his hand.

"I'm from Dilbert, Idaho," Bolan responded as he shook hands.

"You don't sound like you grew up picking potatoes," Tilton commented.

"I didn't." He left it at that.

Tilton proceeded to introduce the other men, and Bolan shook hands with each of them. "What's on for tonight?" he asked after the introductions.

Tilton grinned. "After dinner they're going to teach us how to get lost in the woods at night."

"I don't think I need any help with that," Bolan declared. "I do that pretty good as it is."

"They'll just show you how to do it with a compass."

BOLAN QUICKLY FELL into the old, familiar military routine of the camp.

Although the camp was set up on military lines, as Williams had said, the extraneous military rules and regulations were kept to an absolute minimum. Salutes weren't exchanged, no one ever stood at attention, there were no formations and everyone was expected to act like a soldier without being forced to be one. It was a boot camp for motivated adults, not teenage recruits.

The only trouble Bolan had with the training they offered was that he had to try to forget things that had been second nature to him for years—things that most civilians, and even many ex-military men, had never learned. Having been a soldier of one kind or another for most of his adult life, it was difficult for him to act like a raw recruit. But his cover of having been a Marine for four years accounted for most of his lapses.

The only place he let it slip was on the firing range. His unerring marksmanship attracted comment.

"You're pretty good with that thing, Vance," the range instructor said after Bolan had burned through a mixed-range submachine course with an Uzi. He had always liked the Israeli-designed subgun and had not been able to hold back.

Bolan shrugged. "I've been shooting all my life," he said. "And I guess it just comes naturally."

"What did you qualify on in the Corps?"

"I fired expert with everything they'd let me get my hands on," Bolan answered. "M-14, M-16, M-60."

"Most troops don't get much range time with submachine guns," the instructor said suspiciously, eyeing the smoking Uzi in his hands.

"It shoots just like an M-16 on full-auto."

There was some truth to that, so the instructor backed off.

When Bolan went back to the range the next day for an assault-fire course with handguns, he made sure that he missed more than his share of the pop-up targets.

"I see that you do need to practice on your handgun work," the instructor said with some satisfaction.

"I've never been much good with pistols," Bolan lied. "I'm more of a rifleman."

"I'll schedule you for a little extra time with the handguns," the trainer replied.

"Thanks, I can use it."

"You sure as hell can," the man replied, grinning. "Missing that last target was a crime."

The last target had been a blue-painted, man-shaped silhouette with a white ATF logo across the chest. Since the target had been only some fifty feet away, he should have had it cold. He had pulled the round, however, and hadn't even come close.

"I'll get it next time around."

"See that you do. When the call comes, every round will have to count."

WHILE MOST of the training at the camp was first-rate, the same couldn't be said about all of the men who were undergoing that training. While there were none of the psychos and professional losers that the TV talk shows liked to portray as being the average militiaman, not all of the trainees were the dedicated, quiet patriots that Bolton Grey liked to talk about, either.

Many of the men were there because the Brotherhood was their social club, and they had to go through the initiation. This was the impulse that had created the original militias that had fought America's first wars—friends and neighbors arming themselves to stand together against the danger, whatever it might be. It had been those armed friends and neighbors who had borne the brunt of the fighting in the Revolutionary War and the Civil War. Now they were standing again to fight what they saw as an even more deadly threat to their freedoms, their own government.

Others had joined the Brotherhood, however, because they liked guns and liked running around the woods thinking that they were Rambos in training. These were the men who thought that carrying a weapon made them dangerous, and they liked feeling dangerous. They hadn't yet learned that it was what was in a man's mind, not what was in his hands, that truly made him dangerous.

How any of these men would stand up in a real fight, Bolan had no way of knowing. Most of them had no idea what they would have to face if what they feared ever came to pass. Combat was the ultimate pragmatism, the greatest test most men would ever face. A man had to have a good reason to lay his life on the line, and Bolan wasn't sure that many of these men had actually sat down to think it out.

This didn't make them any less dangerous, however. Men had fought and died for less than the approval of their friends and neighbors. Others had fought for little more than their curiosity. No man could ever know how he would react to combat until he actually got shot at, and the lure of facing the ultimate test was strong—particularly among those men who weren't too sure of themselves.

If the second American Revolution came as the Brotherhood wanted it to, some of its members would cut and run. Others, no less afraid, would stand and fight. The result would be dead Americans on both sides.

CHAPTER TEN

By the middle of the twelve-day training program, most of the dozen and a half men in the camp had accepted Bolan into their ranks without question. His abilities in the field and on the firing range made him a good man to team up with when the going got rough. He was also always willing to help anyone who was having difficulties with any part of the training. On his off-duty time, however, he kept pretty much to himself. His cover was tight, but the less they knew about him, the less chance there was for him to slip up.

Most of the men, particularly the older ones, seemed to understand Bolan's desire to be left alone when they weren't training. One of the younger trainees, however, decided that he could raise his self-esteem by confronting Bolan, a man he saw as an outsider because he kept to himself. Under normal circumstances, that wouldn't have been a problem for Bolan. Better men than the young trainee had tried it and had been left bleeding in the dust at the Executioner's feet. This time, though, regardless of how much Bolan wanted to, he wasn't free to indulge himself and hammer the kid into the ground.

The commandant had warned him about that, and violating the camp rules at this point in time wasn't smart. Plus, as in the bar fight with Red, for him to unleash his full combat abilities would raise questions that he didn't want to answer. But the kid kept pushing hard for a confrontation.

Rob Bannister was one of those men who had joined the militia because he liked to think of himself as a dangerous man. The feel of a rifle on his shoulder and a holstered handgun on his hip made him feel taller than his six feet one inch and made him walk with a swagger. He had once been a small-town high-school football hero, but his inability to get even halfway decent grades had kept him from going on to college to play more football. Now he worked in his father's irrigation business in eastern Washington and dreamed of his bygone days of glory. But proving himself in the camp was almost as good as making a touchdown, and he saw taking Bolan down as just one more score.

The squad members were in the tent one evening cleaning their weapons after a muddy exercise when Bannister called out to Bolan, "Hey, Pops!"

Bolan ignored him and continued cleaning his AK.

"Hey, Pops!" Bannister called out again. "I'm talking to you!"

Bolan looked across the aisle in the tent. "The name's Vance," he said slowly. "Jack Vance."

"I didn't know that you old farts could even re- member your names." The young man snickered. "I thought that was always the first thing you forgot."

"Why don't you leave him alone, Bannister?" Til- ton suggested.

Bannister turned on him. "Butt out of this, Tilton," he snapped. "I'm not talking to you."

Tilton was the kind of men who just wanted to get along, and he wasn't up to facing a bigger, younger man who wanted to fight, so he shut up.

"Pops," Bannister said, standing, "since you're doing such a good job on that gun of yours, why don't you come over here and do mine when you're done?"

"This isn't a 'gun,'" Bolan replied, patting the breech of the weapon across his lap. "It's an assault rifle. Specifically it's a Russian AK-47, one of the simplest assault rifles in the world, and even someone like you ought to be able to take it apart and clean it."

"Are you calling me stupid, old man?" Bannister countered when the other men chuckled.

Bolan's eyes stayed cold as he shrugged and smiled. "I just call them as I see them."

Bannister walked across the tent. "I don't like peo- ple laughing at me, old man, particularly someone like you."

"I can understand that," Bolan replied in a neutral tone. "Now, can you step back out of the light so I can finish what I'm doing?"

"I'm talking to you, dammit!"

Bolan snapped the receiver cover back on his AK and put his right hand on the comb of the buttstock right behind the pistol grip. His left hand was around the barrel right ahead of the hand guard.

When Bannister reached down to grab him, Bolan snapped the AK around, pivoting the butt into the pit of Bannister's stomach in a classic boot-camp-style horizontal buttstroke. It had always been a favorite move of his.

Bannister grunted as the wind was knocked out of him, and he staggered backward until he hit the tent pole. When he saw that Bolan was still sitting on his bunk as if nothing had happened, he recovered and charged back across the floor.

Bolan met him halfway and didn't give his adversary a chance to hit him. Using a takedown hold, he put Bannister facedown on the floor, pinned him with his knees and had his head in a right-armed lock.

Leaning close to Bannister's head, he spoke softly, "Never mess with a man who wants to be left alone, son. You don't know what's on his mind. He might have something troubling him, and he just might get the idea that you're the source of his problems. A man like that can be dangerous.

"Look down," Bolan ordered.

Bannister looked down as he had been commanded and saw the bayonet in Bolan's left hand for the first time. The point of the blade was poised at the pit of his stomach. He was closer to death than he had ever been.

"I don't like killing a man unless I have to," Bolan continued. "But I don't let punks like you mess with me, either. Got that?"

When Bannister nodded, Bolan released him and stepped back. The young man was as pale as a ghost as he backed out of the tent. The Executioner sat back down on his bunk and started to clean his AK's magazines.

THE NEXT DAY, Bolan was called in from the classroom tent where he had been listening to a lecture on field fortification, and he was told to report to the commandant.

Williams was seated behind his field desk when Bolan walked in.

"You wanted to see me, sir?"

"I understand that you had a confrontation with one of the trainees yesterday."

"Yes, sir," Bolan replied. "It got sorted out quickly, and there was no harm done."

"I've heard the testimony of your tent mates, Vance," Williams said, "and they all say that you were only defending yourself. If Bannister hadn't come whining to me, I wouldn't even be talking to you about it now."

Bolan understood that. A good commander let his men iron out their differences as long as the situation didn't get out of hand. He had made sure that he hadn't injured Bannister beyond giving him a few bruises. He considered it to have been a good hand-to-hand combat lesson.

"His father is a good Patriot," Williams continued. "One of our founders in fact, and he wanted his son to join us. I, however, have down-checked him. We can't afford to have men in the Brotherhood who don't have any more common sense than he seems to have. He's already on his way home, and I have spoken to his father. I'm not sorry that this came up, because it exposed a weak link in the organization. However, I don't expect anything like that to happen again."

"It won't," Bolan promised.

Williams gave him a long look. "Just make sure it doesn't, Vance."

"Yes, sir."

AT THE END of the twelve-day training period, the men who had completed the cycle were gathered in the big tent for a brief graduation ceremony. No certificates were handed out, and no trophies were awarded for best shot, just as there were no rank badges or secret signs in the Brotherhood. Williams simply congratulated them on a job well done and delivered a fifteen-minute lecture on the need for true patriots to be ever vigilant in these troubled times. He then shook hands with each trainee, and they were dismissed.

After promising to keep in touch with one another, the men changed into their civilian clothes and were driven out of the forest to the gravel road where their vehicles were waiting for them. One by one, they drove out onto the state highway and back to their homes to await the call to action by their unit leaders. They were trained militiamen now, but most of them would never do anything more criminal than getting a speeding ticket.

When Mack Bolan was reunited with his van, he threw his duffel bag in the back and drove east out of the mountains for an hour before pulling off in a roadside rest stop. There, he thoroughly checked all of the hidden compartments in the vehicle and found everything intact. Assured that his cover was still intact as well, he got back on the road for Idaho.

Dilbert, Idaho

WHEN HE PULLED into Dilbert the next day, he parked his van in front of Mac's Grill and Tavern. Now that he was back in town, he wanted to check in with Samantha and let her know that he had returned. Even though he was on the inside now, he still needed her as an unwitting informant.

Whiting was at her station and she gave him a long look as he walked in and took a stool at the bar. "So, you're one of them now," she said as a statement, not a question.

"I guess you can say that," he replied, not wanting to play dumb with her.

"And I guess that means that you'll be spending

your weekends running around in the woods playing soldier boy with the rest of those damned fools.''

"Not me," he answered. "I had my fill of that crap when I was in the Marines."

"We'll see," she said knowingly, ending that conversation. "What can I get you?"

"How about a draft?"

"Coming up."

"What's the special?" he asked after she set the beer in front of him.

"Same as it always is, chicken-fried steak, but with fries and beets today."

"Sounds good."

Bolan nursed his beer while he waited for his dinner to cook and tried to figure out Sam's apparent disappointment with his having joined the local militia. For all of Grey's vaunted security, his unit, as he called it, was apparently an open secret in Dilbert. But then, in a place like this, it was difficult to keep anything secret very long. In small-town America, everyone's business was always everyone else's business. The wives, sweethearts, poker buddies and co-workers of the Brotherhood members were sure to know of the organization, and they were even more likely to talk about it with one another.

They were just as unlikely, however, to mention anything about it to outsiders. If Bolan hadn't been recruited by Grey himself, it wasn't likely that he would have been able to even hear about the Brotherhood, much less get inside of it. But now that he was in, he hoped to be able to get the leads he needed before much longer.

And once he had what he had come for, he would set the wheels in motion that would put an end to this so-called Brotherhood of Patriots.

Until then, Jack Vance had a job to go to and a place to live. He even had a friend.

After eating his dinner, he made small talk with Sam for a little while before driving out to the fuel yard. He left the bar early, though, because the following day was a work day.

CHAPTER ELEVEN

Bolton Grey was glad to see Jack Vance back in town. The reports on his training had been good, and he was ready to put him to work. "What did you think of the camp, Vance?" he asked when he stopped by the fuel yard the next morning.

"It was very professional," Bolan replied. "If the Marine Corps had been more like that, I might have stayed in a little longer."

"What did you think of the men you met?"

"Most of them were good men," he answered honestly. "With all the bullshit you see about the militias on television, I have to admit that I wasn't quite sure what to expect."

"The Brotherhood of Patriots isn't like some of the other so-called militia groups you've heard about," Grey said. "We don't ask Nazis or religious wackos to join us. We're also not trying to establish a 'whites only' society. We just want to return America to the values that made her strong, and we want to get the federal government off the back of the common citizen. Democracy is a fragile thing, and if the average citizen no longer has a voice in the way the country is run, America is no longer a democracy.''

Bolan had heard all of this before at the camp, but he knew that he would hear it many times again. To make sure that the militiamen stayed true to the cause, they had to hear it repeated often by their leaders.

"Now that you have been through the training," Grey said, "I can let you in on the Brotherhood's operations and give you a chance to make your contribution to our efforts."

"I'm ready to do what I can."

"First off," Grey started, "I want to give you an outline of what we do and don't do. We do not, and I mean do not, operate against the citizenry. Nor, if we can at all help it, do we go up against state or local agencies. Our enemy is the federal government and the federal government only. It's the one who's attacking democracy, so it is our enemy and we can show it no mercy."

"And that includes not showing mercy to federal agents?" Bolan asked.

Grey turned and looked hard at Bolan. "Do you have a problem with that, Vance?"

Bolan shook his head. "No, I just want to know the score up front."

"But," Grey said. "I fully realize that federal employees are Americans, too, even though it's sometimes hard to tell, and we don't target them indiscriminately. FBI. ATF and Justice Department agents,

however, are another matter. They are the main enemies of democracy, and it's open season on them.

"After what they did at Ruby Ridge and Waco,
every American owes it to himself and his children
to do everything he can to see that those agencies are
disbanded as soon as possible. As long as they exist,
democracy in this country is threatened. And if they
aren't defeated soon, this nation will soon become a
dictatorship.

"That is why I formed the Brotherhood, Jack. I
love this country, and I won't sit on my ass while it's
threatened. When I was drafted into the Army, I
swore to defend this great nation of ours from all
enemies foreign and domestic. As far as I'm concerned, that oath is still binding on me.

"Now," Grey said, dropping the preaching tone,
"down to the business at hand. I need someone to
pick up a shipment that's waiting for us in Seattle."

"What kind of shipment?"

Grey looked at him for a moment. "Heavy weapons."

When Bolan didn't respond, Grey continued.
"While you saw that we're pretty well equipped with
small arms, we don't have much in the line of heavy
weapons—antitank, mortars and that sort of thing.
This is the first of several loads we have coming, and
I want to get them out to the units as soon as possible."

"If you don't mind my asking, where are you getting weapons like that?"

"Since you're one of us now, I'll answer that question. But I want to caution you about asking too many questions. Curiosity isn't a valued trait around here unless it directly applies to the mission at hand."

Bolan understood that; it was right out of the insurgency manual. The less you knew, the less you could reveal if you were captured.

Grey stood and turned to look out the window of the office. "We have friends, foreign allies actually, in the battle that's coming. They're helping us get weapons and equipment that are impossible for us to obtain any other way. I had my concerns about foreigners getting involved at first, but I came to see that it was shortsighted of us to refuse help from anywhere it was offered."

He turned back to Bolan. "You'll be picking up a shipment of RPG rocket launchers and ammunition from them. As you know, the RPG is one of the best all-purpose weapons in the world, and they'll go along to protect us from the armored vehicles the Feds are using now."

"When do I leave?" Bolan asked.

"Tomorrow morning," Grey replied. "A man will come by the fuel yard and pick you up."

"I'll be ready."

"And don't take any firearms with you. The truck's main shipment is legitimate, so there should be no problems."

Dilbert, Idaho

THE TRIP to Seattle was completely uneventful, but it gave Bolan a better idea of how extensive the Brotherhood's network was. In Seattle, the tractor-trailer rig simply pulled up to a warehouse loading dock. Crates marked with customs clearance stamps were quickly loaded, and they drove away. When the semi pulled into Dilbert the next day, certain crates were off-loaded into one of Grey's warehouses, and the truck drove off again with the rest of its cargo manifested for Montana.

It was clean, it was simple and Bolan wondered how many more such deliveries had been made to other communities like Dilbert. It wouldn't take many semi loads like that to outfit a sizable force.

He didn't have a clue as to why the Feds hadn't caught on to the delivery system yet. From the location of the warehouse they had loaded from, the weapons had to be coming in by ship and they should have been detected during the customs inspections. The obvious reason they hadn't involved money changing hands, which was the same reason why drug shipments routinely entered the country.

Knowing Brognola the way he did, Bolan was confident that as soon as the Justice Department Fed learned about the pipeline, it would be cut off. So would the careers of the Customs people who were allowing the weapons to get through. But that still left who knew how many heavy weapons in the hands of the militias.

Dilbert, Idaho

BOLTON GREY WAS on hand to receive the shipment, and as soon as the driver was gone, the two men opened the first of the crates to check the weapons inside.

Bolan immediately saw that these rocket launchers were RPG-7s, the improved version of the older Russian designed RPG-2 launchers that had caused the American Army so much trouble in Vietnam. Since then, both versions of the RPG had seen service on almost every battlefield the world over, particularly in the hands of irregular and Third World forces.

The 85 mm antitank rocket it fired wasn't guided to the target in any way. But the launcher was light, it was accurate, it was easy to use and the warhead it fired was powerful for its size. It was the perfect anti-armor, antipersonnel and antibunker weapon for insurgent operations. In a pinch, it could even be used as short-range artillery.

One smaller crate contained the sight optics for the launchers and infrared night scopes. The rocket ammunition was packed six rounds to a crate, and every other crate had a six-pack canvas ammo carrier packed with the rockets.

"These look like the Red Chinese RPGs I saw in Nam," Bolan commented when he saw the first launcher.

"They're from China," Grey confirmed. "They're cheaper than getting them from Eastern Europe, and they're fresh. A lot of the European stuff has been sitting in leaking warehouses for the past ten years and has a high misfire rate. If we ever have to use these things, they'll work.

"They're all here," Grey announced after each crate had been opened and inventoried. "Now we need to get them out to the Brotherhood units. I want you to set aside four launchers and a dozen rockets apiece for the Dilbert unit, and the rest will go out."

"How do we do that?"

"I'll need you for that again," Grey said. "I'll have you make some drum-fuel deliveries and drop off some of the crates, as well."

That was about as good a clandestine delivery system as Bolan had ever encountered. Farmers and small businessmen always needed fuel, and no one would take notice of a fuel-delivery truck making its appointed rounds.

BOLAN WASN'T the only one in Dilbert who knew that the weapons shipment had come in. Samantha Whiting had been on the lookout for it, as well. She had picked up hints of something big coming in a long time ago and had patiently waited for it to arrive, as she had patiently waited all of these years since her sister's death.

She had still been at home when her sister, Kate, went away to school and fell in love with the handsome Juan Carlos Menendez. She had witnessed Bolton Grey's rage when Kate came home for Christmas and told him that she wanted to break off their engagement because she had fallen in love with another man. Grey stormed out of the Whiting home that night, swearing that she would live to regret her foolish decision.

It had been Grey, though, who had brought the news of Kate's death to the house the morning her body had been found under a tree on the Boise campus. He said that he had been having coffee with the town sheriff when the call came in and volunteered to bring the message.

He had been properly shocked, as had they all been, but he had stepped right up to help the family. He had driven them to Boise in his new Cadillac and had arranged for them to be met by a representative of the chief of police's office. After the body had been identified, he had arranged for Kate to be brought back to the funeral home in Dilbert. At the funeral, he had been on hand to take care of the details that the family had forgotten in their grief.

Long after the funeral, when Sam had time to think over the events of that sad weekend, she began to wonder why Bolton had been so solicitous of her family. For a man who had been so angry at being spurned, he had more than gone out of his way to help them.

Her suspicions had first been raised when she had learned that the man Kate had gone out to see that evening hadn't been her boyfriend, Juan Carlos. According to Kate's dorm roommate, she had simply said that she had to take care of some old business and wouldn't be long. That was the last anyone had spoken to her, except, of course, for her killer.

Also Juan Carlos's disappearance at the same time had always been suspect to Samantha. She had never believed that he had killed her sister. He had been from a well-to-do family and had been a gentleman of the old school. Even figuring in the legendary Latin temperament, something like that had simply not been in his makeup. Also he, too, had received a mysterious phone call that night before leaving his dorm room never to return.

She didn't know exactly when she had decided that Bolton Grey had killed her sister and Juan Carlos, but something he had said right before she left for Seattle had burned into her brain. "Make sure that you don't end up like Kate," he had said. "I don't want to have to bury you, too."

She had been so anxious to leave Dilbert that she had let the remark pass then. But when her marriage failed, her father fell ill and she came back to Dilbert, she remembered what he had said and started wondering. When she returned, Grey had tried to court her at first. But after making it abundantly clear that she wasn't at all interested in him, he backed off. He had, however, seen that she got a job at a living wage working for him.

Since then, she had seen Bolton go from being a wealthy man in the community to being the virtual owner of the town and most of the surrounding county. She had also watched him create his own private army, the Brotherhood of Patriots. At first it had been composed of men like him, prosperous property owners who met in the late seventies to discuss local politics. By the late eighties, the group had grown to two dozen or so men who spent a lot of time practicing marksmanship with military-style weapons.

She hadn't seen the men display any of the traditional trappings of the military. They hadn't worn uniforms, nor had they designed an identifying insignia or called each other by military titles. But Bolton Grey had clearly been the man in charge of what could be called an impromptu gun club.

By the early nineties, however, the organization seemingly ceased to exist. She knew, however, that it hadn't disbanded. It had simply gone underground. This occurred about the time that the new gun-control laws went into effect and the federal agencies started cracking down hard on violators.

Her job in the bar was the perfect place to pick up bits and pieces of conversations and put them together. It didn't take long for her to realize that Bolton's old gun club had become a private army. Since that realization, she had quietly gathered as much information as she could about the Brotherhood's activities. She didn't know what she was going to do with it, but she had it if she ever needed it.

BY THE TIME Bolan had finished making the RPG deliveries, he had a much better grip on the extent of Bolton Grey's Brotherhood of Patriots, but his mission in Dilbert wasn't completed. There were still key elements to the Brotherhood's operation that he didn't know.

The main thing he hadn't uncovered was the reason he'd been sent there in the first place. He had seen no signs of foreign advisers to any of the groups. Beyond Grey's one reference to foreigners helping him obtain weapons, there was nothing he could report. Also he still didn't know how the operation was being financed.

The shipment of RPGs he had escorted had cost someone tens of thousands of dollars. Grey was wealthy, but it was mostly rural wealth—land, equipment and properties. Bolan didn't think that he had the kind of liquid assets that would allow him to spend that kind of money. Plus moving legitimate funds on that scale would involve banks, and banks were required to keep records of large transactions as part of the war against drug trafficking. This weapons trafficking had to be set up like a drug running operation where the payments were always made in cash. The question was, where was the cash coming from?

Hal Brognola had said that the Cali cartel was reportedly involved in this operation. If that was true, Grey would be paying them up front. The cartel wasn't known for extending credit. But, he could also be transshipping drugs for them in exchange for the weapons.

Bolan had learned much of what was going down. But he still didn't have enough to report. He would remain undercover until he did.

CHAPTER TWELVE

Boise, Idaho

Dan Butterfield felt like a character in a Sunday-school Bible story. The hand of God had suddenly appeared and saved him from destruction, both personal and professional. For some obscure reason known only to the director, and maybe the National Security Council, he hadn't been put on the rack in front of Congress for the screwup in Lewiston. In fact he had received a promotion for it.

Even so, he knew he wasn't out of the woods yet and probably wouldn't be until he was dead and buried. Nonetheless, Butterfield was now the West Coast man in charge of cracking the militia case, as it was being called within the Bureau. And even with the bank robberies and the death of the salesman in the van in Lewiston, the true nature of the FBI's investigation hadn't been leaked to the press. Yet.

The only thing surer than death or taxes was the fact that the details of this highly classified operation would get out sooner or later. And when the media did get a hold of the rumors, it would hit the fan. The plan to curb the militias would be used against the Bureau as yet another example of federal "thugs" trampling the people's rights under their "jack boots."

Why was it that the public couldn't understand that the Bureau was simply trying to protect them from criminal crazies who were armed to the teeth? There was a big difference between citizens owning shotguns for hunting and military assault rifles. Back when the Constitution had been written, there hadn't been a lot of difference between hunting and military weapons. In fact eighteenth-century hunting weapons had been more accurate than their military counterparts. That wasn't the case these days.

Butterfield vowed that no one under his command was going to make a move unless it was by-the-book. When they ran these bastards to ground, he would starve them out before he risked the life of a single one of his agents. Let them hole up somewhere, and they could rot for the next five years as far as he was concerned. There would be no John Wayne charges or Patton-style tank attacks as long as he was in charge of the operation. And the media would be kept as far away as possible, as well.

Let them scream about their so-called First Amendment rights all they liked. He had authority from the director to keep them out of the line of fire for their "own protection." As far as he was concerned, that meant that they would be kept out of TV-camera range at all times. And that included the helicopters too. The director had had a little chat with the head of the FAA, and he would be able to close airspace when ever he felt he needed to.

Butterfield had everything in place he needed to bring this operation to a successful conclusion. All he needed now was to find the bastards. But that wasn't going well at all.

He pushed the intercom buzzer on his desk phone. "Get Barker in here," he growled.

Special Agent Alvin Barker, the man who was working the informants, was at his door in seconds. "You wanted to see me, sir?"

"What in the hell is happening with your informants?"

"Not a lot," Barker admitted. The one thing he knew about Butterfield was that the man didn't like being lied to. If you didn't have anything, you'd better tell him up front. If you fudged and he found out later, you were in deep trouble. "We have them out there, but they're not finding out what we need to know."

"Why not?"

Barker paused, then plunged right in. "I think that we're on a wild-goose chase, sir. I don't have any indication that there are foreigners involved with the militias in this area at all. And I'm not too sure that there are any militias here, either. We have people in every gun club, every wacko separatist church, every biker gang and even in the state Republican Party, and we have dick so far."

Butterfield looked pained. "You have people in the Republican Party?"

"Not paid informers," Barker said, quickly calming his fears. "I know better than that. We just have 'friends' there."

"Not anymore you don't," Butterfield snapped. "And I hope to hell that you haven't been recording anything you've gotten from those people."

"Not officially, no."

Butterfield took a deep breath. "We do not have FBI informers in political parties, not even the anarchist party. Never have and never will. Got that?"

"Yes, sir."

"And as far as your people not coming up with anything because there's nothing to come up with, that's bullshit. They're out there. We have hard evidence on that, and I want you to find them for me. Got that?"

"Yes, sir."

"Good." Butterfield leaned forward. "You might think Idaho is the asshole of the lower forty-eight, but always keep in mind that there are worse assignments in this Bureau. I understand that there's an opening in Kodiak, Alaska. They need someone to track down drug-running sled dogs."

"Yes, sir."

When the door closed behind the departing agent, Butterfield took the top piece of paper from his desk and reached for the phone. Headquarters wanted to know why his gasoline usage was so high. He was going to recommend that someone in Washington buy a map of the United States and take a look at the northwestern section. Towns that were only fifty miles apart were considered to be suburbs of one another out here. It took a lot of gas to go from point A to point B.

SPECIAL AGENT Alvin Barker had been perusing the L.L. Bean mail-order catalogue looking for cold-weather clothing when he got a call from one of his informers. Willie Lotter, a minor drug dealer who protected himself by working for the FBI, claimed to have developed a lead on a local militiaman.

"You know," Barker said when they met at a Denny's restaurant on the outskirts of Moscow, "if you're jacking me around on this, I'll jerk your ass in on a parole violation so fast that your eyes will water."

"No, I swear," Lotter protested. "This is no bullshit. I saw the guns myself. He's got at least two AKs, and he was working on one of them in his shop. He's got that book, you know, the one they sell at the gun shows that tells you how to convert it to firing full automatic. He's also got a Nazi flag, and he's always bitching about all the damned 'wetbacks.'"

"But does he belong to a militia?"

"I guess." Lotter shrugged. "He's got camouflage uniforms and is always talking about how he'll be able to survive with just a knife and a canteen when everything goes to hell.''

"I need to know if he meets with other men for target practice or that sort of thing.''

"Sure." Lotter brightened. All he wanted was to get this federal agent out of his life, and if it meant doing a number on old Bob Green, it was no skin off of his nose. Green was a pain, and as soon as this was over, Lotter was heading south for L.A. anyway. "There's guys at his house all the time. They sit around, drink beer and then shoot at the cans.''

Barker had never liked this particular snitch, but none of the Bureau's informants were sterling citizens or they wouldn't be working for the FBI. But he had to give this information to Butterfield or risk freezing to death north of the Yukon.

"I'll take this to my boss and we'll check it out.''

"When do I get paid?''

"Like I told you before, you only get paid if the information pans out.''

"But I got to make the rent, man.''

"Tough," Barker said, sneering. "Try working for a living.''

LOTTER FINISHED his cup of coffee alone after the FBI man left. He had a small pot deal going down a little later, then he'd drop by Green's place and plant the AK full-auto conversion book he'd picked up a couple of weeks earlier. He'd wanted to convert his own AK, but hadn't been able to make heads or tails of the damned book, so he might as well get some use out of it. The book had cost him thirteen bucks, and he wasn't about to waste the money. Not when he needed every dollar he could scrape up to move to California.

Out in the parking lot, Lotter got into his pickup and headed for his drug buy. The kid only needed enough grass to get him and his cheerleader girlfriend stoned, but it would be enough cash for him to get a case of beer to take out to Bob's place and still have enough to live for the next week. If, that was, his mother didn't get after him again about buying food.

When he really thought about it, getting the hell away from his old lady had a lot more to do with his wanting to move to California than being a snitch did. In fact he rather liked working for the FBI. Barker treated him like shit most of the time, but as soon as Bob went down, he'd show more respect.

He laughed out loud when he pictured the look Bob would have on his face when the FBI surrounded his house and told him to come out with his hands up.

And since all Barker seemed to want to know about were those people who ran around in camouflage and had what the Fed called assault weapons in their closets, he could come up with even more names for him. There were some other assholes who had pissed him off that he could turn over to the Feds. He might have to sell a couple of them an AK, but that was okay because he still had the three rifles he had ripped off from that gun-show guy. He could sell two of them and still have one for himself.

"WHAT DO YOU HAVE on the suspect?" Butterfield asked when Barker brought his report in. "What's his name?"

"Bob Green," Barker replied. "He's got a rap sheet, but nothing too serious. Several DUIs, an assault or two, unauthorized use of a motor vehicle and possession of less than an ounce."

He looked up from the printout. "Just your average redneck, white-trash rap sheet. Never did any serious time."

"Do you think your information is good?"

"It's the first thing I've gotten from this informant," Barker said, "so I don't have a track record on him. But he mentioned specific things that might show a profile. Our man's got cammies, he's got a Nazi flag, he's got that full-auto book on the AK and he has a couple of AKs to go with it."

"Has your snitch ever seen this guy fire it on full-auto?"

"No, but he saw him working on it."

Butterfield thought for a long moment. "Okay," he said. "I'll declare it probable cause and start working on the warrant request and see if I can get a wiretap. Is there any chance of you getting your boy to wear a wire and have a long talk with this guy?"

Barker shrugged. "I can ask him."

"Lean on him. I want to have this cold, and I don't

want anyone screaming entrapment on this one. I need someone we can sweat and this is the first chance we've had.''

''I'll see what I can do.''

''Don't see, do!''

''Yes, sir.''

It only took a day for Butterfield to run everything through Washington and the regional federal judge. When he was done, he had the warrant, he had the phone-tap authorization and Barker had talked his snitch into wearing a wire. He was a little surprised at how fast everything had been approved, but this was a hot project and the director was tired of not making any headway.

''WHY THE HELL are you yelling?'' Bob Green asked Willie Lotter. ''I'm not deaf, so hold it down a little.''

''Sorry, old buddy. The Fed had told Lotter several times that the wire would work if he talked normally. But he didn't know how that small microphone buried under his shirt and the bulletproof vest could pick up the sound of his voice. Still he lowered his voice when he offered Green another beer.

Green had not been particularly pleased when Lotter showed up on his front porch, but he'd been carrying a full case and the man liked his beer.

''When are you going to take me to one of your militia meetings, anyway?'' Lotter asked out of the blue.

Green looked at the small-time dealer like he had

two heads. "Militia, what militia, Willie? Who the hell ever told you that I was in a militia?"

Lotter shrugged. "You know, I just figured that a guy like you would be in a militia. You know, you like guns and all that stuff."

"Jesus!" Green shook his head. "You've been smoking too much of that loco weed you sell, man. A guy would have to be out of his mind to be in a militia right now. After that Oklahoma City thing, every Fed and his brother are chasing those guys down. Plus, except for having to pay too much taxes to dickheads who don't want to work, I don't have any bitch with the Feds as long as they leave me alone. I've got my pension from the power company, and I don't need anything from Washington."

"But you're always talking about the Mexicans."

"Okay, I don't like Mexicans. So what? It's a free country, and I don't have to like the bastards. I just want them to get out of Idaho and go back to Mexico, big deal."

Lotter was getting nowhere fast with this exercise and started to panic. If he didn't get something on tape, this whole thing would blow apart and Barker would be all over him. The high-school kid he had sold the dope to had gotten caught having sex his girlfriend and had blamed it on the pot he'd smoked. To keep the girl's father from tearing him apart, he'd gladly told him where he'd gotten it. The Fed had found out about it and was threatening to pull him for a parole violation if he didn't produce.

Lotter picked up the AK he had brought and cracked the bolt. "Like I said when I called, can you convert this thing for me so it'll fire like a machine gun?"

Green shook his head. "I don't do that shit, man, I already told you that. It's worth ten years of your life to get caught with a full-auto and no class-three license."

"What's a class three?"

"It's a full-auto weapon, and they aren't legal unless you have a special license from the Feds. I can't get one because I've got an assault charge on my rap sheet."

"But you know how to do it, right?"

"Any idiot can go to a gun show, buy a book and do it, right. But I told you, man, I don't mess with that shit. It's just not worth it."

Seeing his future going down the drain, Lotter played his trump card. Palming a 7.62 mm AK round he had in his pocket, he slipped it in the breech of the rifle and snapped the bolt shut.

"That's too bad," he said, turning to the window behind him. "I was looking forward to being able to rock and roll with this thing."

Aiming the AK out the window, he pulled the trigger.

CHAPTER THIRTEEN

Special Agent Alvin Barker sat in the FBI command-and-control van that had been parked well out of sight of Bob Green's house. This wasn't going down the way Lotter had claimed it would. So far, all he had on tape was a citizen disavowing anything to do with illegal activities. He was about to call the whole thing off when he heard the shot through Lotter's wire.

"Gunshots!" he warned the FBI tactical team surrounding the house over the radio link.

"I have a target in sight!" one of the tac-team marksmen shouted over the radio. "The subject is struggling with the informer."

"Fire," Barker snapped.

The heavy barrel .308 Remington M-700 rifle in the hands of the marksman barked once, and the 168-grain full-metal-jacket slug crossed the three hundred yards to the window at over 2500 feet per second. The glass shattered as the bullet struck home.

"Target down," the marksman's spotter reported.

"Go! Go! Go!" Barker sent the tac squads in. Checking to make sure that the 9 mm Glock pistol was in his holster, he opened the rear door of the van and jumped into the waiting Jeep. The best way he knew to get Butterfield off his ass was to be in on the bust.

When the FBI tac team stormed the house, Bob Green was down with a .308 bullet hole in his chest. The marksman had been aiming for his heart, but shooting through glass was always tricky, so he had missed his aiming point by some six inches. But the heavy, full-metal-jacket slug had done its job. Green was bleeding profusely and was unconscious.

"Why did he fire at us?" Barker asked. "It didn't sound like he knew we were out there."

"Oh. He didn't shoot, I did."

Barker stopped cold. "Green didn't fire that round?"

"Nope," Lotter said proudly. "I did. I thought that it would piss him off and give you guys a chance to take him out."

The FBI man just stared at him while visions of Arctic landscape flashed past his eyes.

"I did good, didn't I?" Lotter whined. "It worked, didn't it?"

"Shut up!" Barker snapped as his eyes were dragged back to the paramedics working over Green's body. "And get the fuck out of here!"

Lotter left, but on the way out he slipped the AK full-auto conversion book from his jacket pocket and laid it on Green's coffee table. He told the Fed he had seen the book, and he had to make good on it.

EVEN THOUGH Special Agent Barker had had an ambulance standing by, Bob Green died on the way to the hospital. The paramedics tried, but it would have taken a trauma-room team to save him.

Dan Butterfield had received a preliminary report on the raid over the radio and was waiting for more when Barker choppered in to give him the wrap-up.

"Green had two semiauto AKs," Barker said, reading from his notepad.

"Which are perfectly legal," Butterfield reminded him.

"And he had the conversion book just like Willie said."

"Which is also perfectly legal—the First Amendment and all of that."

"And," Barker concluded, "that's the upside of the incident."

"The downside?"

"That's a little more complicated."

"It always is." Butterfield wasn't sure that he wanted to hear it. Only an act of God had saved his butt the last time, and he wasn't sure that the deity was going to be on duty for this one.

"Apparently," Barker said, "Green didn't fire that round at us. Willie did."

"I really didn't need to hear that," Butterfield replied.

"And," Barker continued, "neither one of Green's AKs had been converted to full-auto. Both of them, however, had had the magazine-feed ramps worked on so they'd feed better. That's always a problem with those Chinese AK copies. You usually don't have to do that to the Russian or East German ones, though.''

"Thank you, Mr. NRA," Butterfield said dryly. "I really needed to know that fascinating piece of technical trivia. And fixing that was probably what Willie saw him doing to the AKs."

Butterfield leaned back in his chair and looked out the window to the parking lot. A cordon of agents and state cops was holding several TV crews at the boundary of the federal property line, but he knew he'd be on the six-o'clock news anyway. Washington had authorized a press briefing, and he had been ordered to give it. This wasn't something he could slough off onto a subordinate, not this time.

"So—" Butterfield's eyes fixed on Barker "—before I let those assholes in to take a statement, let me make sure that I understand this. Your marksman killed a man who had done nothing wrong except for getting on a small-time drug dealer's shit list for some obscure reason, is that it?"

"More or less," Barker admitted. "But he was seen attacking the informant."

"Which was after this sterling citizen had popped off a round in his living room. Even a first-year law student, or a public defender for that matter, will be able to make a good wrongful-death case out of this. You humped the pooch on this one, Barker, and now I've got to go out there and try to make it go away."

"Can't we fry the informant on this one?" Barker tried one more time.

"And have to answer questions about why we were using a not-so-bright, small-time pusher as our main source of information on a major case? No fucking way. We're in deep enough as it is."

"But we use scum like that all the time."

"True," Butterfield agreed. "But we usually get better information than you got from Willie boy. If we get good information and pop the bad guys, it's okay to use scumbags as informants. Your man's information led us to killing a citizen who admittedly had a rap sheet, but who looks to have been clean this time."

"But he attacked our informant."

"We've been over that." Butterfield was rapidly losing patience.

"Okay." Barker surrendered. "Tell them that I fucked up and let them hang me."

"I can't do that, either." Butterfield shook his head. "Washington won't let me. But you can bet your sweet ass I'd do it in a New York minute if I could."

Barker felt a thousand pounds lighter now that he wasn't going to go down for this. "So, what's the party line?"

"We're going to play up the weapons-conversion angle. Green had a machine shop out back, he had the book and he had two AKs. He started a fight, and our marksman feared for the informant's life."

"That ought to work."

"It had better."

"And," Butterfield said as he stood, "you'd better look into putting your boy somewhere that the locals can't get their hands on him."

"The program?"

Butterfield nodded. Usually the Federal Witness Protection Program was used for big-time hoods, men who had told all to stay alive. Using that level of protection for a man who had either lied or who had invented information was a complete waste of the tax-payer's money. But to keep this from unraveling, it had to be done. If for no other reason than to keep Butterfield's career alive, this had to be declared a righteous shooting.

THE NEWS CONFERENCE went as well as could be expected. Since the deceased hadn't been a Rotary Club member and had an impressive rap sheet, no one really cared if he lived or died. The FBI side of the incident was plausible, and no one questioned the story.

Willie Lotter, the drug dealer turned federal snitch, however, never made it out of town, either to L.A. or into the Witness Protection Program.

Two days after Green's death, he was found tied to a fence post and gunned down firing-squad style. Again, though, no one seemed to mind that Lotter was no longer polluting the earth. Drug dealers, even small-time pushers, weren't very popular in Moscow, Idaho.

"I told you that Willie's information wasn't all bullshit," Barker triumphantly said as Dan Butterfield read through the preliminary report of the death of their ex-informant. "He was executed military style. Green had to have had connections with a militia unit, and they popped Willie in retaliation."

"I have to admit that it looks that way," Butterfield said, relieved to have this confirmation of his decision to seek probable cause for the raid. "This may come in handy later."

He looked up at Barker. "Too bad about your snitch. He might have had more information for us."

"It's good riddance actually," Barker admitted. "The bastard was pushing to high-school kids."

"You have a point."

DAN BUTTERFIELD WASN'T the only one who made a connection between Lotter's death and the militias. A young investigative reporter from the *Seattle Intelligencer* was working eastern Washington and northern Idaho trying to put together an exposé showing that in the wake of the Oklahoma City bombing, the threat of armed militias hadn't diminished. If anything, what little information he had been able to get indicated that the movement was growing. Lotter's execution-style death only confirmed his suspicions.

Brad Goldblum wanted more information to confirm what he suspected before he started writing. But he wasn't having an easy time of it. He wasn't enjoying himself in Idaho, and he didn't particularly care who knew it. It was impossible to get a decent cup of coffee anywhere, and the closest bagel was back home in Seattle. On top of that, he hadn't even seen the word *vegetarian* on a menu since he left Spokane. These people were cultural barbarians, and they ate like animals. When he got home, he'd have to check into a cholesterol clinic to get his blood chemistry back under control.

But it looked like the time he had spent in this cultural outback was finally paying off. He felt like a war correspondent in Bosnia, with danger lurking around every corner. And as far as he was concerned, there was a war going on here, a war against everything that he thought was good in America.

This wasn't a way of life that he would have chosen. People drove around with rifles and shotguns openly displayed in the rear windows of their pickup trucks. Hunting was considered to be some kind of sacrament instead of being the slaughter of helpless animals. Every town, no matter how small, had at least one gun store. Nearly everyone he talked to owned more than one gun; some owned dozens. This wasn't the America he knew, and it shocked him.

The worst for a man with his beliefs, though, were the gun shows. The first gun show Goldblum went to stunned him. Never in his life had he ever seen anything like it. There had been everything from miniature pistols to antitank guns for sale, and the place had been so crowded that there had been a fifteen-minute wait just to get in the door. Once inside, he had been amazed to see all of the people openly carrying guns on their hips or slung over their shoulders. Even some of the women had been walking around armed.

The whole concept of unregulated flea markets openly selling weapons of every description frightened him, but he kept going to them. The reason he kept going back was the number of tables that were peddling a so-called political agenda. There was everything from the infamous NRA to groups wanting to eliminate immigration completely and to pull the United States out of the UN. It was a right-wing freak show the likes of which he had never even dreamed of.

Most of the people at the shows looked more or less normal for the so-called working classes of Middle America, but occasionally he saw businessmen in three-piece suits fingering handguns and well-dressed women buying ammunition.

Since his editor had told him to put it all on the expense account, Goldblum gave a small donation and signed up for every right-wing wacko publication he could find at the shows. He even joined the NRA. When he got home to Seattle and had the time to go through all this stuff, he was going to blow the lid off the gun threat to America. The Second Amendment be damned. There was no way that these kinds of people could be allowed to walk around with weapons.

The thing that puzzled him was that even though he had gone to almost a dozen shows in the past several weeks, he had yet to see anything about the militias at any of them. He had seen plenty of men in camouflage uniforms, but there was no way to tell who were militiamen and who were guys just after the look. He had come up with a theory that wearing camouflage got you in the door at a cut rate, but he couldn't bring himself to buy the gear and test it.

There were also no militia-recruitment booths or even handouts at any of the shows, either. All the TV exposés of the militia movement after the Oklahoma City tragedy had claimed that the militias were base-camped out of the gun shows, but he wasn't finding that to be the case.

Surely, if the militias were actively recruiting, gun shows would be the place to do it. That they weren't only told Goldblum that the militia problem was worse than it had appeared at first. If the militias were as law-abiding and as innocent as they claimed, why weren't they there with the rest of the right-wing lunatic fringe selling their wares? That they weren't only told him that they were deeply underground, and that was a danger sign.

And now that an FBI informant had been gunned down, it was time to quit scouting gun shows and investigate that.

BOB GREEN'S DEATH hadn't gone unnoticed by the Brotherhood, either. Green hadn't been a member, but he had provided a useful service to certain select members. The reason that Willie Lotter had had to plant the AK-conversion book on Green was that the amateur gunsmith had had no need for such a book. He could convert a semiauto AK or a Colt AR-15 to full automatic in his sleep. Unknown to Lotter, his machine shop was perfect for doing the work, as well as other general machine tool jobs. Had this been known, the FBI would have trumpeted the operation instead of playing it low-key.

Had the Brotherhood known that the FBI didn't have proof of Green's illegal gunsmithing, the Patriots might have let Willie the snitch live. But as far as they were concerned, the Feds had struck down one of their brothers, and that couldn't remain unanswered. A good man had died, and there was a blood price to pay.

Willie the snitch had been the first to pay the price, but he wouldn't be the last.

CHAPTER FOURTEEN

Dilbert, Idaho

When Bolan saw Bolton Grey drive up to the fuel-yard office at closing time, he could see that the businessman had something more than the day's gas receipts on his mind. He looked worried and angry at the same time. Bolan hoped that it was militia business that had him concerned, not girlfriend problems. He was tired of pumping gas and wanted to get on with the action.

"Is something wrong, Bolton?" he asked as the businessman stepped out of his car.

"Nothing's wrong, Jack, but I need to talk to you."

"Sure."

"Inside."

As soon as Bolan followed Grey into the office, the businessman got right to the point. "I've got something going down, and I'd like your help on it."

"Sure thing," Bolan answered. "What is it?"

"The FBI killed one of the Brotherhood on a raid. You might have read about it in the papers."

"That guy over in Moscow?"

Grey nodded. "Yeah, Bob Green. We used him as a gunsmith, and some drug-dealer scumbag fingered him to the Feds. And even though Bob was real careful not to have anything illegal at his place, he was killed anyway."

He shook his head in disgust. "He was shot by a sniper in his own living room, and he wasn't even threatening the Feds. Shit, he didn't even know they were out there until they opened up on him."

"You want me to help you deal with the snitch?" Bolan ventured.

"No," Grey replied. "That part of it's already been taken care of. You'll be reading about his sorry ass in the paper tomorrow."

"What's the mission, then?"

Grey locked eyes with him. "We want to send the Feds a message that they've gone too far. We're going to hit their regional office in Boise. A couple of the Brotherhood units are going in together on this to make sure that they get the word."

"Have you thought how they're going to react to taking a lot of casualties?"

"The casualties will be kept to a minimum," Grey reassured him. "We're planning to hit them at night, and we won't target the radioroom or the duty officer, and they're the only two men on duty at night. But, yes, I do expect them to react to it. I want them to think twice before they decide to gun down another man in his own home."

"Isn't that a bit risky? I mean taking them on on their own ground. That's going to really cause a stir up on Capitol Hill."

"Yes, we're taking a risk. But, as Patriots, we can't stand by and allow this sort of thing to happen without doing something about it. A citizen has been wrongly killed, a patriot, and he must be avenged. And if we do cause a stir, maybe we won't have to wait for two or three years until some congressman gets tired of dicking his secretary and decides to look into it."

"What do you need me to do?"

"You're an experienced man, a combat veteran, and I want you on one of my assault teams."

"How're we going to do it?" Bolan asked, being careful to say "we."

"Remember that shipment of RPGs you picked up?" Grey replied. "We have enough ammunition now that we can spare a dozen rounds for a stand-off attack. We won't have to get any closer than three or four hundred yards to blow that place apart. We have a lineman who's going to cut their phone lines right before we hit, so they won't be able to call for help. Then we're going to rocket the building, the motor pool and the helicopter landing pad. We should be able to take out the choppers, as well as enough vehicles to keep them from following us."

"How many men are you taking?"

"We're only going to use ten men. You, me, Dick Jones, the guy who runs the feed store, and his partner, Jim Howard, from our unit. The other six will be from other Brotherhood units. We'll meet in Boise, hit them and then disappear."

"When's it going down?"

"Tomorrow night," Grey said. "We'll drive there tomorrow and I'll talk to one of my bankers and the oil company to give us a reason for being in town. Then we'll recon the area, finalize the plan and hit them around midnight. We'll be back here by morning with no one being the wiser."

"It sounds good." Bolan nodded. "You can count me in."

"I knew I could." Grey smiled. "You're that kind of man. I'll be by to get you tomorrow at seven."

"I'll be ready."

Bolan had wanted to get on with the investigation, and this was as good a way as any. So far, while he had evidence of weapons violations, the Brotherhood hadn't crossed the line into overt criminal activity. If this went as planned, the militia situation was about to become a crisis.

SAMANTHA WHITING KNEW that something was up; she just wasn't sure what it was. She had seen Bolton Grey and several of his henchmen go into his office on the other side of the street, and they looked serious. She, too, had read the newspaper accounts about that gunsmith over in Moscow getting gunned down by the FBI, and everyone was talking about it in the bar. Most of the talk was the usual barroom, macho stuff, but some of Grey's soldier boys had been talking quietly in the corner and looking around to make sure that they weren't being overheard.

Anytime the Feds did something stupid on one of their raids, Grey and his men got antsy. But this time, the looks on their faces told her that something was going down. She only hoped that Vance had the brains to not get involved with whatever it was. There was no doubt in her mind that he was a honorable man, but she also knew that even honorable men did stupid things when they got together.

Maybe she was hoping for too much, but it would be nice if just once the man she was interested in did the right thing. It would be some kind of change. But she also knew that if Jack Vance had given his word to the Brotherhood, he would be true to it. Unfortunately he was an honorable man.

EARLY THE NEXT MORNING, Bolan dressed in the clothes he would wear on a normal trip to the big city. But he also rolled up a dark blue jacket, a knit cap and a pair of thin leather gloves to take along. Grey had said that their equipment and weapons would be waiting there for them, but he wanted to have his own gear available just in case.

When Bolton Grey showed up at the fuel yard in his Cadillac, Bolan was waiting for him. Dropping his bag behind the front seat, he got in and Grey drove off.

All the way to Boise, Grey kept up a steady commentary on the state of the country and the remedies that he felt were needed to bring it back to what he thought it should be. Bolan limited his part of the conversation to agreeing with Grey at the right places.

It was a long drive.

Boise, Idaho

AFTER GREY TOOK CARE of his legitimate business in Boise and established his alibi, he drove to the street closest to the FBI regional headquarters on the southern edge of town and parked where he had a good view of it. The compound sat all by itself in the middle of a field with good approaches from all sides. Apparently the land around it was also owned by the federal government, because there were no other buildings close to the cyclone-fenced enclosure. Sitting all by itself as it did, it was a perfect target.

"Where would you place the RPGs?" Grey asked as he looked at the main brick building with the flagpole and parking lot in front.

Bolan surveyed the area with an expert's eye. It was a simple tactical problem—get close enough to have good lines of sight to fire the rockets, but still be far enough away to have a good withdrawal route.

"I'd hit them from three different sites," he said, "but all on this side of the compound. You've got better routes out from here. And I'd do it in three volleys. Hit the main building first, the motor pool and chopper pad next and use the last volley to take care of anything you missed with the first two shots.''

"That makes sense," Grey said as he took notes and made a crude map of the layout. "And that's the way we'll do it tonight."

"Let's go get something to eat," he said as he hit the Cadillac's ignition switch. "We have several hours to kill before we meet up with the rest of the men."

AFTER DINNER, Grey and Bolan drove to an all-night supermarket on the edge of a new mall on the western side of town and parked close to the entrance of the lot. After locking the doors, the two men walked to a van parked a few yards away in the middle of a cluster of other parked cars.

Inside, Grey introduced Bolan to the other Patriots and assigned him to work with Dick Jones and Jim Howard, also from Dilbert. The men made little small talk as one of them opened two packed duffel bags and brought out night-black coveralls and webbing assault harnesses, ski masks and thin leather gloves.

Once the men changed into the coveralls and donned the harnesses, two footlockers were opened to issue the weapons and ammunition. Along with the RPG launchers, each team was taking two automatic AK-47s and full magazine pouches. They didn't expect any trouble, but they would be prepared if it came.

After Grey went over the attack plan several times

and pointed out the priority targets as Bolan had picked them that afternoon, he had the driver move out. A short drive later, he ordered the man to take the van in behind the buildings closest to the FBI compound to make a final recon of the area.

When there seemed to be no unusual activity from the compound, Grey pulled his ski mask down over his face. "Let's go."

The ten men got out and quickly formed up into their rocket teams. With Grey leading the way, his AK at the ready, they crossed the street to the fields surrounding the compound.

BOLAN MOVED like a shadow across the open field toward the lighted compound. The other two men in his assault team moved quietly, but not with the skill that the warrior showed.

Jones, the team leader, and Bolan carried the AKs while Howard cradled the RPG launcher in his arms. The area that had been chosen for their launch site was roughly four hundred yards from the main building. When they reached it, Jones and Bolan took up security positions to one side while Howard took the three RPG rockets from his backpack and prepared them for firing.

The RPG rounds came packed separately from their prop charges. To make the rocket ready to fire, a metal end cap had to be taken off the rocket and the prop charge screwed in its place. After that, the rocket was loaded into the front of the launcher, the hammer thumbed down and the weapon was ready to fire.

The simplicity of the RPG was what made it such a good weapon on battlefields all over the world. There were no delicate electronic circuits to short out if the launcher was knocked around and no batteries to fail at the wrong time. It was as easy to use as a single-shot rifle—just fix the charge on the rocket, stuff it down the front and shoot.

"Make sure that all the trash is picked up," Jones whispered after all the prop charges had been screwed onto the backs of the rockets. "We don't want them to find anything here to trace to us."

"I'll get that," Bolan replied.

Opening his assault pack, he picked up the plastic prop charge tubes, the paper packing material, the rocket end caps and stuffed them inside. One of the metal end caps, however, he slipped into the side pocket of his coveralls.

"Ready!" Jones whispered as he watched the digital numbers clock off on his lighted watch dial. "Fire!"

Howard pulled the trigger, and the RPG fired. The prop charge in the end of the rocket ignited with a whoosh, sending the 85 mm rocket downrange. A hundred yards out of the tube, the main rocket motor cut in and sent the round on to its target.

The night was shattered by the flash and thundering detonation of the first volley of rockets. Howard's RPG had been aimed at the second story of the side of the building, and when the smoke of the detonation cleared, they could see that it had blasted out a huge hole.

Howard excitedly loaded the next rocket into the front of the launcher, picked his target and waited for Jones's order to fire again. "Fire!"

As had been planned, the second volley of three rockets was aimed at the motor pool and chopper pad area. The missiles all hit their targets, and the antitank shaped-charge warheads devastated the soft-skin vehicles and aircraft. A Bell JetRanger helicopter exploded in a ball of flame when an RPG hit its full fuel tank. The flames instantly spread to the chopper next to it and engulfed it, as well.

The third volley was free fire. Howard picked out a five-hundred-gallon tank at the far end of the motor pool that looked like it might contain fuel. The flash of the rocket warhead detonating against the side of the tank was lost in the resulting blinding flash as the gasoline inside exploded. The blast sent a broiling fireball high into the sky that rained fire to the ground.

"That's it," Jones yelled over the sound of exploding fuel tanks. "Pull back to the van."

Bolan had the drag position and, as he quickly walked away, he slipped the rocket end cap out of his pocket and let it fall to the ground. If the FBI investigators weren't totally blind, they'd find it in the morning, and it should give them a clue as to what had happened here. It wasn't much, but it was the best he could do.

As the militiamen drove away in the van, they quickly stripped off their night suits and assault harnesses and stuffed them back in the duffel bags. The weapons went into two footlockers that would be transferred into the private cars the militiamen had used to get to Boise when the stolen van was abandoned at the supermarket.

When they stepped out of the van in the supermarket's parking lot, they were in their civilian clothes again and walked to their cars as if they didn't have a care in the world. As they drove away, they could see the flashing lights of the fire trucks, police cars and emergency vehicles heading toward the burning FBI compound.

BOLTON GREY HAD LITTLE to say to his passenger on the long trip back to Dilbert. Bolan had gotten used to getting a lecture on the dangers to freedom and democracy every time he was around the man, and he was a bit surprised at the silence. Maybe Grey was going through a postcombat depression caused by coming down from the adrenaline high. Or maybe he was having second thoughts about having declared war against the federal government.

Even if he was, it was too late to turn back now. As Caesar had said, the die was cast.

Normally Bolan would bail out of the investigation at this point. His undercover work had given him enough information to break up the Brotherhood and put a couple dozen people behind bars for various violations and crimes. Usually that would be enough to eliminate a threat like this. But putting Grey and his people in jail wouldn't put an end to it this time. There were hundreds if not thousands more like them all over America, and he still didn't have a handle on the foreigners who had supplied the weapons and, he felt sure, the idea for the attack.

But he didn't think he would have to wait much longer now. The FBI would have to respond to the attack on its headquarters, and that would put pressure on the militia to answer. It was a classic escalation scenario, and when things got hot enough for the Brotherhood, he felt certain that the mysterious foreigners would surface. Brognola would just have to wait a little longer.

CHAPTER FIFTEEN

FBI Special Agent in Charge Dan Butterfield looked around in shock at the ruins of what had been a perfectly good regional FBI office when he had left work the evening before. Less than twelve hours later, the place was smoldering wreckage.

The holes in the main office building didn't look as spectacular as the destruction of the motor pool, but the damage they had done to the interior was massive. The sprinkler system had put the fires out, but the deluge of water had only added to the damage. It would take weeks just to put the water-soaked files back in order.

No one had had any idea that the militias were armed with this kind of weaponry. To make it even worse, no one had had any intelligence indicating that they had finally decided to start an open war with the federal government. This time, at least, the devastation wasn't the result of an FBI operation gone bad, and he didn't have to fear losing his job. He knew, however, that he was in for a rough time. Even though he wouldn't be blamed for this mess, the pressure would be on him like white on rice, and the chance of his ending his career here was still strong.

BRAD GOLDBLUM WAS shocked at the destruction at the FBI compound, and he couldn't believe that no one had been killed in the attack. Two of the night crew had been slightly injured.

The holes the RPGs had blasted through the side of the main brick building were beyond his comprehension; they were big enough to drive a small car through. He didn't think that anyone except the military had weapons that could cause that much damage to a solid structure. The story he would write about this made his exposé of the gun-show culture look like a high-school book report. This was the story that would bring him fame, not a piece about rednecks swaggering around clutching their prized rifles, pistols and shotguns to their beer bellies.

The entire compound had been cordoned off to keep people like him away while the ruins were sifted through for evidence. But he managed to buttonhole a power-company worker on his way out after having checked the compound for hot lines on the ground.

"Just how bad is the damage in there?" the reporter asked him.

"It's bad. They really did a job on that place. I haven't seen anything like that since Tet."

"What's Tet?"

"What's Tet?" The man looked at the young reporter like he didn't believe he had heard the question. "You know, the Tet Offensive during the Vietnam War?"

"Oh, yeah, that Tet," Goldblum answered, even though he didn't have the slightest idea what the guy was talking about. "What do you think caused that kind of damage?"

The power-company man laughed. "That's simple. They got rocketed. From a set of tail fins I saw, they probably used RPGs on them."

When Goldblum's face went blank again, the man explained. "RPG—it's a Russian antitank rocket launcher. They make a pretty big bang when they hit."

"But where would anyone get a Russian rocket launcher?"

"Beats the hell out of me, buddy." The man gestured behind him. "But it looks like they sure as hell did."

When one of the FBI agents left the cordoned-off area, Goldblum moved to intercept him. "I understand that Russian rocket launchers were used in this attack. Can you confirm that?"

"No comment," the FBI man said as he stepped past the reporter.

"But the American people have a right to know what happened here," Goldblum yelled after him.

The agent stopped and turned. "When we have something the American people need to know," he said curtly, "we'll hold a news conference."

Since he knew he wasn't going to get anywhere

trying to question the FBI, Goldblum took out his camera and started to take photographs of the destruction. If nothing else, he could get the film to his editor and file his impressions of the damage to go with whatever story the FBI released.

After snapping several shots, he noticed a group of men in blue jackets with the letters ATF in yellow on the back walk out into the open lot on the side of the fenced-in enclosure. Holding his camera prominently in his hand, he walked over to join them. He expected to be told to clear the area, but it was worth a try.

One of the ATF men was holding what looked like a small metal screw-on lid with a nipple on the top. The lid was painted an odd shade of glossy green and had a red rubber gasket on the inside.

"You the photographer?" The ATF men looked up when he saw him approach.

"Ah, yes," Goldblum said, thinking fast.

"Good." The ATF agent put the lid back on the ground where he'd found it. "Take a picture of this."

"What is it?"

"It's the end cap off an RPG rocket round. Chinese manufacture, I think."

"It's not Russian?"

The ATF man shook his head. "Not unless they've started using Chinese writing on their stuff."

After Goldblum took several shots of the lid and the area around it, the ATF man picked it up again and held it so the Chinese writing on the top could be photographed.

After pocketing the evidence, he turned to the other three ATF men with him. "Is that it for here?"

"Yeah, that's all they left behind here."

"Let's go check the other launch sites."

"How many other sites are there?" Goldblum asked.

"At least two."

The reporter started after the ATF guys, but he saw another man in a dark blue jacket with a camera bag slung over his shoulder walking toward them.

"Hey," he told the ATF men, "I'll catch up with you in a minute. I've got to get some more film out of the van."

Lost in thought, the man answered with a vague wave of his hand, and the reporter raced for the parking lot.

Back in his car, Goldblum headed straight for the airport and a pay phone. If he played this right, he could be back in Seattle in two hours and the story could run in the morning edition. And he was sure as hell going to get the front-page headline. He could see it now—Red Chinese Rockets Destroy FBI Idaho Headquarters.

There could even be a Pulitzer nomination in this if he worked it right. And every reporter's blood ran faster when the Pulitzers were involved. Even a nomination for the coveted award could get him noticed by the East Coast papers, and he had always wanted to work in New York or Washington. For the West coast, Seattle was a nice place to work, but the East Coast was where careers were made.

SINCE DAN BUTTERFIELD didn't have an office to go to now—it had taken a direct hit from one of the rockets—he set up temporary shop in what had been the motor-pool dispatch office. As soon as the phone service had been restored, he got on the phone to update the director behind a closed door. His earlier calls had been made from a cellular phone, and sensitive information was never to be transmitted over a cellular phone. You could never tell knew who might be listening in.

When Butterfield walked out of his makeshift office almost an hour later, his face was grim. As he had expected, he wasn't being held accountable for the attack, but it had happened on his watch and at least some of the blame would stick to him. Understandably the director expected him to bring the criminals to justice. And how much blame stuck to him would depend on how quickly he took care of that. The term "maximum effort" had just taken on a new meaning for him.

Butterfield wouldn't be alone in his effort to solve this crime, however. He had been given carte blanche to call on anyone or anything in the Bureau to assist him. Without even being asked, the director was sending him a fifty-man rapid-response team equipped with armored cars and heavy weapons. Butterfield really didn't know what in the hell he was going to do with what was in effect a company of armored infantry shock troops, but he couldn't turn them down. Not if he wanted to keep his job long enough to try to redeem himself.

But before he could do anything, he had to develop some Intel. Regardless of Alvin Barker's efforts, he still didn't have squat to work with. The shadowy militias were out there; he now had graphic proof of that. But if he was going to dig the bastards out before the headlines made the Bureau the laughingstock of America, he had to have some new leads that would tell him who and where.

Walking out across the blasted compound, he stopped the first man he saw. "Have you seen Barker?"

"Not in the last hour or so."

"Find him and tell him to report to me immediately."

"Yes, sir."

"I'll be in what's left of my office."

"Yes, sir."

Seattle, Washington

THE MILITIA RAID on the FBI headquarters in Idaho made the headlines, all right. Every TV news agency from ABC to CNN ran top-of-the-hour stories on the attack. But Brad Goldblum's Seattle newspaper was the first to break the story that the destruction had been caused by Red Chinese RPG antitank rockets.

Even though Goldblum had the proof on film, it hadn't been easy for him to get it printed.

Fortunately for the young reporter, he had been able to catch an Alaska Airlines commuter flight from Boise back to Seattle without having to wait too long. Less than two hours after taking off, he had been at his word processor in his cubicle at the offices of the paper, converting his scribbled notes into a lead story.

Even more fortunately for him, some of the older men in the newsroom had known the difference between an RPG rocket launcher and a crowbar and had been willing to share the arcane knowledge. They explained to him what the rockets were, how they worked and why they had done so much damage to a brick-and-concrete building. Someone even found a file photo of an RPG launcher to run with his story.

It was the picture he had taken of the metal rocket end cap that showed the Chinese characters that had clenched the deal, however. It was the proof that there was a foreign connection to the militias and was the only reason that the editor had passed his story.

WHEN RAMON DE SILVA read about the attack on the FBI headquarters in the Seattle paper the next morning, he knew that the time he had worked so hard for had finally come. The key elements were all in place, and the first shot had been fired. Now the war could begin.

It had been easy enough for him to convince Rick Cummings to talk his fellow Brotherhood members into making the attack on the FBI compound in Boise. Unlike Bolton Grey, Cummings was impressed by Silva's résumé and, more importantly, he didn't harbor a personal grudge against Hispanics. He was also more interested in striking a blow for freedom than he was in playing it safe like Grey did. The fact that he had lost over half of his family farm to an EPA ruling probably had something to do with it.

It was also important that the Brotherhood was flushed with the outstanding success of its first large-scale operation. It had been carried off without a hitch, and except for the stray end cap from that one RPG rocket, the Feds didn't have a clue what had happened. With that success under their belts, the militiamen were emboldened. They had confronted the dragon in its lair and had come back unscathed. Now they would be ready to go on to even bolder operations against their federal enemies.

The FBI had reacted to the attack as Silva had expected it. According to the newspaper, shock troops and armored cars were being rushed into the area, as well as fleets of helicopters and aircraft. The senior officers would be under great pressure to come up with the perpetrators of the attack. The FBI had lost great face, and it would be eager to regain its honor, maybe a little too eager, and that would play into his hands.

The third leg of the tripod was the media, and getting them to play their role was going to be more difficult, but it was no less important. Without proper media coverage, World War III could start in Idaho and no one would even know. By the same token, with the media on his side, an insignificant incident could be twisted and manipulated until it was seen as a major event. And it was so simple to manipulate journalists. They strutted around like children, patting themselves on the back and telling one another that they were the first line of democracy's defenders, the champions of the American people's right to be informed. In real life, they were less than they told one another, much less.

In one way, it was too bad that these so-called journalists were as badly flawed as the rest of humanity. And from what Silva had seen, most of them were deeply flawed. There was no lie they wouldn't tell, no fact they wouldn't ignore or twist and no bribe they wouldn't take if it suited their purposes. America's freedom of the press was an international bad joke. Rather than being truly free, whatever that might mean, the American media was an activist unit of the left wing of American politics. And all too often, the radical left at that.

After his long experience in the secret service of Castro's Cuba, Silva harbored no illusions about liberal politics. He well knew the corruption and blissful ignorance of reality that fueled the liberal thinking process, both in his own country and in America. Anyone else who ignored reality the way they did would simply be called idiots. Only in a country like America could such complete fools be held in such high esteem. They might be idiots, but as Lenin said, they were useful idiots. And he was going to use them to destroy the United States.

The forces were all in place, and it was time for the games to begin. The next move on this live chessboard needed to be made by the FBI, so the Cuban needed to leak something to them that would be guaranteed to bring a response. The question was, what would send them in, guns blazing?

The answer to that was simple. Thanks to that reporter, Silva knew that the FBI was aware that Chinese RPGs had been used to attack its headquarters. Therefore, anything about RPG rocket launchers would bring the Feds running. And if one of the Brotherhood was fingered, the rest of the militia would spring to his defense. Then all it would take would be for the media to be alerted, as well, so they would be on hand when the operation went down.

CHAPTER SIXTEEN

Boise, Idaho

When Dan Butterfield saw the story on the attack on his headquarters in the Seattle newspaper, he was fuming. The idiot who ran his mouth off to that reporter about the RPGs was going to be in deep trouble. Leaking information was hampering Butterfield's investigation, and he had to close the leak.

Butterfield called the paper's editors about his problem, but all he got was that tired journalistic line about a reporter never revealing his sources. When were they ever going to learn that in the battle against terrorists, you either told what you knew or you were a part of the problem, not part of the solution?

There was nothing he could do about the article now. But he made a mental note to make sure that no reporter from any Seattle paper got within a hundred yards of another FBI office or operation in his jurisdiction. Then, when the bastards screamed about their First Amendment rights and the American people's sacred "right to know," he'd tell them to take their complaints to Washington.

The director had already been on the phone to him about the article, and the man wasn't happy. He also wasn't happy that beyond the one shipping plug—what the metal lid was officially called—and the tail fins of several exploded rockets, nothing else had been found that might help them crack the case. There had been no eyewitnesses to the attack, no identifiable tire tracks, no readable footprints, no cigarette butts, no notes proudly claiming responsibility, no nothing. Whoever the raiders were, they had come, made the attack and had vanished without a trace.

Even with no clues, Butterfield knew that the attack had to be tied into the killing of Bob Green and the murder of the informant they had used against the gunsmith. Apparently Willie Lotter had been on to something real. Unfortunately, though, he didn't have the slightest idea what it was.

Even though a complete search of Green's house had found nothing to tie him to any militia, someone had taken offense at his death. And it could only be one of the militias. That was further evidenced by the fact that Lotter's body had borne more than a dozen AK bullet holes, as well as the traditional final pistol shot to the head.

Beyond that, though, the coroner reported that Lotter had shown no signs of having been beaten or even roughed up. It had been the professional execution by firing squad that one would expect to get from the military, and Butterfield knew it had been done by one of the militias.

The odd thing about Lotter's unfortunate death was that it had actually helped relieve the building pressure generated by the more unfortunate Green shooting. Now Butterfield could point to Lotter's demise and use it as further evidence of Green's involvement in the armed underground. If it hadn't been the militia, he had told the director, who had offed him?

The problem was that beyond that circumstantial confirmation of militia involvement, as shaky as it was, he didn't have a single lead to follow. All of Green's known acquaintances, from his old beer-drinking buddies to the people he had worked with at the power company before his retirement, had been rounded up and questioned. But so far, they had all claimed not to know of any illegal activities such as weapons conversions, bomb building or anything like that, that their old buddy had been involved in.

Butterfield was sure that some of them knew something, but he didn't have any legal way to drag it out of them. The last thing he needed right now was to face charges of police brutality on top of everything else.

He desperately needed another snitch to replace Willie Lotter, and he had given Alvin Barker orders to develop one ASAP. But Lotter's death had also served as a graphic warning to any other local would-be loudmouths. Even law-abiding citizens were being very careful about what they said to the FBI now. No one wanted to end up tied to a fence post and riddled with bullets.

He remembered reading about the resistance movement in Nazi-occupied France during World War II and realized that he wasn't the only one who had found the topic interesting. The militia leaders had obviously taken a page or two from that book and were applying it to their operations in Idaho. The Resistance had made graphic examples of informers, leaving their bodies in places where they were sure to be found to give a warning to other Frenchmen who might be tempted to talk to the German occupiers.

The Germans, however, had been able to crack much of the Resistance because of the effectiveness of their questioning methods. The problem Butterfield had was that he couldn't put people though those kinds of interrogation techniques. American law frowned on torture. There were those times, though, when he really wished that he could apply a little pressure. A little electricity in the right place did wonders for awakening a man's memory.

The worst thing about the RPG attack was that no one had claimed responsibility for it. Sure, there had been a few crank calls—one old woman even called to say that it had been God's way of announcing the end of the world. Each and every one of the calls was being checked out, and there were a few people who wished that they had kept their mouths shut. But none of the callers had panned out, and this bothered Butterfield more than the actual attack.

Usually a terrorist group made a big deal out of its attacks. Terrorists listed their ridiculous demands and took great pride in their handiwork. This, of course, always made it easier for the Feds to track them down. The New York World Trade Center bombing investigation had revolved around the boasts and threats of the Arab fanatics who had pulled off that job. This, though, wasn't the work of amateurs.

Whoever was behind this was smart enough to know that a terrorist attack was more effective if it remained completely anonymous. If you didn't know who was after you, it could be anyone, who could strike anywhere at anytime. Also, making sure that no one had been killed was more chilling than if there had been a dozen bodies in the ruins. The men and women who would return to work after the mess was cleaned up would always know that it could have been them.

Butterfield had done everything he could to increase security at all the FBI offices and operations in his region, but he knew that security alone wasn't really effective against determined terrorists. Just ask the Israelis.

AS IF HE DIDN'T have enough on his plate, Butterfield was starting to have personnel problems with his agents. A wave of requests for transfer and leave had come across his desk since the attack, mainly from married men with families who were having second thoughts about their chosen profession. Busting down doors on redneck recluses who were accused of sawing the barrels off shotguns was one thing. Going up against terrorists armed with RPGs who were coldly professional enough not to leave a calling card behind, was entirely another matter.

FBI agents weren't used to being the targets. Occasionally one of them was in the wrong place at the wrong time and ate a bullet. The famous shoot-out in Miami a few years earlier was a good case in point; several agents had been killed that day. But for the most part, they were used to being the guys that even hardened drug-cartel criminals feared to come up against. Being targets was a new experience.

Never before had the FBI been singled out for an attack in this manner. The Boise attack had brought home the fact that they were in a dangerous profession. Dying in the line of duty wasn't just something that happened to another agent. Now it was up-close and personal, and it could happen to each of them and they didn't like it.

One of his most senior agents simply put in for an early retirement. The man had looked embarrassed, but explained that his wife really wanted to go back to their hometown in southern California to be with her aging parents. Butterfield understood only too well that the man had lost his guts and wanted out before he lost his life, as well. He had approved the request, however. He didn't want to have a man on his team that he couldn't depend on.

And, speaking of depending on his people, Alvin Barker had come through again. The hard-working intelligence officer—Mr. Snitch, as he was being called now—claimed to have developed a lead on someone who might have been involved in the shipment of the RPGs that had been used in the attack. Again the lead had come from a drug informer, but as with the late and unlamented Willie Lotter, drug scum were often good sources. They went places no one else wanted to go to, and they heard things that you could only hear in those places.

Barker was on his way in now to brief him on what he had uncovered. And after Butterfield cleared the operation with Washington, he'd take this new suspect into custody and see what he knew.

Dilbert, Idaho

THE RETURN to the sleepy little town of Dilbert after the rocket attack had been anticlimactic for Bolan. After Bolton Grey dropped him off at the fuel yard early the next morning, he had slept for a few hours. When it was time to open the business, he had gone back to work pumping gas and diesel for the farmers and truckers as if nothing had happened. Grey had said that he'd be in touch if he needed him, but until then, he had work to do.

The attack on Boise was the talk of the town, as it

was all over America. But in small-town America, it was more than a one-day topic. Even completely law-abiding citizens who wouldn't even think of joining a militia secretly enjoyed seeing someone take on the federal government and get away with it clean.

Beyond two minor injuries, the only thing that had been hurt was the high-and-mighty federal government that many Americans saw as a threat to their freedom and liberties. To have hit the arrogant FBI was also seen as being a good choice. To most Americans, only the universally loathed IRS or the intensely hated EPA could have possibly been a better target.

The days when FBI agents had been the good guys were long past in most people's minds.

As Bolan listened to the talk at Mac's Grill and Tavern about the attack, he came to realize just how far apart the thinking of the American people was from that of the politicians. He was confident that he would finally be able to break the back of this latest challenge to peace in the United States, but he wasn't all that sure that anyone would be able to stop the next one. Or the one after that.

If the average American's perception of government didn't change, and change soon, it wouldn't be long before there would be nothing left to save. But he also knew that the change needed to come from both directions. Both the American people and the American government needed to stop looking at each other as the enemy.

Lewiston, Idaho

FLUSHED WITH the success of his story about the attack on the Boise FBI headquarters, Brad Goldblum was almost glad to be back in Idaho. This time he had enough prepared food and bottled water stashed in the back of his Volvo that he wouldn't have to choose between eating the swill the locals ate and going hungry.

Now that he knew what an RPG was, he was determined to find out where they were coming from. He knew that the FBI, the ATF and most of the rest of the federal government was looking for them, as well. But if the Feds couldn't stop the drug trade, he knew they sure as hell weren't going to be able to stop this trafficking in military weapons, either. And being a longtime recreational user of controlled substances, he casually wondered if the established drug-smuggling network was somehow involved.

However they were getting into the country, though, that would be the thrust of his next series of articles—the failure of the federal government to protect the public from this new menace.

Like most people of his political leanings, and profession, Brad Goldblum usually held the federal government in amused contempt. Unlike the militiamen, though, he didn't fear it at all. As far as he was concerned, the federal system was populated with slackers, second-raters and incompetents who couldn't hold down a job anywhere else, so there was nothing to fear from them. He had a liberal's traditional contempt for everyone in government, except of course, when he felt that they should be doing something that was near and dear to the liberal agenda.

For instance, the reporter didn't particularly want to see the DEA become more effective in the so-called war on drugs. He didn't want the flow of cocaine or grass halted because he liked a harmless snort or a toke every now and then as much as the next guy. He did, however, want to see them completely eliminate the tar-heroin trade because it turned the users violent and made them a danger to society. As far as he was concerned, the DEA wasn't doing enough to stop the Mexican traffic in that particular drug. They needed to get tough and the hell with the so-called rights of drug traffickers.

By the same token, he screamed every time he thought that anyone in the government was getting in the way of his exercising the First Amendment rights he held sacred. But his reverence for the Constitution didn't extend beyond the First Amendment.

For instance, he wanted the federal government to crush gun owners wherever and whenever they were found, and to silence their voices. As far as he was concerned, the Second Amendment to the Constitution was a serious mistake. It might have made sense for Americans to have guns back when the pioneers had been invading the Indian lands. Today, though, the Second Amendment was an anachronism that modern society could no longer afford.

Although the gun-control issue had been raging for some time now, this use of the RPGs in Boise made it only more important that the nation be disarmed. And he would do everything in his power to make sure that this came to pass. He saw himself as a crusader in a holy cause, and his pen would be mightier than the sword.

GOLDBLUM'S FIRST COUP in his renewed crusade came at another gun show in Lewiston. He had seen a sign advertising it as he drove into town and made it his first stop. He was scanning a tableful of do-it-yourself gun books when he saw a slim volume claiming to show you how to make RPG-like rockets at home. Thumbing through it, he saw step-by-step instructions telling one what to use and how to use it to make a primitive, but apparently effective, antitank rocket launcher.

Suddenly he got an idea. He would buy the book, pick up the necessary ingredients, make an RPG himself and take lots of pictures of the process. Then, he would have the ingredients of a world-class exposé.

If he, a man who had never even handled a firearm in his entire life, could make a dangerous antitank weapon in his motel room, then anyone could.

CHAPTER SEVENTEEN

Now that he had fine-tuned the focus of his next great exposé, Brad Goldblum went back to the gun-show circuit to do his research at the bookseller's tables. His collection of how-to-do-it weapon books was rapidly growing. And by faithfully following the directions in the books, he had put together a large collection of homemade grenades, rockets and other explosive devices. In the manufacture of each example, he had carefully photographed each step of the process before testing the device.

In the process, he had become fascinated with the explosives he was making. Beyond the legally sanctioned, and thereby tame, fireworks of his youth, he had never been around explosives. The more devices he made, the more he wanted to make. Long after he had enough data for his story, he was still buying books on the subject. He had finally found the book on homemade time fuses and, after he made and tested several of them, too, he told himself that he would be ready to show the country the danger it was facing.

He was returning to his car in the parking lot of the Lewiston gun show when two men wearing sunglasses with suits suddenly appeared on each side of him.

"Brad Goldblum?" one of them asked as he flipped open a leather case to flash a gold badge. "Thompson, FBI. Do you mind if we ask you a few questions?"

"About what?"

"You are Brad Goldblum from the *Seattle Intelligencer,* aren't you?"

"What if I am?"

"We'd like to talk to you."

"About what?"

The agent backed off a step. "Mr. Goldblum, the first thing I need is for you to confirm that you are who we think you are. Once you have done that, we will continue."

"I don't have to tell you guys a damned thing."

"Wrong, Mr. Goldblum," the first agent said as the second one drew his pistol. "You're under arrest. Please step away from the door of the car."

"But you can't do this to me!"

"Wrong again." The agent almost smiled. "We can and we are. Put your hands on the hood of the car, or we'll do it for you."

Frozen with fear, Goldblum stood there. When the agent spun him and slammed him against the side of the car, he panicked and tried to break free. He didn't make half a step before both of the agents jumped him, wrenching his arms behind his back.

He fought to free himself, but it had no effect. In a flash, he was facedown in the parking lot with his hands handcuffed behind his back.

"You can walk," the agent said as he stood, not even breathing heavily, "or we'll carry you. It doesn't matter to us."

Goldblum decided that further resistance was futile. "I'll walk," he muttered.

Leaving his Volvo station wagon in the parking lot, Goldblum walked to the agents' sedan and got into the back seat. "What's going to happen to me?" he asked.

"The same thing that would have happened if you had cooperated with us in the first place," the agent said. "We want to talk to you."

"About what?"

"We'll talk about it at the office."

The reporter leaned back against the seat. He tried to raise some righteous indignation at having been treated like a common criminal, but he was too scared to put on much of a macho front. It was one thing to talk contemptuously about the "Feds" at a cocktail party while passing a joint. It was completely another to be handcuffed in the back of one of their vehicles.

Ever the reporter, though, he carefully noted the details of the car for the article he knew he would write. It was the only way he could control his fear.

Boise, Idaho

GOLDBLUM WAS DRIVEN to the local airstrip and put into a helicopter. Every time he asked where he was being taken, his question remained unanswered. When the chopper finally reached its destination, Goldblum instantly recognized where he was—the regional FBI office in Boise. The damage the motor pool and outbuildings had sustained in the militia RPG attack wasn't visible now, but the main building hadn't been completely repaired yet.

Still handcuffed, Goldblum was led into the main building. But instead of being taken to a booking desk like he saw in all the TV shows, he was taken up to a second-floor office that still showed the effects of the RPG attack. The sign on the door read Regional Director.

The middle-aged man behind the desk in the office didn't bother to get up when the two agents hustled Goldblum into the room. He did, however, identify himself as Dan Butterfield, special agent in charge of the Idaho regional office.

"What's the meaning of this?" Goldblum said after the introductions had been made. "Why have I been dragged in here like a criminal?"

"But you are a criminal," Butterfield said. "We have reason to believe that you are in violation of several federal weapons laws. Conviction on even one of those charges can put you in a federal correction facility for ten years."

"What are you talking about?" Goldblum could feel himself going into shock.

"You have been making illegal hand grenades and other explosive devices."

"But I'm just researching a story," the reporter protested. "I've been following the directions in books I've been able to buy on the open market. I'm going to show that they are dangerous books and should be banned."

Butterfield smiled. "I thought that you journalistic types were always ready to go to the wall to protect your First Amendment right to print any damned thing you wanted to. Doesn't that right apply to everyone, or is that just for guys like you?"

"But this is different," Goldblum tried to explain. "These books are really dangerous. Children can use them to make hand grenades and antitank rockets."

"I know," Butterfield replied, "and they do. But let's get back to the issue at hand—the warrant for your arrest. First, I want to read you your Miranda rights so you won't be able to say that we deprived you of said rights."

Taking a card from his pocket, Butterfield began to read the famous rights of the accused. "'You have the right to remain silent. Anything you say may be used against you in a court of law. Further, you have the right to...'"

When he was done, he looked back up at Goldblum. "Do you understand those rights as I have read them to you?"

"Yes, but I—"

"Do you understand your rights?"

"Yes."

"Good." Butterfield leaned back in his chair. "Now we can get back to talking about the laws regarding explosive devices and fully automatic weapons."

"But I didn't use them on anyone," Goldblum said. "All I did was test them so I could prove that they worked. I had to do that to write the article."

Butterfield was enjoying himself immensely. For a so-called investigative reporter, this man wasn't so smart. He had just confessed to a Class A federal felony and was looking at doing hard time in a maximum-security unit with the scum of the earth. Weapons violators didn't do their time in one of the famous federal "country club" prisons; that was only for political prisoners and white-collar criminals. He'd get ten years, do five inside and come out with a severely traumatized anus.

"You realize, of course," Butterfield explained, "that you have just confessed to the crime you have been accused of. You were read your rights and you subsequently freely confessed. That, and your connection with the attack here, makes you a high-risk suspect and—"

"What connection with the attack?" Goldblum blurted out.

Now Butterfield had the snotty little bastard on the mat, and he couldn't stop the smile that formed at the corners of his mouth. He'd think twice the next time before he tried to piss on the Federal Bureau of Investigation. There had to be something in the water of the Northwest that made people like him think that they could get away with making the Bureau look bad.

"What connection?" the FBI man asked. "Aren't you the smart-ass who proudly printed that Chinese RPGs were used in the attack? That information hadn't been made public before you got in on the act. So, from where I sit, mister, it looks like you have some kind of contact with the attackers."

Goldblum felt his heart stop. This had been shaping up to be the best story of his career, and now it was blowing up in his face like one of his home-made hand grenades.

"Look, sir," he said, trying to stay calm, "I don't have any connection with the attack, I really don't. I only found out about the Chinese RPGs because I saw a metal thing from one of the rockets and it had Chinese writing on it."

"And just where did you happen to see that? In a militia meeting?"

Goldblum violently shook his head. "No, that's not the way it happened. I was here the morning after the attack, and I walked up when that metal thing was found. One of your men asked me to take a photo of it. I guess he thought that I was part of the investigating team."

"So," Butterfield said, jumping on him, "you were

impersonating a federal officer. That's worth another ten years.''

The reporter closed his eyes and willed this nightmare to go away. He had no idea that his problems had just started.

"If you're at all interested," Butterfield said in an offhand manner, "there's a way that you might be able to make this all go away."

"What's that?" Goldblum couldn't say the words fast enough.

"But," the FBI man continued as if he hadn't heard, "I understand if you don't want to cooperate with our investigation, journalistic freedom and all that bullshit. But I can tell you that you're not going to do well in the maximum-security facility you're going to find yourself in. Unless, of course, you're gay and go in for what I think they call 'rough trade.'

"You know," Butterfield went on. "I've seen big guys, football players and weight lifters, come out of those places needing emergency surgery for—"

"You said there was something I could do." Goldblum's voice was wavering.

Butterfield leaned back in his chair, knowing he had him. "However, if you were to volunteer to assist us in our investigation, become an unpaid informant as it were, this would be taken into consideration if your case goes to the federal grand jury."

Even in a state of blind panic, Goldblum heard the word "if" and knew that he was being offered a way out. He also knew that if anyone at the paper learned of this, he'd be fired so fast his head would spin. Being a snitch, paid or unpaid, was considered to be a serious violation of journalistic ethics and was cause for dismissal.

"You understand, of course," Butterfield continued, "that the weapons charges against you aren't being dismissed at this time. At the end of this investigation, your file will be reviewed and a decision will be made then to proceed with indictments or not."

"I understand," Goldblum said, and he did.

WHEN THE REPORTER was taken downstairs to be fingerprinted and photographed, Butterfield turned to Alvin Barker with a big grin on his face. "Damn, that felt good! It was almost worth getting rocketed to be able to grind that arrogant bastard's face in the dirt."

"What do you want me to do with him?" the intelligence officer asked.

"Link him up with your best snitch and send him out to get a story. I want him out there in the small communities hustling to find leads for us. He can tell them that he's writing a story and wants to get his facts straight. There's enough assholes out there who are dying to get their names in the paper that he should be able to come up with something we can use."

"Do you think they'll buy that line?" Barker asked. "If he runs into any real militiamen, they'll probably just kill him like they did Willie."

"That would be even better," Butterfield said. "If they off a reporter, every newspaper and TV station in the nation will scream their heads off, and maybe we'll get some sympathy from the media for a change."

"Fat chance of that," Barker scoffed. "It will take more than one dead reporter before we become the good guys again."

"You've got a point there."

BRAD GOLDBLUM FELT like a character in a bad made-for-TV spy movie as he sat in a fast-food restaurant outside of Lewiston. After being processed, as the FBI had called it, he had been given his instructions by Agent Barker before being flown back to Lewiston and driven out to the parking lot where he had left his car. Now he was waiting to meet his contact, an FBI informer. Or he should say, a fellow FBI informer.

He had sold his soul to the Feds to save his butt, so that made him the same as all the rest of the snitches and rats that inhabited the lowest levels of what was laughingly called law enforcement. But he'd had no choice but to become a snitch. He had no illusions about the reality of his surviving a maximum-security federal prison. Just the thought of having to become some drug-dealing biker's "bitch" to save his life filled him with gut-wrenching horror.

But while he was buying time and maybe even a pardon for doing something he hadn't known was against the law, he had to make sure that none of his friends or fellow reporters at the paper found out about his deal with the FBI. His friends would scorn him, and his boss would simply fire him and blackball him from the profession.

He was caught between the proverbial rock and a hard place, and he hoped that he could carry it off. If not, he might as well just shoot himself and get it over with. A quick death was better than spending even a day in prison. He had done a story on the Washington State lockup at Walla Walla, and he knew the hard-core federal joints were even worse.

The man who walked up to his table looked like an Hispanic bad guy in an action-adventure flick. "Are you Brad Goldblum?"

When the reporter nodded, the man sat down. "I am Ramon de Silva," the Cuban said, not afraid to use his cover name for this mission. The name wasn't even close to his real one, and it was clean. "Our mutual friend said that I should break you in, teach you the business, so to speak."

"I appreciate it."

"Don't thank me yet. This is a dangerous job."

CHAPTER EIGHTEEN

FBI Special Agent in Charge Dan Butterfield was a little surprised when Alvin Barker called the next day and reported that their reporter claimed to have turned something up. Even by the best expectations, it was much too soon for him to have found his own car in the gun-show parking lot, much less anything of value to the investigation. But stranger things had happened, so he called his intelligence officer in for a conference.

"Our man Goldblum claims that your man Ramon de Silva just laid a hot one on him."

"What did he say?"

"He claims that Silva gave him the name of a farmer who's been acting as a militia weapons shipment point. What do you have on this Ramon snitch, anyway?"

Barker shrugged. "He was passed on to me by a contact in the DEA. Apparently he's been doing odd jobs for them in Seattle for a long time, and he wanted to clear out of town for his health. He has a relative who owns a Mexican restaurant in town here, and he moved in with him. The DEA boys say that his stuff's usually pretty good."

"Did he ever tell you how he got his pipeline into the militias?"

"He didn't say, but I think he's still keeping his hand in his old business. It's nothing serious. He's just moving a little of the local grass, wholesale. And he might be involved with a Seattle chop-shop operation, their roving salesman, as it were."

Butterfield shook his head. "So he's another scumbag that we're protecting because he feeds us."

"That's about it," Barker admitted.

"And he says that there's this farmer who's been letting the militia store weapons in his barn?"

"Apparently Silva told Goldblum that he got his tip from a feed salesman who saw some crates that could have come from an RPG shipment."

"Why do you think Ramon talked to Goldblum and not to us about this?"

Barker shrugged. "It could be a number of things. One is simply that Goldblum told him that he'd get anonymous credit for the tip in the newspapers. Everybody wants their fifteen minutes of fame, even snitches. Maybe we'd get more out of those assholes if we instituted a regional Snitch of the Month award."

"Nonetheless, I want to move on this now," Butterfield said. "We need some good news about now."

"Who do you want to use?"

"Let's put Ron Brown on it." Butterfield went

through his mental list of available senior agents. "He's been after me to give him something useful to do."

"I'll brief him."

Dilbert, Idaho

WITH THE NEW FBI directive about not involving local law enforcement until immediately before a federal raid, Sheriff Frank Banner didn't have a clue what was going on when several grim-faced FBI and ATF agents walked into his office early the next morning. But he knew that the presence of the Feds only meant trouble.

Like county sheriffs in most rural areas, Banner spent most of his on-duty time doing things that urban law officers saw as public relations, not law enforcement. In fact, beyond a few Saturday-night punch-ups, a little drunken driving and the occasional domestic squabble, crime wasn't much of a problem in Dilbert. Stray livestock and teenagers drag racing on the country roads were much more of a problem than crimes that would involve the Feds.

In fact he couldn't remember the last time a federal crime had been committed in his county. Unless, of course, it had to do with some old boy making moonshine in his barn or poaching on federal lands. He didn't consider the presence of the Brotherhood unit in town to be a federal crime because, as far as he knew, they had broken no laws.

"Sheriff Frank Banner?" the lead FBI agent asked as he flashed his badge. "I'm Special Agent Ron Brown."

"I'm Banner," the sheriff said, standing up behind his desk. "What can I do for you?"

"We need you to come with us."

"What's going on?"

"We're following a lead on the Boise attack and we need a local officer to come along with us."

"Who're you going after?"

"We'll let you know when we get there."

Like all local sheriffs, Banner hated being ordered around in his own jurisdiction by the high-and-mighty FBI. "I need to know who you are going after before I move out of this office," he said flatly.

The FBI agent stared him down. "Do you want to talk to Washington about obstructing a federal investigation?"

Knowing how much trouble could come from that, Banner reached for his hat. "Okay, okay."

Outside his office, he started for his patrol car parked at the curb when the FBI man stopped him. "We'd like you to ride with us."

"Sure." Banner shrugged. Obviously they were afraid that he'd get on his radio and alert whomever they were after. And he had to admit that was a likely possibility. He had been reelected time and again because he took good care of the people in his county. And that included warning them that the Feds were coming.

AFTER AN HOUR'S DRIVE through the countryside, the three FBI cars pulled off the county road a quarter mile from a farmhouse and outbuildings. This was the dairy owned by Bill Grissom, a man Sheriff Banner had known all of his life, and his wife. There wasn't a reason in the world he could think of for the Feds to be investigating Grissom.

Agent Brown spoke to someone on the radio, and a few minutes later, two blue vans emblazoned with the FBI logo on the door pulled up alongside and black-clad tac-team troops got out.

"You didn't say anything about making a raid in my jurisdiction," Banner said in complete amazement when he saw the SWAT team.

"We aren't 'making a raid,' as you put it," the agent replied. "We're conducting an investigation of a possible violation of weapons laws."

"But why all the guys in the SWAT gear? I don't want a war going on here."

"They're here because federal regulations say that I have to have tac teams on hand anytime we investigate a weapons violation."

Banner knew enough about federal regulations to know that there was no point in his saying anything more. The Feds were going to do whatever they liked, and he was going to have to pick up the pieces when they left.

As Banner watched in amazement, an unmarked moving van drove up next and parked behind the two blue vans. Three men in FBI blue jackets got out of the cab and, after opening the rear door, let down a vehicle ramp. One of them walked inside the van and the sheriff heard the sound of an engine firing up. A second later, he saw the back end of some kind of armored vehicle start down the ramp.

"That's a tank!" he said in complete bewilderment. "What in the hell are you going to do with that?"

The agent turned to him, his eyes unreadable behind his mirrored sunglasses. "We're going to make sure that no one gets hurt here today."

"Jesus, Brown!" Banner exploded. "You don't need a tank here. Bill Grissom's a good man. I know him from a long ways back. He might have violated some federal gun regulation, but you don't need to do this to him. Let me go in and talk to him."

"The time for talking is over," Brown said. "If he's as clean as you say he is, he can come out and let us take him into custody so he can be questioned. If he doesn't—" the agent shrugged "—we're going in after him, and that vehicle is going to make sure that no one gets hurt doing it."

"Please," Banner said. "Let me talk to him."

"Maybe on the bullhorn," the FBI agent conceded. "But you're not going in there. I don't need a hostage situation here, as well."

By now, the FBI and ATF tac teams had moved in unseen and had the Grissom farmhouse surrounded. The armored car was still out of sight, but the sheriff had a sinking feeling that this was quickly getting out of hand and was a disaster in the making.

"Hand me the phone," Brown said.

An agent gave Brown a cellular phone, and he quickly dialed a number. "William Grissom?"

"Yes."

"This is the FBI. We have a warrant for your arrest, and your house is surrounded. Come out with your hands up, and you won't be hurt."

"What in the hell are you talking about?"

"Look out your front window, Mr. Grissom."

The agent signaled, and the armored car started moving toward the house. Banner saw Grissom's face appear at the window and then jump back in fright when he saw the armored car and the black-clad troops.

"Damn," Brown said. "He hung up on me."

Imagine that, Banner thought.

INSIDE THE HOUSE, Bill Grissom was in a state of blind panic. He was a middle-aged dairy farmer living on the farm his grandfather had built up well before WWII. He had lived there all of his life and, unlike many of his high-school classmates, hadn't gone into the military, but had stayed on the farm. In fact the farthest he had been away from it had been one trip he had taken to Seattle.

He didn't have the slightest idea what an army of Feds was doing in front of his place, but he feared the worst. The previous year, he went through an IRS audit and a hassle with the EPA about environmentally correct cow-manure disposal, and he'd had about all of the government helping him that he could stand.

In frustration, he had joined the Brotherhood of Patriots after hearing Bolton Grey talk about the need for Americans to band together against the encroachments of the federal government. And sure, he had guns in his house; almost everyone in rural America had a gun of some kind. He had hunting rifles, shotguns and varmint guns and he even had a handgun, an old Colt .45 his father had acquired after coming back from WWII. But he didn't have an assault rifle or a sawed-off shotgun, and he had never fired a weapon at another human in his life. He had done nothing to warrant the Feds sending a tank and a SWAT team after him.

Bolton Grey had promised that he and the other Patriots would come to the defense of the Brotherhood if anything ever happened. Grabbing the kitchen phone again, he quickly dialed the sheriff's number.

"This is Bill Grissom," he said as soon as the sheriff's office in Dilbert answered. "Is the sheriff in? I've got an emergency out here and I need to talk to him."

"He's not here," the deputy answered. "He left with some FBI boys and—"

"Those damned Feds are out here," Grissom exploded. "And they're—" The phone went dead.

WHEN THE DEPUTY TRIED to call Grissom back, a male voice came on the line. "This number is out of order until further notice."

That didn't make any sense to the deputy. He had just been talking to the farmer, and Grissom had said that the Feds had gone to his place. With Sheriff Banner with the FBI, he didn't have anyone to turn to, but maybe Bolton Grey would know what was going on. The deputy quickly dialed his number.

"HE SAID WHAT?" Bolton Grey asked when the deputy told him what was happening at the Grissom farm.

Grey frowned when the deputy repeated his short conversation with the farmer. Bill Grissom was in the Brotherhood, but he wasn't an active member, nor was he part of the inner circle. He was just someone who had joined because he was angry at the government, not because he really wanted to do anything about it.

He was sure as hell not anyone the FBI would have any reason to want to talk to. But the gunsmith, Bob Green, hadn't had any direct connection with the Brotherhood, either, and look what it had gotten him. He'd been killed in his own living room.

Grey had expected a reaction from the Boise attack but not anything like this. It was beginning to look like someone was selling out the Brotherhood so the Feds could take it down. If this was the case, it couldn't go unchallenged.

Grissom lived well out of Dilbert and was actually closer to the neighboring town of Caryville. Dave

Gardener ran the Caryville Brotherhood unit, and he was closer to Grissom's farm. He could get there faster and find out what was going on out there.

After Grey placed a call to Gardener, he ran through the Brotherhood's notification list. He called three men, briefed them and told them to stand by. Each of them would call three more men and so on until every one of the Brotherhood of Patriots in western Idaho knew that the federal government was raiding one of their neighbors and a fellow Patriot.

It was a call to arms like the one Paul Revere had ridden to deliver over two hundred years ago, and it could signal the beginning of the Second American Revolution.

AT THE DAIRY FARM, Special Agent Ron Brown tried to call Grissom on the phone again, but as soon as the farmer heard his voice, he hung up on him. The agent turned to Frank Banner. "Your Mr. Grissom just hung up on me again, Sheriff. If he's as clean as you say he is, why doesn't he come out and talk to me?"

"He's scared shitless," Banner tried to explain. "He's just a farmer, and he's not used to dealing with the government. Plus, I think you'd be scared shitless, too, if a fucking tank showed up in your front yard."

"I'm going to give him a little more time to think this over." Brown's jaw was clenched. "Then we're going to go in and get him out of there."

"Please," Banner pleaded. "Let me talk to him on the bullhorn. He's not a criminal, he's just scared."

When Brown turned away without answering, the sheriff exploded. "Goddammit, Brown, I'm talking to you!"

Brown spun. "And I'm talking to you, Sheriff. This is an FBI operation, and I want you to go over to the commo van and stay there until I call for you. Got that?"

"You know, Brown, I've been trying my best to cooperate with you on this, fellow law-enforcement officers and all that shit, but that doesn't seem to be working. When you're done here, I'm going to be talking to your boss about your attitude."

"If you're done, Sheriff, I have a job to do."

"Go to it, G-man," Banner said, sneering. "But if you blow it, I'm going to be all over you."

When Brown ignored him and walked off, Banner had no choice but to stand by helplessly while this went down.

CHAPTER NINETEEN

Militiaman Dave Gardener made sure that his four-wheel-drive rig was well below the crest of the hill overlooking the gravel pit at the edge of the Grissom farm when he stopped. The farmhouse was in the middle of open ground, so there was no way that he could have driven close enough to recon the situation without being seen. The gravel pit, however, was only a little more than a quarter of a mile away, and it looked down over the dairy.

Gardener had been working on his farm equipment when he had gotten Bolton Grey's call, and had been able to respond to the crisis immediately. He was one of the men who had gone on the Brotherhood raid on the FBI compound in Boise. In fact he had been one of the RPG gunners who had rained destruction on the Feds, and he was damned proud of it. Now, if Grey's information was correct, he might have another chance to strike a blow for freedom.

After he hung up, he'd quickly put his RPG launcher and three rockets in the toolbox in the bed of his pickup and now, fifteen minutes later, he was at the gravel pit. Grabbing the launcher and the rockets, he crawled to a position between two large boulders that gave him an unimpeded view of the farm below.

Through his powerful Russian-army-surplus field glasses, Gardener could clearly see the Grissom farmhouse, the black-clad tac teams surrounding it and the armored car parked at the end of the driveway. Grey had been right; the Feds were moving in to attack the farm in what looked like a Fort Benning textbook mech-infantry assault. As he watched, one of the tac teams rushed forward to take up positions against the side of the house. They were about to move on Grissom, and that was Gardener's cue to defend a brother Patriot.

Taking the glasses from his eyes, he quickly scanned the skies overhead to see if the Feds had brought their secret air force with them. When he couldn't see any planes or choppers in the distance, he smiled. As a Vietnam Air Cav vet, he knew that you should never commit ground forces without proper air support on hand. It was a lesson that had been brutally taught to the VC and NVA during the war, and it would be taught to the FBI today.

Loading a rocket into the front of the RPG launcher, he estimated the range to the armored car to be a little over four hundred yards from his hilltop position. The first part of breaking up any armored assault was to take out the armor. When it was taken out, he would start working on the black-uniformed troops.

Since the scout car wasn't moving, Gardener had all the time in the world to make sure that he had it lined up properly in the sights of his RPG. Since he only had the three rockets with him, he wanted every one of then to hit home. He took measure of the direction that the wind was blowing and even took into consideration the fact that he was shooting downhill.

When he was satisfied that he had a perfect sight picture, he took a deep breath, held it and slowly squeezed the RPG's trigger.

The antitank rocket left the launcher with the whoosh of the prop charge. When the main motor ignited fifty yards out he saw that it was going to be close to, if not right on, the target.

Not taking his eyes off of the trail of dirty smoke from the speeding rocket, Gardener loaded the next round into the front of the launcher and thumbed back the firing hammer. The second RPG round was on the way before the first one hit the scout car.

He decided to hold his fire of the last rocket until he saw what the first two had done, and ducked behind cover to reload again.

SPECIAL AGENT Ron Brown was about to give the order for the tac team to gas the house when the rear of the V-100 scout car exploded with a roar that sounded like a thunderclap hitting an iron wall.

The RPG's 85 mm shaped-charge antitank warhead

efficiently performed its job as it had been designed to do. The cone of white-hot explosive gases it projected had been calculated to punch through twelve inches of homogenous steel tank armor. The half-inch-thick armor plate on the rear of the scout car might as well have been thin cardboard for all the protection it offered.

Since there was nothing to slow down the warhead's destructive blast, it penetrated to the vehicle's rear-mounted engine and spent its remaining force destroying it. Droplets of molten metal sprayed around the engine compartment like red-hot machine-gun bullets ripping open the fuel tank.

The second explosion was even more destructive than the first. A fireball filled the air behind the scout car, sending shards of metal flying. Protected by the engine compartment's quarter-inch firewall, the car's three-man crew wasn't hurt. But they exited the vehicle in great haste and hit the ground running for their lives.

Everyone had hit the dirt when the scout car exploded, and they were looking around in a daze when the second rocket hit. This time there were casualties.

Although the RPG had been designed as an anti-tank weapon, it was widely used as an antipersonnel round, as well. Many Vietnam veterans carried scars to prove that it was equally effective in that role. Several of the FBI men took hits from the razor-sharp sheet-metal shrapnel from the exploding round.

Since the tac teams had been briefed that the suspect was believed to be involved with the shipment of RPGs, they jumped to the conclusion that the rockets were somehow coming from the farmhouse. Their rules of engagement allowed them to shoot if lives were in danger, and they opened up on the fifty-year-old shingle-and-frame house with everything they had.

INSIDE THE FARMHOUSE, Bill Grissom was hugging the floor as a steel storm of automatic fire ripped through the walls of his home. By sheer good fortune, he had been standing behind the sturdy overstuffed couch in the living room when the first RPG rocket hit. He ducked for cover right before the tac teams opened up.

Curled up in a ball, the farmer had his eyes squeezed shut and his hands pressed against his ears, but it did no good. The roar of gunfire couldn't be shut out. Neither could the rain of glass shards and wooden splinters. He was too much in shock, though, to know that he was bleeding in a dozen places. All he wanted was for the noise to stop.

WHEN DAVE GARDENER raised his head to take a look at his handiwork, he was stunned to see the Feds firing into Grissom's house. Even from where he was, he could see the windows shattering and pieces of the wooden shingles flying off under the concentrated barrage of full-automatic weapons fire. He had no idea why they had started shooting, but he would do what he could to fight back.

He sighted his last RPG rocket in on a clump of black-clad federal troops and squeezed the trigger. The RPG round flew true again and impacted in front of the tac team. The warhead converted itself into deadly shrapnel and blast, bowling over several agents. Their issue flak vests and Kevlar helmets saved them from most of the damage, but several of them took hits in unprotected arms and legs.

This time, though, someone had been looking his way and spotted the signature puff of smoke from the launcher. He saw men pointing at him and saw a sniper aim his rifle at his hiding place.

Ducking back down, Gardener crawled back down the slope to where he had left his pickup. Tossing the RPG inside, he fired up the truck's engine and was moving before the first shots were fired.

When the FBI sniper told him that the rockets had come from the ridgeline over the gravel pit, Ron Brown realized that he had screwed up. "Cease fire!" he screamed over his handheld radio. "Cease fire!"

It took a while before everyone stopped firing. In the stunned silence that followed, the cries of the wounded could be heard.

"Get the medics over here!" Brown radioed. "We have wounded."

In the confusion, no one bothered to look in the house to see if Bill Grissom was still alive.

While the medics were evacuating the wounded, a shaken Brown got on the radio to Boise to report.

DAN BUTTERFIELD'S JAW was locked when he stepped out of the borrowed Bureau of Land Management helicopter at the Grissom farm an hour and a half later. Washington had promised replacement aircraft for the ones he'd lost to the earlier attack, but typically they hadn't arrived yet, and he'd had to call on a brother agency to help him out when he got the call about the firefight at the Grissom farm.

He was really getting tired of seeing his law-enforcement operations turn into combat scenes. If he had wanted to be in charge of a war, he'd have gone to West Point, not the FBI Academy.

He was looking around for Ron Brown when a man in a local sheriff's uniform walked up to him. Sheriff Frank Banner was wearing a crude bandage on his left cheek and looked the worse for wear. "Who's the asshole in charge here?" he snarled. "I want to file a complaint."

"I'm Dan Butterfield from the regional office," the FBI man said as he extended his hand.

The sheriff ignored the offered hand. "Who's your boss, Butterfield?"

"I'm the boss, as you put it, at least here in Idaho. But if you've got a complaint about me, Sheriff, you can talk to the director in Washington."

"I'll do that later," Banner promised, "but for now, I guess you'll have to do. First off, how many other farms in my jurisdiction do your boys want to shoot up? Maybe I can pick a couple out for you, places where the poor bastard working the land has enough insurance to pay for the damage after your boys in black are through using it for target practice.''

"Sheriff," Butterfield said wearily, "there's no one who is more sorry than I am about this."

"I think Bill Grissom might argue that point with you. This used to be where he lived."

"How is he?"

"He's alive, no thanks to your boys."

"I want to talk to him."

"He's sitting on what's left of his porch."

Bill Grissom hadn't been seriously wounded in the barrage of fire that had torn his small house to splinters. When the firing stopped, he cautiously walked out with his hands up. When no one immediately jumped up to arrest him, he simply took a seat on what remained of his porch and sat with his head in his hands.

Everything he had ever owned was in the house behind him and it was in shreds. His wife's neat little kitchen looked like a bomb had gone off in it. The oak dining-room table his grandfather had made had been reduced to well-polished kindling. The family albums, the trinkets, the mementos of three generations of Grissoms were gone, as well. Now he knew what the people in the Old South had felt like when Sherman had marched through Georgia.

Fortunately his wife was away visiting her sister in

Pocatello, and he should be able to get things cleaned up at least a little bit before she could drive back. He knew, though, that there was nothing he could do to make it the same as it had been just that morning.

"Mr. Grissom?"

The farmer looked up to see a man in a shirt and tie standing in front of him with two goons wearing sunglasses standing on either side of him. "Yeah?"

"I'm Dan Butterfield from the Regional Office of the FBI."

"Are you going to arrest me now—is that it? You've torn up my house, tried your damnedest to kill me and now you're going to arrest me?"

Grissom shook his head and looked around his still intact outbuildings. "You know, for a long time I thought that I was living in the United States of America, but I guess not. This ain't Idaho anymore, not if I can be treated this way, so it's got to be Russia."

He stood, looked Butterfield straight in the eyes and defiantly held his hands out in front of him. "Okay, Mr. FBI, go ahead and put the cuffs on. If I'm in jail, at least I won't have to try to explain to my wife what in the hell happened to her house."

He glanced down in front of the porch and back up to Butterfield. "Or to her flower beds. She loves those flowers, you know."

"Mr. Grissom, please put your hands down. We're not going to arrest you."

"That's not what that other fella said before they started shooting."

"There's not going to be any more shooting," Butterfield stated. "A mistake was made here, and I assure you that we will put all this right for you."

"I'm not going to be arrested for some crime I don't even know about?"

"No."

Now Grissom got mad. "Then get your ass off my property, mister, and take the rest of your Nazis with you. If I'm still in America, I've got some rights and I ain't seen no warrant yet, so get the hell out of here!"

Seeing that Grissom was on the edge of hysteria, Frank Banner moved in to keep the farmer from making this situation any worse than it already was. As far as he was concerned, the old boy could shoot Butterfield right where he stood, but he knew that really wouldn't help.

"Bill," Banner said, "I called a couple of your neighbors and they're on their way over here right now. Bud Rogers and his wife said you and Ella can stay with them until this gets taken care of. Ralph Hodges and his kid are coming over to help you get your things together."

"But what am I going to tell Ella, Frank?" Grissom's eyes started to tear up. "I don't know what to say to her."

The sheriff smiled grimly. "I'm sure that Mr. Butterfield here will be able to explain all this to her. Or if he's at a loss for words, I have the number of the director of the FBI, as well as the home phone number of Governor Thorpe."

Banner turned to face the FBI man. "I'm sure that between the three of them, they'll be able to come up with something, won't you, Mr. Butterfield?

"And," the sheriff went on, "one of my wife's nephews is the editor of the Boise paper. I'm sure he'd love to talk to you about this, too."

Butterfield winced. This was going to be worse than getting his office rocketed. "We will talk to your wife for you," he said, "and we will do everything we can to make this right."

Grissom looked at him as if he had two heads.

Butterfield turned away to find Ron Brown and located him at the commo van where he was talking on the radio. Brown was mussed up a little, but he hadn't been wounded in the attack. He had hit the dirt at the first RPG explosion and had stayed there facedown until it was all over.

"You're flying back with me," Butterfield told him. "And when we get back to the office, clean out your desk and pack your bags."

"Where am I going?"

"Washington. The director wants to talk to you."

CHAPTER TWENTY

Dilbert, Idaho

As soon as Bolton Grey heard from Dave Gardener about the battle at the Grissom farm, he put his unit of the Brotherhood on full alert. If the Feds were shooting at the citizens, he wanted to be able to shoot back. After making the phone calls, he drove out to the fuel yard and found Bolan topping off the fuel tank of a livestock truck full of cattle.

"As soon as you're done here," he said, "I want you to close down early today."

"What's up?"

"There was a raid on a farm to the north of here this morning. The FBI hit the place with an armored car and a twenty- or thirty-man SWAT team."

"Was anyone hurt?"

"I don't know yet. One of our men took out the armored car with an RPG. But before he got out, he saw them shooting up the farmhouse and we don't know the outcome."

"Was the farmer a Patriot?"

"He's a member," Grey stated, "but he doesn't come to the meetings or anything like that. There's nothing to connect him to us."

"Then why the raid?"

"I'm damned if I know." He shook his head. "Old Bill was in trouble with the EPA a little while back about too much cow shit getting into the creek. But I can't see even the Feds sending in armor over a few cow pies."

"How many raids does that make where there's been no real reason for it?" Bolan asked. "You know, no evidence or activity that would alert them. It's starting to look to me like someone's selling us out."

"We know who fingered Bob Green," Grey said, "and we took care of him. But you may have a point. There was another operation that went bad right before you got here."

"What was that?" Bolan asked.

"I'll tell you later." Grey evaded the question. "Right now we've got to see what we can do about the situation at the Grissom place."

"What're we going to do?"

"I want to get a couple of the assault teams suited up and ready in case they decide to hit someone else. I also want to get someone tracking them so we know where they're going next. Can you handle that?"

"No problem," Bolan replied. "How many of them are out there?"

"Dave Gardener took care of the armored car, but

he said that there were twenty or thirty of the black-suited bastards and a fleet of vehicles.''

"If I'm going to track them, I'll need to be in contact with you. What do we have for commo gear?"

"We've been using cell phones."

"That's better than CB radio," Bolan said. "But the Feds can intercept cell-phone calls, too."

"I know, but it's all we have right now. We don't have military-style tactical radios. That's something else that's on my wish list, and I'd better move it to the top of the list ASAP."

"If you can show me on the map where this place is, I'll get going."

Grey had a gas-company map ready and pointed out the Grissom farm and the quickest way to get there.

"Let me take that with me, and I'll throw a fuel drum in the back of my van so it looks like I'm making a delivery. Also, I'm not going armed, I'll just make a recon."

"Good point. Get going."

IT TOOK A COUPLE more hours before the FBI was ready to leave the Grissom farm. Bill Grissom's neighbors came and helped him pack some clothes and essentials before taking him away. The neighbors were as outraged as the farmer was, but they got him away before he assaulted anyone.

Sheriff Frank Banner stood by and took notes while the FBI took pictures and documented the damage done to the property. When this came to court, if it did and wasn't settled out of court, the sheriff wanted to be ready to testify on Grissom's behalf. And testify he would. Butterfield's promises that everything would be made right were not reassuring, not coming from a Fed.

This wouldn't be the first time the FBI had screwed up and then had tried to cover its ass. The Bureau would drag poor old Grissom through the mud and come up with a dozen snitch reports, all of which would point to probable cause. But their agents sure as hell couldn't blame him for the loss of the armored car or the casualties they had taken. That honor belonged to the mysterious RPG gunner in the gravel pit, whoever he had been. How he had gotten involved was anyone's guess.

But figuring that out wasn't Banner's problem. He had been told that the FBI would be investigating that as it was the rocketing of its headquarters in Boise. He wished the Bureau good luck.

THE FBI RETREAT from the farm that afternoon was a near route. The convoy of cars, vans and the now empty truck that had brought the armored car looked like the remnants of a defeated army. Several of the vehicles bore the marks of RPG fragments or bullet holes from panicked firing.

Bolan used his map and his eye for terrain to position himself where he could watch the withdrawal without drawing attention to himself. The Brotherhood's phone-alert network had done a good job of telling the citizens what had happened to one of their neighbors. The men and women of the county were out in force to watch the Feds retreat. Cars, four-wheel rigs and pickups dogged them the entire way. Several times, they blocked the road completely, forcing the convoy to stop until Sheriff Banner's deputies could convince them to disperse peacefully.

It was civil disobedience at its finest American expression. The tactic had been used for years by civil-rights groups, environmentalists, war protestors and others who were unhappy with the status quo. When they had used it, they had been applauded, but Bolan knew that this demonstration was only going to raise fears on Capitol Hill.

All along the route, the retreating Feds were being treated to catcalls, a few rocks being thrown at them and the din of honking horns. Fortunately, though, no one fired on them, and a bloodbath was averted. The FBI had been bloodied, but they were still heavily armed and they were completely spooked. Had anyone taken a pot shot at them, they would have fired back.

Overhead in his borrowed helicopter, Dan Butterfield kept an eye on the slow-moving convoy. By now, dozens of Idaho State Police cars had joined the Feds convoy to protect them from the outraged citizenry. Once they were back on the freeway, Butterfield used the chopper's radio to contact Alvin Bar-

ker. He told him to find Goldblum and to get the
reporter to his office ASAP.

Boise, Idaho

"YOUR INFORMANT set us up," Butterfield said
coldly when Brad Goldblum was brought before him.
The reporter looked as scared as he had the first time
he had been dragged in. Barker had briefed him on
what had gone down at the farm, and he was afraid
that he would be somehow blamed for it.

"But, he's not 'my' informant," Goldblum argued.
"You were the one who told me to meet that guy and
to find out what he knew. I just did what you said
and told you what he told me. There was no way I
could have confirmed any of the information. I didn't
have enough time."

Butterfield was many things, but "a fair man"
pretty much summed it up. He was ruthlessly using
Goldblum as a pawn, but the reporter had set himself
up to be used by breaking the law several times.
Nonetheless, the FBI man knew that he wasn't being
fair to him.

"Okay," he conceded, "that's a point well made.
We have to share the blame on this one. The next
time you report to us, though, I want you to assess
what your informant's saying and give us that assessment."

"How the hell do I do that?" Goldblum couldn't
believe what he was hearing. "I'm not a lie detector.

I can't tell if a guy's telling me the truth about this stuff.''

"Just give us your gut feelings, okay?"

"I guess."

"Next," the FBI man said, "I want you to take your reporter persona on the road and chase down a story on these militiamen. You can square it with your editor yourself, or if you like, I can give him a call."

"I'll take care of it," Goldblum said instantly. Newspaper editors considered working with the police or the Feds as getting into bed with the enemy. Nothing sold papers like a story of a cop gone bad, so a good reporter had to keep his distance rather than cooperate with them in any way.

"To lead you into the situation," Butterfield continued, "Alvin will give you access to all of our reports on known or suspected militia activity in Idaho and the surrounding states for the past several months. I'd like you to read them over so you'll know what's been going down, and then we'll work up a plan of action for you."

Every fiber of Goldblum's liberal sensibilities wanted to protest against this organizing of his betrayal of everything he held sacred. It was bad enough that he had been forced to become an informer for the FBI, a spy for the government. Being given his assignment as if he were some fourth rank bureaucrat unable to think for himself added insult to injury. If he had to spy for the bastards, he wanted it to be some casual thing so he could tell himself that he had undertaken it because he believed that he should.

But he wasn't even being given that shred of self-deception. He was a snitch now, pure and simple, until Butterfield let him off the hook. He couldn't even think of what his life would be like if he didn't.

"Yes, sir," he said.

WHEN GOLDBLUM READ through the compiled FBI reports on militia activities in Idaho, however, it turned out to be enlightening. While there had been scattered incidents throughout the state, as well as in the neighboring states of Washington, Oregon and Montana, most of the suspected militia activity had occurred in the northwestern sector of Idaho in an area running roughly from Lewiston north through Coeur d'Alene to the Canadian border.

That was the area he had first gone to when he thought he had been writing a great exposé, but he'd had no luck getting any of the locals to talk to him about much of anything, much less militias. This time he would have to change his tactics. He wasn't unaware that he stood out among the locals like a nun in a whorehouse. Everything about him from his car to his Nike running shoes screamed big-city.

There was little he could do about his Volvo; he couldn't afford to buy a pickup. But he could tone down some of the other things that marked him as a stranger. He could lose the Nikes, the Rolex watch and the Gore-Tex ski jacket, cut his hair so he looked like the weatherman on a Boise TV station and buy some no-name blue jeans.

He would never be able to pass for an Idahoan, but maybe he wouldn't stand out too badly. It was worth a try at least, because this time he had to come up with something.

Washington, D.C.

HAL BROGNOLA LOOKED OUT of the window of his Washington, D.C., Justice Department office at the snarled traffic on the streets below. From where he sat, it didn't look any different than the rat race in any other overcrowded American urban area. Only those who didn't live inside the Beltway thought that it was glamorous to work in the District.

His gaze fell to the fax report on his desk about the latest screwup in Idaho. In just a few short weeks, there had been a fatal shootout with bank robbers that had resulted in the loss of an FBI aircraft and two pilots, as well as the bank robbers. Next the FBI had killed a gunsmith under questionable circumstances, and its informant on the case had been executed military style, apparently in retaliation for the gunsmith's death. After that, the FBI regional office in Boise had been almost blown off the map in a military-type attack. And now there was this bloodbath at a dairy farm, with an armored car taken out with an RPG and several FBI agents wounded. That was to say nothing of a farmer's house being reduced to kindling wood.

What was next, a shoot-out at a barn raising or a quilting bee?

What was going on in Idaho? And even more importantly, what was Mack Bolan's role in this, if anything?

The big Fed hadn't liked sending in his old friend without a firm commitment for Bolan to keep in touch on a regular basis about what he was doing, but he'd had no choice. The soldier had been his last resort, and as he usually did, Bolan had insisted on playing the game by his own rules. Brognola knew that the man's instincts were always right on things like that, but it didn't make his job any easier when he didn't know what was transpiring.

Brognola had a meeting with the President in half an hour, and the Man wanted a briefing on the situation in Idaho. Brognola didn't want to have to tell him that he didn't know diddly squat about his own intelligence operation except what he was getting secondhand from the FBI. The special agent in charge, Dan Butterfield, seemed to be trying to do the right things, but it obviously wasn't working. Even worse, the FBI intelligence on the situation was pathetic. They really didn't have a clue about what they were facing.

Even though RPGs apparently were as common in Idaho as BB guns, there was nothing in any of the FBI reports about the foreigners who were reportedly supplying the militias with the rocket launchers, as well as other up-to-date military weapons.

This debacle at the dairy farm was the last straw. After having their headquarters blasted by RPGs, the Idaho FBI should have figured out that the natives were restless. To have gone in full force with an armored car to talk to a man—who by all standards was an upstanding citizen—had been criminally stupid. It would have made more sense to wave a red flag at a bull. That the farmer turned out to have well-armed friends should have been anticipated and planned for. A smart man would have gone in with a little less fanfare.

Brognola was going to strongly recommend to the President that a Justice Department task force be sent to Idaho to oversee any further actions of the FBI and ATF in the region until this situation was brought under control. The way it was escalating, the northwestern United States would be in open rebellion against the federal government by the following week unless something was done and done quickly.

He wished again that he had something from Bolan; even one report would help. He'd be in a better position if he could give the Man something positive; good news never hurt. But he could wish all he wanted for all the good it was going to do him. He hoped against hope that Bolan would get a handle on the situation as soon as possible. But as always, the Executioner was doing things his way, and there was nothing Brognola could do about it except wait.

Before collecting the papers on his desk for the long trip to the Oval Office, he popped an antacid tablet from the ever present roll in his pocket. After swallowing it dry, he decided to take another one just for good measure. He could tell that it was going to be one of those days.

CHAPTER TWENTY-ONE

Dilbert, Idaho

Ramon de Silva couldn't have been more pleased with how the Idaho operation was going now. For too long he had been lagging behind the Arizona and Florida missions, and that hadn't looked good. Now, though, with the fallout of the FBI attack on Grissom's farm, he had jumped ahead of the other two operations. The number of FBI and ATF agents in the Northwest had doubled in the past few days, and more were pouring in. Washington was even sending in high-level bureaucrats to oversee the operations against the militias. But as far as Silva was concerned, the more Feds that were in Idaho, the better he liked it.

The focus on Idaho had relieved the pressure on the militias in other states and was giving them time to get better organized for the final effort. The massive government response to the Idaho situation had also drawn strength away from other federal law-enforcement activities all over the country. Even though the DEA wasn't directly involved with the militia situation, there had been fewer drug shipments intercepted in the past few weeks. And in general, arrests for a wide range of federal and state crimes were down as everyone hunted for the elusive militiamen in the Pacific Northwest.

The plan was working exactly as the Cali board had intended. The kindling was packed tightly against the firewood of American society, and all that was left was for Silva to strike the match. And that would happen as soon as he held his meeting tonight with the leaders of all of the Brotherhood units in the area. The operation he intended to propose to them, an attack on a National Guard armory, would light that the fire that would consume the United States.

Everything that had happened so far was merely prelude to what would happen after that.

BECAUSE OF THE NUMBER of Brotherhood leaders who had been invited, Silva's special meeting wasn't being held in Bolton Grey's fuel-yard office this time. Instead, a hall outside Dilbert had been chosen as their gathering place. The hall's manager was a Patriot, so no one would ask what the meeting was about.

When Bolan walked in the door behind Grey, he instantly saw that there were three obvious foreigners in the room. The man who appeared to be in charge of the group of advisers was known to Bolan as Victor Cordoba, ex-DGI—the Cuban Intelligence service—and former leader of a brutal Communist insurgent group in Guatemala. He was now believed to be working—under a cover name—in some capacity for the Cali cartel. Seeing Cordoba here made it crystal clear what that capacity was now.

Thinking back to the night he had spied on Grey's late-night meeting at the fuel yard, Bolan thought he recognized the Cuban as one of the two men who had been there. The light had been too poor for him to make a positive ID, but from the back, he looked familiar. That meant that Cordoba was the conduit for the RPG shipment Grey had received, and the pieces were now in place.

The Cali cartel was employing Cordoba to run an insurgent operation in the United States, using the Brotherhood of Patriots as its guerrilla fighters. With the government of the United States busy dealing with domestic terrorism and insurrection, the flow of cartel drugs into the country could continue unabated. And increased drug use would also contribute to the destruction of the nation. Bolan had to admit that it was a slick concept. Using the enemies of your enemies always made good sense.

"Jack?" Grey turned around when he spotted the Cuban. "Come over here, I want you to meet someone."

Bolan acknowledged Grey's call and walked over to him. "Ramon de Silva," Grey said, "this is Jack Vance, one of my assault-team leaders."

A fleeting shadow crossed the Cuban's face when

he looked into Bolan's blue eyes as if he recognized the big man. Just as quickly, it was replaced by a neutral smile. "I am pleased to meet you, Mr. Vance," he said as he stuck out his hand. "I have heard much about you."

Bolan shook his hand. "All good, I hope."

Silva laughed, but his face didn't smile. "You could say that."

The Cuban excused himself and walked to the front of the room. "If we are all here, gentlemen," he said, his eyes sweeping the room, "let's get down to business. First off, as the recent attack on the Grissom farm showed, the federal forces are moving into a new phase of repression."

Angry growls answered his words as they rang true to the militiamen.

"And as you saw there, they are willing to bring massive force against you, and you need to be ready for them. If it hadn't been for that one Patriot with the RPG that day, who knows what would have happened there? As you saw, even the vaunted FBI SWAT teams will back down when they are confronted with equal force."

Again there were sounds of agreement.

"You are going to need more heavy weapons to defend yourselves," the Cuban continued. "But I am afraid that I have some bad news for you. My principals are having difficulty securing these weapons for you, specifically the mortars and antiaircraft missiles you need."

"But—" one of the Brotherhood leaders spoke up "—you assured us that you would be able to get them."

"I know I did," the Cuban said soothingly. "But the delay has been caused by things beyond our control. I know that our timing is bad, as you need the weapons more than ever right now to protect yourselves from the federal forces. But I have come up with an idea that will provide you with what you need at no cost."

"And what is that?"

"Right now the National Guard armory at Coeur d'Alene is being used as a shipment point for heavy weapons and ammunition being distributed to other National Guard units throughout the state. There are enough Stinger and TOW missiles and both 81 mm and 4.2-inch mortars to supply all of your units for the foreseeable future. And the price is right. They are there for the taking. A few brave men should be able to overcome the night guards and capture the shipments. That will give you more weapons than we could have ever supplied you."

This was it, Bolan thought, where the rubber met the road. Raiding a military armory was moving up into big-time insurgent warfare. Running minor skirmishes against the FBI was one thing; this was entirely another. If this plan went off as Silva wanted, it could really be the start of a new American Civil War. The government would be forced to take strong action in response, and it would have no choice but to declare martial law at the least. That, however, would only feed the paranoia of the militias and escalate the crisis.

Bolan finally had what he had come for, and he could get in contact with Hal Brognola now. It was time that this charade was shut down permanently.

Americans had the time-honored right to disagree with their government as long as no laws were broken. But this had already gone too far. The Brotherhood of Patriots had gone wrong when they had invited outsiders into what should have remained a domestic difference of opinion. How Bolton Grey and the other Brotherhood leaders could have ever trusted Silva, as he called himself, was completely beyond him. They were so afraid of the federal government that they had let their fears overwhelm their common sense.

Some of their fears were justified, he had to concede that. But why they couldn't see that this course of action could only have one outcome was beyond him.

"I'm not sure about taking on the Idaho National Guard," Grey stated flatly. "They're not involved with this, and we have many friends in their ranks."

"But," Silva said, "if you want to be ready for all emergencies, you are going to need the heavy weapons. Courage, patriotism and determination cannot make up for a lack of firepower."

"I could use the weapons," Grey admitted. "But if your people cannot supply them, I'll just have to turn to someone else. I cannot commit my men to an operation like that without consulting them first.''

Silva had a difficult time keeping his feeling of frustration off his face. He was too close to success to let it get away from him now because one cowardly American didn't want to get his hands dirty. Why couldn't they understand that this was a fight to the death, and that, for them to have any chance of winning, they had to strike first and strike to win.

''This is an opportunity that will not last forever,'' the Cuban argued. ''The weapons are going to be shipped out next week, and you will never get another chance at so much matériel in one place.''

A Brotherhood leader from a small town right outside of Coeur d'Alene stood up. ''I'm willing to go for it,'' he said. ''My people want heavy weapons badly so we don't get treated like that dairy farmer.''

''I'm in, too,'' another said, standing.

After further discussion, the majority of the leaders committed their units to the operation. Faced with being the odd man out, Grey reluctantly agreed to provide an assault team to the group effort.

As soon as the militiamen committed themselves, Silva's two companions opened their briefcases and took out packets. ''I have the information here you will need on the target. My information is that the shipments will start being sent out in four days, so you don't have much time to get ready. Since that is the case, I had my people draw up an attack plan that you may want to use.''

Bolan instantly realized that this was a significant escalation of the foreign involvement with the militias. From the information he had been given before he came to Dilbert, he had halfway expected to find foreigners conducting actual training, but he had found them only supplying weapons. This choice of a target and working up the attack plans ahead of time marked a not-so-subtle shift of the command structure. If the Brotherhood leadership bought it, it would mark the end of the military independence.

It was ironic that men who talked so much about liberty and freedom were giving theirs up to enemies of their country.

WHEN BRAD GOLDBLUM rolled into Dilbert the next day, he pulled his dusty Volvo station wagon to the curb in front of a place called Mac's Grill and Tavern. Coming into town, it had seemed like the obvious place to start looking for antigovernment militiamen in this burg. And now that he had stopped, he could look around and see that there wasn't really a lot of choice.

Dilbert wasn't the smallest town he had ever seen in Washington or Idaho, but it didn't look like it had much going for it. The main street was all of three blocks long, and with the exception of the post office and credit union, the other buildings looked like they had been built back in the fifties and hadn't been updated since. There was a small café, something called a dinner club, and this bar was the town's social center. For the kind of men he was looking for, the bar seemed to be the best place to start. Plus, since it titled itself a grill, maybe he could have a little lunch while he was at it.

The woman behind the bar wasn't as old as the building, but it had been some time since she had been a candidate for the local high-school homecoming queen. There was that no-nonsense hardness about her that he had come to expect from the women in rural Idaho.

"You're new in town," the woman said, giving him a quick once-over.

"Yes, I am," Goldblum replied.

"We don't get too many new faces in Dilbert. You just passing through?"

"Kind of," he said. "I'm a reporter, and I'm trying to get some background for a story I'm working on."

"Well, how about that?" the woman said, her face not breaking into a smile. "Little ol' Dilbert is going to make it into the paper."

"My name's Brad Goldblum," the reporter offered.

"Around here, they call me Sam," she said. "Can I get you something?"

"Ah, how about a cup of coffee and a lunch menu?"

She jerked a thumb back at the chalkboard titled Today's Special. "That's lunch, and you take milk in your coffee, right?"

"Ah…right."

She smiled thinly. "Thought so."

Faced with the choice between a burger special or a big bowl of chili, he opted for the burger. There was no way he was going to risk gastric distress in a town like this.

"What kind of story are you writing?" Sam Whiting asked as she took away Goldblum's half-empty plate. As he had expected, the fries had been first-rate, but the burger had been more grease than he usually allowed himself at one sitting.

"I'm trying to get some background on a story I'm doing on the militia movement in the Pacific Northwest."

Whiting studied him for a long moment. "You're either the dumbest bastard I've ever seen, or they've been putting superstrength vitamins in the yogurt lately. You look like you have the makings of becoming a reasonable man someday, mister, but you're going to have to learn to recognize when something is none of your damned business."

This wasn't the first time that he had faced open hostility on this topic, and he wasn't put off by it. Not when a federal prison sentence would be his reward for failure. "But how can it hurt for me to just talk to people?"

Whiting just shook her head. "No harm at all, I guess. But don't say that I didn't warn you. One thing, though. You'd better be up front about what you're doing with them. You don't want anyone to think that you're a government snitch. If you haven't noticed already, we don't take too kindly to Feds around here. Not after they blew old Bill Grissom's place away the other day.''

Now Goldblum could go into his act. "Ma'am," he said, "I'm a journalist and that's all. I don't have anything to do with any part of any government. I'm looking for facts, and I'm looking for background so I can explain a serious social movement in our part of the country to my readers. The press has an obligation—"

"Save the sermon, bud. You don't have to try to convince me."

She nodded toward the three men at one of the tables in the back. "They're the boys you have to impress if you want to learn anything about what's going on around here. I don't know nothing about militias, and I don't want to. And as long as they don't bring it into my bar, I'm never going to know anything about them, either."

"Fair enough," Goldblum said. "Maybe I'll go have a talk with those guys."

"Good luck."

Whiting watched the reporter walk over to the table and introduce himself. He was either a brave man or a damned fool, and she opted for the latter choice. But it wouldn't be the first time that some big-city boy got his lights punched out in her bar. She just hoped that he didn't bleed all over the place. She had just mopped the floor yesterday and wanted it to last more than one day.

To her surprise, though, she saw one of the regulars offer him a seat and signal for a beer. It only went to show you how dumb some people could be. If Bolton learned that any of his soldier boys were talking to a "gentleman of the press," he wouldn't be amused. But since she kept her nose out of that part of Grey's business, it was no skin off her ass.

CHAPTER TWENTY-TWO

Brad Goldblum hit paydirt in Mac's Grill and Tavern that afternoon. Two of the men at the table he walked up to were in Bolton Grey's Brotherhood unit, and they had just been alerted to get ready for the attack on the National Guard armory. They were a little concerned about making such a bold attack and were drowning their concerns with beer.

While they thought they were being careful about what they said, they weren't being careful enough. The idea of being the source for a Seattle newspaper article appealed to them and overruled their common sense. The beer had something to do with it, as well. Both of the men, though, claimed not to know anything about any militia group.

"There's nothing going on around here like that," the first man said. "We mind our own business out here, and we just want to be left alone. But you should go up to Coeur d'Alene and talk to those people."

"You better make sure that you get there in three days," the other guy said. "Or you'll miss it."

Goldblum was smart enough to know not to directly ask what was going to happen in three days in Coeur d'Alene.

"Tell me about that shoot-out at the farm the other day. Did you guys go out there?"

"We heard about it," the first man said. "But by the time we got out there, it was all over. The fucking Feds had already shot up the place, and they were leaving."

"I'm surprised that the militia didn't do more than blow up that armored car. From everything I've heard, that man out there hadn't done a damned thing wrong. It looks like what you were saying earlier about the Feds doing any damned thing they like and no one standing up to them."

The two men exchanged glances. "They're some people standing up to them," the first man said. "You can bet your ass on that. But they'll wait till the right time, and they'll pick the place like they did when they blew up that FBI office in Boise."

The second man laughed. "Now, that was something I really wished I'd have been in on. And I'd have given anything to see those bastards' faces the next morning. Pow! Boom! All their nice little cars and stuff blown sky-high. It serves the bastards right. It'll take them months to repair all the damage."

"But," the first man said, "remember that it comes out of your tax money, old buddy, and you're always bitching about your taxes."

"That's okay with me." The second man grinned.

"As far as I'm concerned, it's money well spent and they can spend some more of it fixing the armory in Coeur d'Alene while they're at it."

Again Goldblum didn't react, but he realized that he had just been given the next target of militia retaliation. Hitting an armory would be more than a gesture, however. Armories held weapons, and the militias always needed more weapons.

To keep up the pretense, Goldblum didn't run for the door immediately. He bought the next round and listened as the conversation turned to hunting and women. He knew zilch about the first topic, but he contributed a few big-city stories that got sympathetic chuckles from the men.

When he left, he promised to come back and talk to them again if he needed any more background material. He also promised to spell their names right if he quoted them in the article. People always liked to be told that.

Boise, Idaho

SPECIAL AGENT IN CHARGE Dan Butterfield wasn't sure whether or not he wanted to believe the report from Brad Goldblum that Alvin Barker had forwarded to him. According to what the reporter had told the Intel officer, the National Guard armory at Coeur d'Alene was going to be raided for its stock of heavy weapons and ammunition sometime within the next three days. If it was a good tip, Butterfield had a real problem on his hands, to say nothing of a dramatic shift in the balance of power in the Pacific Northwest if it actually took place.

Just a few weeks earlier, he would have considered that kind of a scheme to be just a redneck Rambo fantasy, but not anymore. As far as he was concerned, a virtual state of war existed between the federal government and persons unknown in western Idaho. So far, though, considering that the Grissom farm and Boise attacks were still front-page news all over the Pacific Northwest, the war was being kept as low-key as possible. The governor hadn't declared a state of emergency, and martial law hadn't yet been imposed.

For most of the citizens of the state, life went on more or less as it always did. With the rare exception, like Bill Grissom, their lives weren't being affected by the events that were being played out in their communities. So far the war had been little more than newspaper and CNN headlines. An attack like this, though, would change all that pretty dramatically.

Against that background, the pressure was building for both the state and federal governments to come to grips with the militia crisis, as the politicians were calling it. There was great political theater in progress on the topic on both Capitol Hill and on the TV talking-head shows. Careers were being made as politicians from both the right and the left postured and primped in front of the TV cameras. The leftists wanted the citizenry of the country to be disarmed down to their kitchen knives. The right wing trumpeted the sacred right of the citizenry to own and bear arms as had been written in the Constitution over two centuries earlier.

Not since the issue of slavery had been debated before the Civil War had the lines been so firmly drawn, and *compromise* wasn't a word being spoken. Both camps felt that they had God and the right on their side and weren't going to back down. And the cries of the liberals to disarm America were feeding the already rampant paranoia of the militiamen.

While this political theater was going on, both state and federal agencies in Idaho were leaving no stone unturned to try to discover who was behind the attacks. But they weren't coming up with anything.

The Idaho attacks had been carried out, if not by professionals, at least by men who had been professionally trained. There were no leads in the Boise attack, and whoever had rocketed the tac teams at the Grissom farm hadn't left as much as even tire tracks behind. The FBI had nothing to go on and was getting nowhere fast.

Even though he had been too young to go to Vietnam, Dan Butterfield had gone through a phase of reading everything he could get his hands on about the military art of guerrilla warfare. It may not have done him any good back then, but it was coming in rather handy now. As far as he was concerned, he was dealing with a guerrilla war in Idaho, and he needed to apply counterinsurgency tactics if he was to get to the bottom of this.

So far, though, he had been able to resist suggestions from several quarters that he go to a military option to track down the militiamen responsible for the attacks. He knew that troops in the streets, even the Idaho State National Guard, would only make the situation worse, as it always did in a guerrilla war. The troops would only create sympathizers for the militia's antigovernment sentiments and fuel even more incidents.

Butterfield was afraid, though, that one more big incident would blow the lid off and martial law would be declared whether he liked it or not. And when that happened, he might as well pack his bags and turn in his badge, because it would be all over for him.

While he wasn't yet willing to give up and call in the military, he had do something about this latest report from Goldblum and do it fast. The problem with alerting the National Guard to the threat was that there were sure to be sympathizers within its ranks. The same thing was true of the state and local police. The only troops he could depend on not to tip the militia off were his own FBI tac teams and the ATF men.

But it might be to his advantage to let the militia know that he was aware of the planned raid. In the best of all possible worlds, the armory raid would never take place, not at Coeur d'Alene, nor anywhere else in his region. That way, there would be no confrontation between the militia and the National Guard and no excuse to make the situation worse than it already was.

Butterfield didn't run his idea past the director's office in Washington nor did he even talk about it with his own staff. It was his decision to make, and he would live with the results while he still could. The pressure from Washington was getting more intense by the minute, and he didn't know how much longer he would be in charge of the region. He had just heard that a Justice Department oversight team was being assembled to look over his shoulder, as well as that of every other senior federal official in the Northwest.

This might be the last chance he would have to make a difference in law enforcement in his region before control was taken away from him. It wasn't much of a legacy, but it might save some lives.

Getting on the phone to the Idaho adjutant general's office, Butterfield passed his snitch's information on to the commander of the Idaho National Guard. As he had expected, the general immediately hit the panic button. Almost before Butterfield hung up, troops were being called up, issued weapons and ammunition and were given orders to defend the armories at all costs.

When the troops received their orders, the militia sympathizers in their ranks would pass the word on to their buddies who hopefully would get the word to the militia leaders who would call the attack off. Many of the militiamen were fanatics, but he didn't think they were crazy enough to go up against well-armed troops who were waiting for them. At least he hoped they weren't.

Dilbert, Idaho

ON THE RIDE BACK from the hall meeting two nights earlier, Bolan had decided not to end his undercover operation. Now that Silva was actually calling the shots, he wanted to gather as much information as he could about the Cuban and his associates. When Brognola sent in the Feds, Bolan wanted them all to be scooped up at the same time. And to do that, he needed to know more about the Cuban, which meant staying in the cold.

Nonetheless, he also intended to break his cover just long enough to make a phone call to alert the National Guard. Letting the Patriots rocket an FBI building at night was one thing, but he couldn't allow them to gain access to the weapons of an armory.

Then Bolton Grey drove into the fuel yard two days before the scheduled raid. "The raid on the Coeur d'Alene armory has been called off," Grey said.

"What happened?"

"Someone tipped them off. They went on full alert and are guarding it twenty-four hours a day now with a full company of infantry."

Bolan could detect a note of relief in Grey's voice. The man was a fanatic, but he wasn't stupid. With this change, all the raid would accomplish would be the deaths of Patriots and Guardsmen alike. "Maybe your first impression about it was right," Bolan offered.

"It looks that way," Grey agreed. "But now I have to develop some new weapon suppliers, and that's going to take time."

With the attack called off, Bolan could try to put the last of the pieces together before he left Dilbert. He briefly considered letting Samantha Whiting know what was going on and advising her to think about living somewhere else until the smoke cleared away. When the Feds moved in to break up the Brotherhood, anyone who was at all connected with the militia was going to go down and go down hard. For some time to come, lengthy federal prison sentences were going to be as common in Idaho as potatoes. He didn't think that she was connected with the militia. But like almost everyone else in town, she was sure to have known about it. And while that wasn't a crime, she might get brought up on charges of conspiracy.

On the other hand, while he had spent more time with her than with anyone else in town except Bolton Grey, he couldn't say that he really knew her well. She had to know about the Brotherhood and had hinted as much several times. But he didn't know if she was just a silent observer or a sympathizer, as so many of the townspeople were. He thought that she was the former, but he wasn't positive.

If she was a sympathizer and he warned her, she might warn the others and his work would have been for nothing. It might be safer to keep her out of it and work behind the scenes to see that she didn't get caught up in the dragnet. If she did get swept up, he would get Brognola to release her.

RAMON DE SILVA was enraged when he was informed that the Brotherhood leadership had called off the raid on the Coeur d'Alene armory. He tried to talk the leaders out of canceling, but nothing he said could change their minds about going up against well-armed troops who were ready and waiting for them.

He wasn't about to allow a bunch of halfhearted cowards to defeat his plans. But before he tried to institute another battle plan, he had to find the traitor in the militia's ranks. For the National Guard to have been alerted, someone had to have given the plan away. It was a setback, but if he could find the government informer in the militia ranks, it would have been worth it. But finding the informer wouldn't be easy.

His mind kept flashing back to the meeting when the plan had been announced and he had been introduced to Jack Vance, Bolton Grey's new right-hand man. Something about Vance had nagged at the back of his mind, and since then he couldn't figure out what it was. He didn't think that he had ever seen the man before, but there was something very familiar about him. And now that the plan had been betrayed, he thought he knew what it was.

When he really thought about it, everything about

Vance screamed that, unlike the other Patriots in the room, he was a professional. There had been a steadiness about him, combined with a watchful assessment, that was completely out of place among the rank amateurs of the Brotherhood. His eyes had been too carefully guarded, his movements too sure, and he had shown none of the nervousness of the others when the plan had been announced. They had all been playing macho games with one another, trying so hard not to let anyone see that they were scared. Vance, however, had taken the mission calmly as if he had done it all before, many times.

Grey had said that he had screened Vance, but Silva had no confidence in the militia's security system. No matter how many sympathizers they had in state and local governments, they were still amateurs compared to the cold professionals of the federal government.

Unlike the militiamen, Silva didn't think that the men of the FBI, DEA and ATF were incompetents and second-raters; he knew better. It was true that they had done some unbelievably stupid things, but for the most part, the Feds were worthy opponents—as the Islamic Jihad could well attest.

Dealing with Vance wasn't Silva's only problem. Since the raid on the armory had been called off, he needed to come up with another operation to create the incident he needed to start the war. Since an attack on the National Guard was out, maybe a political assassination would do the trick. Americans always reacted strongly to assassinations. Killing an FBI or state official would bring a violent reaction from the government, which in return would bring a violent reprisal from the militiamen.

Suddenly the Cuban saw a solution to both of his problems. He would request that Grey loan Vance to him for the new operation. Once they were away from Dilbert, he would simply have Rahman cut his throat. Or better yet, he could be killed during the operation and he would become another martyr to the cause of American freedom. Either way, Vance would be gone, and Silva wouldn't have to worry about him.

CHAPTER TWENTY-THREE

Ramon de Silva's problem as to how to lure the man he knew as Jack Vance to his death was solved with the unwitting help of the FBI. Working on a tip, an FBI team accompanied a local sheriff's raid at a remote farm in the southern part of the state. Instead of finding a cache of weapons, however, the officers uncovered a huge methamphetamine laboratory. In the process of the bust, the men who were producing the illegal drug decided to shoot it out with the agents rather than go back to a federal prison. In the ensuing hour-long firefight, two of them died and a third was seriously wounded.

The raid had nothing at all to do with the ongoing countermilitia operation and, in more normal times, it wouldn't have become more than a local story. However, with the recent heightened public awareness of the conflict that was building in Idaho, the raid made both the national and local headlines because the FBI had been involved in another fatal shoot-out.

Even though the raid hadn't occurred in their region, the Brotherhood units in the northern part of

Idaho went on full alert again. The memory of the
FBI raid on the Grissom farm was all too fresh in the
militiamen's minds and had only fed their home-
grown paranoia. As far as they were concerned, any
federal law-enforcement activity was a potential
threat to them.

When Silva heard about the FBI raid and the militia
response, he was confident that he could get the
Brotherhood to retaliate. And again the FBI gave him
the inspiration for his target. A militia informant
within the Coeur d'Alene police department passed
the word that the regional director of the FBI would
visit the city to talk to civic leaders and local police
officials about the militia crisis. The meeting wasn't
being publicized and would make a perfect target for
a retaliatory militia attack. Making the hit in Coeur
d'Alene would also show the Feds that even with the
National Guard on alert, they weren't safe.

Best of all, though, the death of an FBI official or
two should goad the government into making another
major move against the militias. And one more move
might be all it would take.

IN THE FEW DAYS that had passed since the Coeur
d'Alene armory raid had been called off, Bolan hadn't
been able to gather any more information on Silva's
involvement with the militia. Every time he tried to
bring the subject up to Bolton Grey, the man had
backed away from it, and Bolan knew better than to
press the issue. The inaction of this mission was start-

ing to get to him, but he knew that he had to stay loose and wait.

For Silva's plan to work, the Cuban would have to force the Brotherhood into doing something that would cause a government retaliation. So Silva would be back, and Bolan would be waiting when he showed up.

When the word of the drug-lab raid in southern Idaho hit Dilbert, however, Grey was the one who brought up the subject of the Cuban.

"The Feds are moving against the people again," the businessman said the next afternoon. "So Silva and I came up with an operation that will let them know that we aren't going to stand by and let them run rampant over the citizenry. Every time they go in somewhere with their guns blazing, we have to respond."

Grey's voice took on the intense tone of a tent preacher. "To do anything less is to just stand by and watch while they steal our freedoms from us. We have to do something to protect ourselves."

Bolan didn't bother to point out that this latest incident hadn't been a questionable federal raid against a law-abiding citizen. It had been a good bust and had produced evidence of large-scale illegal-drug production. Usually the militias severely frowned on drug activities, and they were known to move against local drug dealers to clean up their neighborhoods. But when Grey started talking this way, he wasn't in a mood for rational thinking.

Bolan really didn't want Grey to be thinking too rationally right now. He needed to get closer to Silva's operation, and with the Cuban behind this latest idea, it was a good way to do it.

"What do you have in mind?" Bolan asked.

"I think that the time has come for us to take the war directly to the Feds themselves," Grey replied. "So far, we've only attacked their installations and their armored vehicles, but they haven't gotten the message. I think it's time that we made it very clear to them that they can be killed when they attack the liberty of Americans."

Grey looked Bolan directly in the eyes. "We have word that there's going to be a special meeting in Coeur d'Alene between the regional FBI boss and local police agencies, where they are going to make their plans to eliminate the militias. We'll have a man inside the meeting who will tell us what takes place. But we want to send the Feds a message that as long as they terrorize the people, they aren't safe. We want to take out the FBI honcho."

Bolan's blood went cold. Grey was talking about assassination pure and simple, and he was certain that the idea had come directly from Silva. The success of the Cuban's program required that the militias and the government go at each other head to head, and this tactic was designed to create a maximum response from the Feds. In turn, the militias would defend themselves even more forcefully, and the war would be on.

"Anyway," Grey said, "this mission is important to the future of freedom in this country, and I'm asking you to undertake this job for us. I've seen your service records, and I have the reports from the training camp. You're probably the best shot we have, and I don't want this mission to fail. And more than just ensuring that the hit is made, I want to make sure that no one else is harmed. We have to make the point that we aren't at war with the state or local agencies, only the repressive federal government."

No matter what Grey said, Bolan wasn't going to kill any federal official. But if he accepted the mission, maybe he could ensure that no one was killed by anyone in the Brotherhood. It should be easy enough for him to make sure that something went wrong, something that would cause the mission to be called off as the armory raid had been. It would be risky, but it would give him a chance to learn more about Silva and his operation.

"You can count on me," he told Grey.

"Good," Grey answered grimly. "I knew that I could. Now, here's the plan...."

SILVA WAS PLEASED to hear that Jack Vance had agreed to be the shooter for the mission. He had planted the idea in Grey's mind, but hadn't wanted to ask for him too strongly. Now all he needed to do was to put together the details of Vance's mission, a one-way mission. He still wasn't sure that he was the government informer, but he didn't want to leave him alive on the chance that he was.

Plus, at this stage of the program, the Brotherhood needed a martyr to rally around. Were Vance to fall in "the defense of freedom," the militiamen were sure to want to avenge his death. And it would be child's play to make sure that Vance was martyred.

Boise, Idaho

DAN BUTTERFIELD DIDN'T like the idea of making the high-profile trip to Coeur d'Alene. Someone in Washington had come up with the idea as a public-relations stunt to show that the Federal Bureau of Investigation had the militia situation in northern Idaho well in hand, but it was pure crap. They had the situation all right, but no one in his right mind would say that it was "in hand." It wasn't even close.

Preventing the armory raid didn't mean that they had made any real progress toward disarming the militias and bringing them under control. The Bureau was still reacting to the militias instead of proacting, and that always left a person behind the power curve. But with the Justice Department bosses breathing down his neck, he had to make the appearance as he had been ordered to. Anything less would be as good as handing in his resignation.

Before he went, though, he wanted to know the lay of the land and went down to his own intelligence office. "Do we have anything new on activity in the Coeur d'Alene area?" he asked Agent Alvin Barker.

The intelligence officer shook his head. "Nothing, boss. I'm not getting a thing from either the state or local boys or even from our snitches in the area. Maybe we scared them off when the National Guard finally got serious about guarding their own stuff."

"I wouldn't bet on that if I were you." Butterfield shook his head. "More than likely they've just hunkered down and are waiting until we get distracted and turn our attention somewhere else."

"Let's hope that doesn't happen for a while then," Barker said. "We've had too much trouble from that part of the state for too long now, and we can use the break."

"I wouldn't count on that, either," Butterfield replied. "It seems that the farther north you go in this state, the more radical the population becomes. We've always had militia wackos up there. It must have something to do with the weather."

"I think it's the potatoes," Barker said seriously. "I've completely quit eating the damned things since I got transferred here."

"That's probably a good move."

Dilbert, Idaho

BOLAN DIDN'T LIKE the way the Coeur d'Alene mission was shaping up. According to the briefing Grey gave him, there were to be four men on the team, which was about right, but two of them were to be Silva's people, not militiamen. When he asked Grey why Silva's people were involved, the businessman had muttered something about the Cuban's concern with keeping security tight on this mission so it wouldn't be leaked the way the armory raid had been.

Bolan understood that concern; it was obvious that someone had leaked the armory raid to the Feds. But he saw it more as an excuse to get Silva's people involved. This was beginning to have the earmarks of a "throwaway" mission, where the operatives were to be sacrificed to make an impression. Although that tactic went against the way most Americans operated, it was common in terrorist groups, and Silva was no stranger to terrorist operations.

In this scenario, the hit would be a high-risk operation requiring the shooter, and any other throwaway, to take up a position that was bound to be instantly discovered. The shooter would make the hit, but then he and any other man with him would be killed in the ensuing commotion. The bodies would be found with evidence that would either lay a false trail or that would connect them with a preselected group that was to take the fall.

It was a complicated tactic, but it had worked well before, and it would work on an FBI official in Coeur d'Alene. Once you were committed to it, the only way to keep from becoming a dead martyr was to know that you were being set up.

Bolan knew the score, and he had chosen to put it

on the line when he agreed to take part in it. The only way he could control events without blowing his cover was if he stayed in the action. If he begged off the mission, someone else would take his place, make the kill, be killed in return and the scenario would still play itself out. The assassins would be identified as militiamen, and the FBI would be forced to retaliate, creating the confrontation Bolan was trying to prevent. To keep that from happening, he had no choice but to take the mission.

The other problem was that he wasn't going to have a rehearsal or even a recon of the target before the day of the hit. Grey said it was because of security concerns, but Bolan saw that as one more sign of this being set up as a one-way mission. If he didn't know the mission area, he wouldn't be able to take his time, and in an assassination mission, haste was a good way to blow the mission.

Then there were the other men who had been assigned to go with him. The two men Silva contributed to the operation were both Hispanics who looked like they had been on the sharp end of the stick more than once. Bolan pegged them as two cartel hitters. Supposedly they were to be the lookouts and drive the getaway van while he and the other militiaman made the hit.

The other militiaman was Don Gooding from Lewiston, known mostly for his hunting expertise and his fearlessness. At another time, he would have made a good field soldier, but now he was a potential assassin. He didn't have any military training beyond what he picked up at the Brotherhood training camp. But what he lacked in experience, he made up for with youthful enthusiasm, and that was going to be a problem.

Bolan would have rather been teamed with an older man, someone who was a little more cautious. That way, he wouldn't have to watch to make sure that his partner didn't do something stupid and endanger him. But he saw Gooding's assignment as one more sign that this was to be a one-way mission. There was no reason to waste an experienced, valuable militiaman when there was a young kid who was so willing to die for the cause.

All told, it was a recipe for disaster, and it was coming on fast.

THE NEXT MORNING, neither of Silva's two Hispanic gunmen had much to say on the ride to Coeur d'Alene. They spoke to each other a little in Spanish which Bolan understood, but nothing of any importance was said. One of the men, however, the one who called himself Rivera, kept looking at him as if he were memorizing his face. Or trying to remember his face. Either one wasn't good.

Bolan knew that the closer he got to Silva's men, the more risk he took in being recognized. The face he currently wore wasn't completely unknown to the Cali cartel. Usually the enemies who got too good of a look at him died. But he knew that a photograph or two of him existed, and his description had been reported hundreds of times.

The upside of that was that his description could fit almost any man of his height and coloring who kept himself in good shape. Nonetheless, the attention Rivera was paying to him wasn't a good sign. If he could work it in, Bolan decided to make sure that Rivera's body got left behind.

If the Hispanics were quiet, Gooding apparently felt compelled to fill the silence and talked almost nonstop all the way. Bolan wanted to tell the kid that chattering wasn't the way of a would-be warrior, that it betrayed his inner tension. But since he figured that the kid's career was going to be cut short by a federal prison sentence, he didn't bother.

He still didn't have a strategy to prevent the planned assassination, but he figured that he would stay loose and wait for an opportunity. Since this mission had been thrown together rather than being thought out, the smallest thing would throw it off. If nothing else, when the time came he would pull his shot and purposefully miss the target. That was lame and would be difficult to explain, but it was better than killing a federal agent to maintain his cover.

The time had finally come for him to end the assignment. He didn't have everything he wanted, but he had exposed himself more than was wise. As soon as he got back from Coeur d'Alene, he would leave Dilbert as suddenly as he had arrived.

CHAPTER TWENTY-FOUR

Coeur d'Alene, Idaho

When Garcia entered Coeur d'Alene, he drove the van directly to the site where the hit was going to take place, the helipad behind the local police station. The setup was like something straight out of a made-for-TV action-adventure flick. But Bolan saw that it had great possibilities, particularly for a one-way mission. Whatever else he was, Silva knew his business.

"This is where it will happen," Rivera told Bolan as he pointed out the helipad through the windshield of the parked van. "See that landing place behind that building?"

Bolan nodded.

"That is the police station where the meeting is being held. The FBI helicopter will land there, and the agents will go in through the back door."

Bolan saw that the agents would have to walk fifty yards to the building, which would put them in the kill zone for more than enough time to identify the target and make the hit.

The target was the man who headed the regional FBI office, and Rivera had a full-face photo of Dan Butterfield for Bolan to study. "This is the man you are to kill. He is a little over six feet tall, he has brown hair cut short and wears glasses. He will be wearing a coat and tie, and he does not wear sunglasses like the rest of them."

The ambush site that Silva had picked was in a parking structure across the street from the empty lot behind the police building. It would be easy to make the shot from there, a mere three hundred yards across an empty lot to the helipad. But that wasn't the problem. The problem was that as with all parking structures, there weren't any good escape routes out of the building. There was only the one entrance and exit for vehicles, and only one elevator to take the drivers down to ground level. He'd seen jails that had more exits than that.

Now Bolan was completely convinced that his earlier suspicions were correct. It was apparent that Silva had purposefully chosen the parking structure because it was a trap. It would be all too easy for him and Gooding to be caught or killed while they were trying to escape. All it would take would be for one police car to block the entrance and they would be in the bag.

"I don't like this place," Bolan stated. "If we make the hit from here, we're going to get trapped.

All they'll have to do is drive just one cop car out front and we'll never get out.''

"But Garcia and I will be parked out on the street," Rivera said soothingly. "And we will make sure the entrance stays clear until you get out."

The setup was a little too pat for Bolan's taste. With him and his militiaman assistant up on one of the parking levels and the two Colombians on the street below in the van, he would be screwed for sure.

"This isn't the first time that I've done something like this," Bolan replied. "And I can tell you that this isn't going to work. There has to be somewhere else that I can set up to make the hit, and you'd better find it. We don't have much time left."

"But this is where Mr. Silva said he wanted the hit to take place."

Now Bolan had his head. "I don't remember your boss as being in the Brotherhood," he said chillingly. "My commander is Bolton Grey, and he told me to use my judgment on this mission. Shooting from that building is too dangerous, and I'm not going to do it from there. You'll have to find another location for me to shoot from."

Rivera and Garcia exchanged glances that Bolan didn't like. But he pressed his point. Throwing Silva's two watchdogs off balance was essential to his survival. Plus, moving to a new site could take quite a bit of time, and the clock was running.

Rivera also knew that the time was running out. Spotting an alley that opened up on the lot facing the chopper pad, he turned to Garcia. "Pull over," he said in Spanish.

When the van stopped, Rivera opened the door and ran into the alley. Bolan saw what the Colombian had seen and realized that he was scouting an alternate site for the kill.

Just then, Gooding pointed through the windshield. "Jesus!" he said. "There's a couple of cop cars over there, and they're watching us!"

Bolan looked down to the end of the block and saw two Coeur d'Alene police cars parked in front of a doughnut shop, one of them aimed each way so the drivers could talk to one another through their open windows. It was the sort of thing you saw every day in any major American city.

"There's another cop coming up behind us," Gooding said with a note of panic as he looked into the door mirror.

Bolan doubted that the police cars they had seen were any more than just the town's routine patrols. But since the guilty run when no man pursues, it was easy to make something more of them than they actually were. This was the opening he had been waiting for. "Go! Go! Go!" he shouted.

Since he was a trained soldier, Garcia reacted instantly to Bolan's command. Dropping into first gear, he pulled out into traffic heading west. At the end of the block, a third Coeur d'Alene police car was stopped at the light on the cross street and, in the background, a siren wailed.

"We gotta get out of here," Gooding pleaded. "There's too many cops around here. They know why we're here, and they're looking for us."

Gooding's nerve had snapped, and he was hovering on the verge of panic. Bolan knew he could snap him out of it with a word or two, but he refrained. Having him panicked ratcheted up the tension, and that was what he wanted right now.

Garcia looked over at Bolan. "We have to pick up Rivera!"

"We'll get him later," Bolan said, keeping his voice tense. "Keep going like we're heading out of town."

A glance in his rearview mirror made up Garcia's mind. The police car was still behind him. It stayed there as he headed directly for the freeway.

In the back of the van, Gooding was going out of his mind. "You just keep going," he told the Colombian. "Don't you even think of going back there."

"Silva is not going to like me leaving Rivera behind," Garcia stated.

"Mr. Grey will understand what happened," Bolan replied. "And Rivera can take the Greyhound back to town."

Once they were on the freeway headed south back to Dilbert, Bolan allowed himself to relax. It was finally over, and he felt a certain satisfaction at how the mission had gone.

RIVERA WAS STUNNED to see the van pull away from the curb. What in the hell was Garcia thinking? He ran back out to the street and started to yell after the van when he heard a car behind him and turned around to see an Idaho State Police cruiser. The officer in the car glanced over at him before he picked up his radio microphone. Concerned that the cop was calling someone about him or the van, Rivera quickly turned the corner and hurriedly walked away.

When he was in the clear, Rivera walked to the nearest phone booth. The number he dialed was Silva's mobile phone in his car. He had just remembered where he had previously seen the man who now called himself Jack Vance, and Silva had to be told about it immediately.

Dilbert, Idaho

BOLTON GREY WAS in his private office at the credit union when his secretary buzzed him and said that a Mr. Ramon de Silva wanted to see him. He frowned but told her to send him right on in.

"I thought I told you never to come here," Grey said as soon as the door was closed.

"I don't have time for your petty Yankee prejudices right now," Silva snapped. "We have a serious problem, and something must be done about it immediately!"

If there was anything he hated, it was the hysterical aspect of the Hispanic personality. But for Silva to have broken the security arrangement they had agreed to, it had to be something out of the ordinary. "And what is it that is so important?"

"The Coeur d'Alene mission. It failed."

Bolton frowned. "What happened?"

"We were betrayed!" the Cuban grated. "That man who calls himself Jack Vance is a government agent. Somehow he passed a warning to the government, and they were waiting there for us. To make it worse, he abandoned one of my men and he was almost captured."

"That's not possible," Grey replied calmly. "Jack Vance couldn't have done anything like that. I had him thoroughly checked out before I brought him into the Brotherhood. We checked everything from his military records to his employment history, and he came up clean."

As a Cuban who had lived most of his life hip deep in international Communist intrigue, Silva couldn't believe the childlike naïveté of most Americans. Even a man in a position of power like Grey, who should have known better, had no idea of the power of misinformation. How could men like him even hope to overthrow the government when they had no concept of what they were going up against? If they didn't get smart quick, they were all going to find themselves dead or in prison.

He really didn't care about the fate of the militiamen one way or the other. They could be slaughtered like sheep for all he cared. But before they were gunned down, he needed their help to accomplish his mission, the disruption of the United States. For them to do that, they had to get smarter fast. More importantly the man who called himself Jack Vance had to be eliminated.

"You say that you had him checked out," Silva said, fighting to keep from sneering. "And who did you check him out with, may I ask, the federal government?"

"Of course," Grey answered. "Like I said, we checked everything through our contacts in the government. Like I told you in the beginning, there are people in all levels of government who are—"

"Using the government to check out your recruits is like asking the fox to guard the henhouse," the Cuban snapped. "Can't you see what has happened here? They misled you so they could plant an agent in your ranks. It is a common tactic of the government."

"It has worked well for us before," Grey said. "We have never had a security problem."

"That may be," the Cuban said, leaning closer to Grey. "But that was before it came to this man who calls himself Jack Vance. Let me tell you about this man. He has been a deep-cover federal agent for many years, and he is probably the most dangerous man in all of your country. He is a thug, a killer, an assassin, and he has more blood on his hands than most armies."

Grey unconsciously moved back from the Cuban. One of the other things he didn't like about Hispanics was their naked intensity. "Are you a hundred percent sure of this supposed identification of him?"

Though he wanted to say that he was, Silva was an honorable man. "I have never seen him myself, no," he admitted. "But I have talked to those few who have seen him and who have survived. I have also seen a photograph that is said to be of him."

Silva leaned over Grey's desk again. "I tell you, he is the one they call the Soldier, and he is well-known to both the Cuban government and to the Cali board. We had heard that he once worked with Mack Bolan, the man who was called the Executioner, and after Bolan's death, Vance started working for your government."

"I have heard of the Executioner." Grey thought hard. "But that was years ago, and he fought the Mafia crime Families, didn't he?"

"Yes, Mack Bolan was the sworn enemy of the Mafia, but he also operated against other enemies of your country even as your government was doing their best to eliminate him."

"And you say that Jack Vance worked with him?"

"His name is not Vance," Silva insisted. "But the name he uses is not important. The only thing that is important is that he must be eliminated before he betrays your entire operation. The government is gathering their forces to crush you, and you must protect yourselves or you will all die."

Put in those terms, Grey had no choice but to grudgingly believe the Cuban. If Vance was who

Silva said he was, he would be taken care of. But he would be tried first by a tribunal of the Brotherhood. You didn't kill a man for treason without a trial.

"Okay," he conceded. "I'll have him taken into custody today."

"I will capture him," Silva said eagerly. "I have some of my men available and we will—"

"No," Grey said firmly. "Vance was taken into the Brotherhood of Patriots, and if he is a traitor, we'll discipline him ourselves."

"What do you mean 'if he is a traitor'?" Silva couldn't believe what he was hearing. "Didn't you listen to what I said? He is a government agent."

"What I mean," Grey said, his voice rising, "is that the Brotherhood will put him on trial for treason. If he is found guilty, we will execute him as a traitor."

"But, he has to be taken care of..."

"He is one of us now," Grey insisted. "And we take care of our own problems."

Silva knew that he had reached an impasse with the stubborn Yankee, at least for now. But he had no intention of giving up. The Cali board had suffered many reverses engineered by this man "Vance." And the man who brought him back to Colombia would be richly rewarded. He would let Grey handle Vance for now, but Silva wasn't finished with him. Not by a long shot.

"As you say." The Cuban smiled. "He is your man, so you take care of him. But I suggest that you do it quickly and get him out of here to someplace where he can be held safely. It is too dangerous to keep him here.''

"On that we agree,'' Grey said. "I'll have him taken to the Washington camp.''

"It must be done quickly,'' Silva insisted. "We're at risk every minute that he runs loose.''

"I said that I will handle it!'' Grey snapped. "And I will.''

"As you say.'' Silva shrugged. "You know what has to be done.''

"Yes, I do.''

"And,'' the Cuban added, "you know where to reach me as soon as it is done. I want to question him as soon as you have him in custody.''

Now Grey bristled. He'd had more than his fill of this bastard telling him what to do. "Until the Brotherhood has determined Vance's guilt,'' he said firmly, "you'll do nothing except to tell us what you know of him. And after the trial, we'll decide what happens to him next.''

"Just get him out of here before it's too late.''

"I told you that I would.'' Grey's eyes were cold. "And I'm a man of my word.''

CHAPTER TWENTY-FIVE

Bolton Grey sat at his desk for some time after Silva left his office. If the Cuban was right, Vance had to be stopped immediately, but the problem was that Grey didn't want to believe him. Deep down, he really wanted to believe that Vance was an honorable man, and an honorable man wouldn't betray his sworn comrades. He wanted to believe that because he himself wasn't so honorable, and he admired the trait when he found it in others. But if Vance was a government agent, he had to be stopped before he could betray them all. And he had to be punished.

He knew that Vance was still returning from the blown mission in Coeur d'Alene and wouldn't get back to the fuel yard for another two hours. That was enough time to put something together.

He reached for the phone and placed several quick calls to Patriots living outside of the Dilbert area. He knew better than to try to do this one alone. From what he had seen, Vance was too good for Grey to go man to man with him. Plus, he didn't want anyone in town to be in on Vance's disappearance. The four men he called would be able to deal with him without gunfire. The last thing Grey wanted was to draw attention to what they had to do.

WHEN THE VAN BROUGHT Bolan back to the fuel yard, he saw Bolton Grey's Cadillac parked in front of the office. Right beside it was another car with four men leaning against it. From the expressions on their faces, something serious was going down.

"Come on inside, Jack," Grey said casually as he opened the door of the office to greet him. "We need to talk."

"Sure thing."

Bolan had no fear of what Grey wanted to talk to him about. He had his story down cold and couldn't be blamed for the mission going bad. He didn't know what the four other men in the car were doing here, but that didn't mean anything. As he had learned, the Brotherhood was widespread, and it wasn't an exaggeration to say that one out of every four men in the region was somehow connected with it.

"We just couldn't do it," Bolan started to explain. "The cops were crawling all over the—"

"That's not what I need to talk to you about," Grey said, cutting him off abruptly.

"What is it, then?"

Grey looked him full in the face. "I just got a report from a reliable source who claims that you aren't who you say you are."

"And just who the hell am I supposed to be?"

"I'm told that you call yourself a variety of names."

Bolan laughed.

"I'm not joking," Grey said.

"Neither am I." Bolan's voice was cold. He had no idea what had gone wrong, but he knew that he had to brazen it out. His only chance to survive was to keep playing his Jack Vance persona to the hilt.

"I can't take a chance," Grey said, almost pleading for understanding. "You know that. I've got to take you into custody until we can get this sorted out."

"I know you're making a big mistake."

When Bolan said that, the other four men closed in on him. They weren't showing weapons, but he had no doubt that they were packing. They wouldn't be here if they weren't. Boxed in as he was, he knew that he didn't have a realistic chance of breaking free, and any attempt would only leave him wounded or dead.

"Now what happens?" Bolan asked.

Grey hesitated before answering. "I'm sending you to the training camp for safekeeping while we investigate this. If it turns out to be true, you'll stand trial for treason."

"You're making a mistake, Bolton."

"I hope so," Grey said. "I really do, but I can't take any chances. Not now."

"Let's go, buddy," the man who appeared to be in charge told him. "You know the drill. Put your hands behind your back."

Bolan did as he was told and felt the handcuffs clamp down over his wrists.

"Out to the car."

Grey watched the car drive off before going around to the room in the back of the building. He had to clear out Vance's things and get rid of his van in case anyone came looking for him. From what he knew, Vance had no family, so anyone who did ask about him would be the enemy and that would be proof of his treachery.

SAMANTHA WHITING WAS behind the bar at Mac's Grill and Tavern when John Nolan came in. Plopping down on a stool, he ordered a draft.

Taking a long drink of his beer, Nolan stared at her breasts and grinned. "I hear that your new boyfriend turned out to be a government snitch."

Whiting's blood turned cold. "What are you talking about, John?"

"You know, that Jack Vance guy." Nolan chuckled. "He's supposed to be some kind of hotshot secret agent."

"I don't believe it."

The man shrugged. "Just ask your boss. He knows the score on him."

"Are you telling me that Bolton Grey's spreading that bullshit story?"

Now Nolan looked concerned. It wasn't healthy to talk about Mr. Grey's business. "I'm not supposed to be talking about none of this," he muttered as he picked up his beer glass.

"You'll talk to me, dammit!" she said.

The man drained his beer, laid a bill on the bar and walked out of the tavern without another word.

Whiting frowned as she watched Nolan walk out. He was a slobbering blowhard, but she didn't know him to be a liar. At the same time, she simply didn't believe that Jack Vance could be a federal agent. He didn't look or act like a man who was spying on anyone. He sure hadn't tried to get any information out of her, and he hadn't asked for the job Grey had given him, either. In fact, if it hadn't been for Red Gillum picking that fight with him, Vance would have probably just drifted through town after a couple of days, and that would have been the end of it.

And to hear that Bolton had turned against him didn't make any sense, either. Bolton hadn't only given him the job that allowed him to stick around, but he had also invited him to join his private little army, as well. Nonetheless, Whiting felt fear. She knew that when Bolton Grey got an idea in his head, it was downright difficult, if not impossible, to get him to change his mind.

But if Vance was in trouble, for whatever reason, she had to see if she could help him. He had helped her when she had needed it, and she would return the favor if she could. But she knew that it was more than just payback for a good deed that made her want to help him.

She was almost embarrassed to admit it, but she thought that she was falling in love with him. It had been a long time since she had met a man who had made her feel that way, and she had thought that part of her life had been long dead and buried. There was something about him, though, his quiet strength for one, that had made her come alive again, and she liked the feeling. It was worth it to her to try to keep that feeling in her life.

She placed a quick call to Thelma, her replacement barmaid, and arranged for her to come in and cover for her.

"What's going on?" Thelma asked when she showed up a few minutes later.

"I'll tell you when I get back."

"You'd better."

WHEN WHITING DIDN'T find Vance or his van at the fuel-yard office, she went around to the room in the back of the building. The door was unlocked and the small apartment had been completely cleaned out. There was no sign that Jack Vance had ever been there. Nothing, not even as much a dirty plate, had been left behind. Vance had seemed like a tidy man, but if he had suddenly left town, he wouldn't have cleaned his room from top to bottom first. This looked more like someone had removed all the evidence that he had ever lived there, and she knew the only man who could possibly have been responsible for that.

Getting back into her car, she drove back into Dilbert to talk to the one man who knew everything that happened in town.

BOLTON GREY LOOKED UP from his desk in the credit union building when Samantha Whiting stormed into the room without knocking. From the look in her eyes, she had discovered that Jack Vance was missing.

"Where is he, Bolton?" she asked.

"Where's who?" he asked, frowning.

"Dammit, Bolton," she snapped, "don't get cute with me. Where's Jack Vance? The word is going around town that he's a federal agent."

Grey's eyes narrowed. "Where'd you hear that?"

"One of your soldier boy wanna-bes tried to hit on me at the bar. He figured that I was available again because he'd heard you were saying that Jack is a Fed."

Grey leaned back in his chair. "Sam, please close the door and take a seat."

"No, I want an answer from you, Bolton, and I want it now."

"I'm sorry that you had to learn about it this way," he said, his voice trying to show concern.

"Learn about what?"

"Jack Vance is a federal agent, and he came here to infiltrate our town. He was here to cause trouble for us, Sam, but we learned about him in time."

"Where is he now?"

"He's gone, Sam, and he won't be coming back."

Whiting felt her heart lurch. "You killed him, didn't you?" she asked, her voice low.

Grey shook his head. "No, Sam, I didn't kill him, and I don't know why you would say something like that. I just confronted him with what I'd learned about him, and he left town."

"You're a lying sack of shit, Bolton Grey. You and your boys did something to him, I know you did."

"You think that he wouldn't have left town without saying goodbye, is that it?" Grey almost sneered. "Well, let me tell you something, Miss Samantha. You may be one of the most eligible women in this town, but you're not Miss America, not by a long shot. Vance wasn't drawn to you because he wanted to share a cottage on the edge of town with you and live happily ever after. He was using you, and you fell for it like an old maid."

Grey shook his head. "I'm disappointed in you, Sam. I thought that you were smarter than that.

"But then," he added, "I thought the same about Kate, as well, and look what she did. It looks like neither one of you girls have a lick of common sense. But then, with the father you two had, I'm really not too surprised. If your mother'd had a lick of sense, either, she'd have found herself a different man and you girls would have been a hell of a lot better off."

Whiting was enraged now. To hear him talk about her family that way brought back all the pain she thought she had left behind, and she exploded. "I've heard some crap flow from your mouth over the years, Bolton, but I don't think that I've ever heard anything like that. My family doesn't have a damned thing to do with this, and you know it."

She leaned over his desk. "I swear I'm going to get to the bottom of this, even if it kills me."

"If you're not careful, it might," he warned her. The last thing he needed was for her to start poking her nose into his business. Although they had never talked directly about the Brotherhood, her working behind the bar guaranteed that she picked up on almost everything that was going on around town.

"Are you threatening me, Bolton?"

"No, Sam, I'm not. But you're in completely over your head on this. If you don't want to end up like your sister, let it drop."

Her eyes narrowed. "Exactly what does that mean, Bolton?"

Now Grey hesitated. "All I mean is that she didn't listen to me, and look where it got her."

Whiting's blood turned cold. "You killed her, didn't you, you bastard?"

"I didn't kill Kate, Sam. She killed herself. If she'd listened to me instead of going off to Boise and running around with that damned Mexican, she'd still be alive today."

"I'm going to find out what you did with Jack, Bolton. I'm not going to let it slide like I did with Kate. Not this time."

"You'd better watch yourself, Samantha, or you're going to learn that Dilbert can do without you, too."

She bit back an angry retort. There was nothing else to say to him and nothing more that she was going to learn from him. Now that Bolton had shown his true colors and she really knew what she was up against, there was no point in making a bad situation any worse. She wouldn't be any help to Jack Vance if she disappeared, too.

Making a sharp about-face, she left the office, but she wasn't done trying to find out what Bolton had done to Jack Vance. Not by a long shot.

BACK AT THE BAR, Whiting fielded Thelma's questions and promised to explain everything to her later. Right now she needed information, and the bar was the best place in town to get it. It had given her the tip about Vance, and maybe it would give here even more. All she had to do was unbutton the top of her shirt, lean over when she served them a beer and these guys would be all over her chatting her up.

When she spotted the Seattle reporter walking in, though, she got another idea. Her plan to find out what Grey had done with Jack Vance would take too much time, and she didn't think that time was on her side. Goldblum, however, might be able to give her search a jump start. There was no doubt in her mind that the reporter wasn't in Dilbert to get background for a story about the militia movement as he had claimed. Had the paper really wanted to do a story on militias, they would have sent a redneck to get it, not a Yuppie.

She had lived in Seattle long enough to recognize a Yuppie when she saw one. Everything about him from his fashionable rustic clothes to his politically correct Volvo station wagon screamed that he was a trendy, status-seeking liberal. Anything he wrote about the militias would be a condescending hatchet job if not openly hostile. She didn't understand why any of the men had talked to him at all.

In fact he might even be a government spy like Bolton had accused Vance of being, and that's what had given her the idea. She was willing to do anything it took to get Jack Vance back even if it meant turning federal snitch on the locals. She had lived most of her life in Dilbert, but when push came to shove, she didn't owe this miserable town, or anyone in it, a thing. All it had brought her was sorrow and a life of quiet desperation. There were worse things than being ridden out of Dilbert on a rail.

CHAPTER TWENTY-SIX

"Coffee?" Whiting asked Brad Goldblum as she walked up to take his order.

"Thanks."

"Listen, sonny boy," she said as she poured, "I know what you're really doing here, and I have some information for you."

"What do you mean?"

She backed away and smiled. "What I mean is that you're no more looking for background on a news story than I am. You're a snitch, but I just don't know who you're working for."

Hearing the magic word, he glanced over his shoulder and started to get up.

"It won't do you any good to run," she said, reaching out and grabbing his arm. "If you do, I'll blow the whistle on you right now and you won't make it to the door. Just sit here, drink your coffee and listen to me."

"Why are you doing this to me?" Goldblum looked panic-stricken.

"It's simple. I need some help, and you're going to give it to me."

Goldblum knew a deal when he saw it. He also knew when it was time to deal, and this was it. "What do you need?"

"I have some information that I need sent to the FBI immediately."

"Why not give it to them yourself?"

"You know why, asshole," she snapped. "After that rat-screw at the Grissom place the other day, the Feds aren't too popular around this place, and I have to live here. At least for now, I have to."

"What is it that you want me to do?"

"The Brotherhood's holding a man prisoner, and I want them to get him released. If they get him out, I'll tell them everything they want to know about what's been going on around this burg back to the beginning of time.

"But," she cautioned, "that's only if they get him back alive and in one piece. Otherwise, I know nothing."

"Okay," the reporter said, activating the small tape recorder in his coat pocket. "What's this guy's name?"

"His name's Jack Vance, and I think he's being held in a secret militia training camp in the Wenatchee National Forest in Washington."

"Do you know where this camp is located?"

"I don't know exactly, but it's not too far from Bender, Washington."

"I'll see what I can do," Goldblum said.

"You'd better do real good, mister," she warned him as she looked over his shoulder at the locals sitting at the other end of the room. "And do it quickly. If I tell the boys here that you're a snitch, they'll track you to the ends of the earth to kill you."

Knowing that her threat was real, Goldblum swallowed hard. He was getting tired of people threatening his security, but he had to live with it for now.

"I'll get right on it," he said as he reached for his wallet.

"Do that," she said. "And the coffee's on me."

Going out to his car, the reporter pulled out onto the street and headed out of town. There was no way that he was going to step into a phone booth and call the FBI from Dilbert. There were easier ways to commit suicide.

Boise, Idaho

DAN BUTTERFIELD FROWNED when he read the transcript of the latest telephone report from Brad Goldblum. There was something naggingly familiar about the name the reporter had given of the local who was reportedly being held prisoner by the Dilbert militia unit.

The Department of Justice put out a list of people who were to be immediately reported any time they were encountered in any fashion. Some of them were escaped or wanted criminals, some of them were known or suspected foreign spies, some were persons of interest in ongoing investigations and some weren't identified at all. They were always at the top of the list, though. This list was updated weekly, and he had read through it just the day before.

He punched the button on his intercom to Alvin Barker's office. "Do you have the latest Justice Department notification list?"

Barker had to think a moment before he realized what his boss was talking about. "Yeah, it's right here."

"Bring it up."

When Barker appeared a few minutes later, Butterfield snatched the list out of his hand. There it was, Jack Vance with a bare-bones physical description that could fit almost any dark-haired Caucasian older than thirty and of better than average height. Only the color of his eyes, blue, was mentioned. Behind his name was the AAA-1 code that meant any mention of him, no matter how tenuous, had to be reported as a priority.

"It looks like I'd better call this guy in ASAP."

"Do it," Butterfield agreed. Considering the events of the past few weeks, he didn't want to fail to do anything that Justice wanted him to do.

Washington, D.C.

HAL BROGNOLA WAS working late in his Washington, D.C., office when he was notified that Jack Vance had been reported from the Idaho regional headquarters of the FBI. "What are the particulars?" he asked.

"We don't have them yet."

"Get them immediately and send them up to my office!"

"Yes, sir."

That Bolan had surfaced this way wasn't good. He didn't want to get too worried until he got the full report, however. A few minutes later, Brognola read the FBI report, and his blood went cold. He punched the intercom button to the secretary outside his office.

"Yes, sir."

"Kelly, get me Dan Butterfield, the regional FBI director for Idaho on the line. Tell him it's urgent."

"Yes, sir."

"Butterfield," the voice on the phone said.

"This is Hal Brognola at the Justice Department, and I'm calling about Jack Vance, the man from Dilbert that your office reported has been taken prisoner by the militia. How good is that report?"

"As far as we know," Butterfield said, "it's really good. Our informant got it from a local woman that Vance is apparently involved with. She's concerned about him and asked our man to try to get our assistance to find him."

Brognola thought fast. Bolan didn't usually involve women in his operations, but since he had been playing the role of a drifter in town, he might have used her to help build his cover, as well as getting information from her. Either way, her report of his having gone unaccountably missing had to be taken seriously.

"I want you to focus on finding out what happened to Jack Vance," Brognola ordered. "You can consider this a direct order, and the backup paperwork will catch up with you later. Nothing is more important right now than finding him. Use any assets necessary and feel free to call me if anyone gives you any static."

"Yes, sir."

Butterfield hated it when the Justice Department ran an operation in his jurisdiction and didn't inform him what was going down. Obviously this Jack Vance guy was a hotshot Justice operative who had gotten himself in over his head. That's what happened when amateurs were used to do a professional's job. This wasn't the first time the Bureau had bailed out a Justice hotshot, either. If they'd get out of fieldwork and stick to political ass-kissing on Capitol Hill, everyone would be better off.

"I want to be informed of your progress on a regular basis," Brognola said. "And any information you learn about him is to be phoned in to me personally as soon as you get it, day or night, without delay."

"Of course."

"I'll be talking to your director as soon as I hang up here to confirm these instructions. But I expect you to act on them immediately."

"Yes, sir."

"And Butterfield?"

"Yes, sir."

"Don't screw up on this," Brognola cautioned. "So far, your career is still intact. Find Vance for me and you'll still be able to retire."

"Yes, sir."

When Brognola hung up, Butterfield just sat and stared at the wall for a moment. Jesus Christ! He was used to having his job threatened by Washington ass-kissers, but there was something about Brognola's tone of voice and the way he hadn't directly threatened him that made it serious this time. Who in the hell was this Jack Vance guy anyway?

Realizing that he was wasting valuable time, he punched his intercom. "Alvin," he said, "get your ass in here ASAP."

"Yes, sir."

As soon as Hal Brognola got off the phone with the director of the FBI, he punched in the number of Stony Man Farm in Virginia. "Let me talk to Aaron," he told the operator abruptly.

"Kurtzman."

"Aaron, this is Hal, we have a problem with Striker."

"What is it?"

Brognola quickly and concisely filled in the Stony Man computer expert on the FBI report.

"That's not much to go on," Kurtzman said. Like

Brognola, he had worked with Bolan long enough not to panic over his disappearance.

"That's why I lit a fire under the FBI," the big Fed said. "I'm hoping they can develop a lead."

"What's this about a militia training camp hidden in a national forest?"

"All I have is that it's somewhere in the Wenatchee National Forest."

"I'll get the NRO to make a satellite run over the area. I'll have them do a full-spectrum run and see what I can develop from that."

"Also," Brognola suggested, "have Phoenix Force suited up at the closest secure facility and have them stand by for a rescue mission. Also, get Able Team on the ground in the area as soon as you can identify it. I want to be able to move on this as soon as we can develop a lead. I have the FBI going all out to find out what happened to him, and I built a fire under the regional director."

"Will do."

"Keep me informed," Brognola said, ending the conversation.

When he put down the phone, he decided to cut the President out of the loop until he had something good to tell him. Having the White House breathing down his neck would only make this more difficult.

He had no doubts that Bolan would surface safely this time, as he had done countless times before. This wasn't the first time he had been taken by the enemy. And as long as he lived the life he did, it wouldn't be the last. But Brognola also knew that some day, the soldier's luck would run out.

Dilbert, Idaho

SHERIFF FRANK BANNER SAW the trouble coming before it hit the door of his office that morning. Three dark sedans with FBI insignia on the doors parked in front of his office, and a dozen men got out. All of them wore the suit-and-sunglasses uniform of senior agents.

He also noticed that Special Agent Ron Brown, who had screwed up so badly at the Grissom farm, wasn't among them. And that was a good thing; Brown wasn't a popular man in the county right now. In fact he was the subject of a lawsuit that was being filed today on Grissom's behalf to recover damages for the destruction his farm had suffered from the FBI raid.

"I'm Agent Alvin Barker—" the FBI agent introduced himself "—from the Boise office."

"Frank Banner. What can I do for you?"

"We're looking for a man named Jack Vance. What can you tell us about him?"

"Come on into my office."

Once the door was closed, Banner asked, "What's this about Vance?"

"We have a report that he's missing, and we have been ordered to find him immediately. What can you tell me about him?"

While Barker took notes, Banner quickly told him what little he knew about Vance—that he had appeared in town, had gotten into a fight with a local who had abused a barmaid and had been hired on to work for a local businessman.

"Tell me about the fight."

After Banner did, Barker asked, "And where is this Red Gillum right now?"

"I don't know," Banner said honestly. "He left town right after that."

"And the woman Vance defended, where can we find her?"

Whatever Vance had done, Banner didn't want to drag Samantha Whiting into it if he could help it. "Do you mind my asking what this is about?"

"I don't mind your asking," Barker replied, "but all I can tell you is that Vance is a person of importance to a national-security investigation, and we have to locate him ASAP. Any attempt to impede this investigation will fall under the provisions of the National Security Act and will be treated accordingly. Now, what about the woman?"

Realizing that he had no choice, Banner gave him Whiting's address and place of employment.

"And this man who hired Vance, who is that?"

"His name is Bolton Grey, and you can find him in his office at the credit union."

"Where is that?"

"On the other side of the street, one block north."

"That's all I have for now, Sheriff, but I'd like

your home phone number in case something comes up."

"How long do you plan to be in Dilbert?"

Barker locked eyes with him. "We'll be in town until we locate Vance."

"You'll need a place to work, then," Banner said. "You can use one of the empty desks out front."

"Thanks," Barker said.

"Anything to help get you people out of town."

"I understand."

WHILE THE FBI agent was questioning Sheriff Banner, one of his deputies slipped out the side door and walked to the phone booth on the corner. Deputy Jim Dodge was a full-fledged Patriot and a member of Grey's inner circle. Most of the time he stayed in the background and fed Grey information from the sheriff's office. Frank Banner wasn't a Patriot, and Grey needed someone in the department, so Dodge served as his inside man.

"The FBI is here looking for Vance," Dodge said when Grey picked up the line. "They sent a dozen guys, and they look serious."

"Did they say why they were looking for him?"

"Not that I heard," Dodge said. "But I saw Sam talking to that reporter guy yesterday afternoon, and maybe she had him report that Vance was missing. If he's a snitch like you think he is, they would come looking for him. What do you want me to do?"

"Just keep your ears open," Grey replied. "I'll take care of everything else."

CHAPTER TWENTY-SEVEN

When Bolton Grey hung up the phone, he grabbed his jacket and told his secretary that he was going out. In the parking lot behind the office, he opened the trunk of his Cadillac and took out a small aluminum case. Getting in the car, he put the case on the seat beside him and opened it. Nestled inside was a 9 mm Smith & Wesson Model 59 pistol with an extended barrel threaded for a sound suppressor. After screwing the device in place, he put the pistol in his belt and closed the case.

Starting the car, he pulled out onto Main Street and headed for Samantha Whiting's house on the edge of town. He had warned her not to get involved with the Vance situation, but she hadn't listened to him. He didn't know what was wrong with her and her sister. Both of them were hardheaded bitches—rather Sam was, and Kate had been. But it was time to put Sam in the past tense, as well.

He had been a sentimental fool to have given Sam a job when she came back to Dilbert after her divorce. He should have known that she would turn out to be the same kind of woman her sister had been, and now she had betrayed him the same way Kate had. She had threatened him, and he didn't take well to threats. But there were ways to deal with threats from traitors.

He pulled up behind Whiting's house and walked up to the back door. Few people ever locked their doors in Dilbert, so he walked right into the house he owned and rented to the woman.

"Bolton!" Whiting said when he came through the back door. "You startled me.

"What do you want?" She backed up when she saw the pistol in his hand.

"Over a dozen Feds came to town this morning looking for your boyfriend," he said. "They said you told them that the Brotherhood had taken him prisoner."

"You killed him, didn't you?"

"I'm getting a little weary of you telling me that I've killed someone," Grey said. "He's not dead yet, and you're going to join him. You brought the Feds into Dilbert, and now you're going to pay the price of treason, too. I can't afford to have traitors living in Dilbert."

"You're just afraid that if someone speaks out against you, you'll no longer be king of the mountain, aren't you? You're pathetic, Bolton. But you're so hung up on being the biggest frog in a small pond that you can't see it."

"I'm not going to stand here and argue with you, Sam." Grey raised the pistol again. "You can walk

out of here on your own two feet or I'll carry you
out. It's up to you."

"I'll walk," she said.

"Get a coat."

"Where are you taking me?" she asked once she
was in the Cadillac.

"Like I said. I'm taking you where Vance is."

"Where's that?"

"You'll see when you get there."

ALVIN BARKER HAD set up shop at an empty desk in
Sheriff Banner's office and was fielding calls from his
men as they systematically canvased the town for
anyone who knew anything about Jack Vance. So far,
though, they hadn't come with much useful information.

Everyone claimed to remember Jack Vance, spoke
of him as being a good man but one who had pretty
much kept to himself. No one claimed to know anything about his alleged disappearance or his whereabouts if he wasn't at the fuel yard. The team that
had gone there had reported that the room behind the
office where Vance had lived had been swept clean,
and his van was nowhere in sight, either.

"I just got a call from one of my agents," Barker
said as he walked into Sheriff Banner's office, "the
one I sent to find this Bolton Grey guy that Vance
worked for. According to Grey's secretary at the
credit union, he got a phone call an hour ago and
immediately left without saying where he was going.

Also, the man I sent out to talk to Samantha Whiting found her house empty, but her car was still there. It's beginning to look like the rats are deserting the sinking ship.''

"I don't know what to say," Banner offered without waiting to be asked. "Normally Grey's in his office, and Sam's either at work or home."

"Do you think they were warned that we were looking for them?" Barker asked.

"I don't know how," Banner answered honestly. "It's a possibility, sure. But I've been here since you arrived, and I sure as hell didn't call them."

"That's a good thing, too. A federal obstruction-of-justice rap is hard to beat."

"Look, Barker," the sheriff said, "I'm doing everything I can to help you people on this. I know I gave your Agent Brown a rough time for that screwup out at the Grissom place, but he deserved it. This has nothing to do with that, or does it?"

When Barker didn't immediately answer him, Banner put two and two together and came up with twenty-two. "Vance is an undercover Fed, isn't he?"

Now it was Barker's turn to think hard. He couldn't remember a time when a high-ranking Justice Department official had ever personally called a regional office to order an undertaking like this. Usually Justice went through the director of the Bureau when there was something they wanted the FBI to look into for them. If this Jack Vance was a deep-cover Justice spook working the militia situation, that would explain the extreme urgency. It would also mean that, more than likely, he had been found out and was dead by now.

"If he is," Banner continued, "it would help if I knew the facts."

"Look, Sheriff," Barker said, "I don't really know who or what Vance is. All I know is that my boss got a call from Washington telling him to find Vance and find him immediately. We really don't know anything about him beyond a bare-bones physical description. I've got to develop some leads on him ASAP and get Washington off of my ass, though, or I'm going to be looking for a new job."

Banner's eyes searched the Fed's face for signs of deceit and concluded that the agent was telling him the truth. "If Vance is an undercover federal agent," Banner said, "and if he got tangled up with one of the local militias, he could be in real danger."

"What can you give me on the local militias?"

"Not much," Banner admitted. "The locals all know that I play it pretty much by-the-book and don't want anything to do with that sort of thing. So," he said, shrugging, "they make sure that I don't learn much."

"But," Barker said, "you know that you have a militia here in town, right?"

"We could have one, yes. But I can't tell you for sure who's involved."

"Just give me the names of anyone who you think is in the militia, and we'll take it from there."

Banner took a deep breath. This was where the rubber met the road. He was a peace officer who had sworn to uphold the law, but he was also elected by the citizens of Dilbert. Since there were no laws banning militias, he had tried hard not to pay any attention to any of rumors he heard about them. Unlike in a big city, the law in a place like Dilbert wasn't always by-the-book.

"I'm not sure that I can do that," he said. "They haven't broken any laws that I know of, and they do have the right of free assembly."

"We have a possible kidnapping here, Sheriff," Barker reminded him. "And since Samantha Whiting is also missing, we might have two of them. The quicker I have some information I can have my people follow up on, the faster we can try to find them."

"Okay," Banner said. "I'll give you a list of possible militiamen in town and in the surrounding area. But I swear that if you send your storm troopers in to bust their doors down and shoot their houses up, I'm going to call Washington myself. Hell, I'll even call the President. Before you do anything more than talk to these people, you'd better have independent probable cause and valid warrants, or I'll do everything in my power to see your asses in jail."

"I'm not a hot dog like Ron Brown," Barker said evenly. "When I send my people in, it's a good bust. And," he added, "you might like to know that Agent Brown has been recalled to Washington and he's being investigated for the federal equivalent of police brutality."

"That's good enough for me."

Taking out a yellow legal-sized pad, Banner quickly wrote out some two dozen names and addresses. Leading the list was Bolton Grey's name.

"Thanks," Barker said as he took the list. "I'll have my people start talking to these contacts."

"Remember, though, no rough stuff unless you really have probable cause."

"You have my word on that."

"I'm counting on it."

Washington, D.C.

EVEN THOUGH IT WAS negative, Hal Brognola was relieved to get the initial report from the FBI team looking into Bolan's disappearance. At least now he knew where the soldier had been and a little of what he had been doing there. It wasn't much to go on, but at least it was a start. The downside, though, was that the barmaid who had reported him missing was now missing herself. Her disappearance could have several interpretations, but he assumed the worst. To him it could only mean that the opposition had learned that she had called the Feds in on them and had silenced her, too.

Also, the FBI hadn't been able to contact this Bolton Grey who had hired Bolan to run his fuel yard and see what he knew about the disappearance. Brognola was having difficulty picturing Striker pulling a nine-to-five pumping gas in a small Idaho town. But Bolan had done stranger things over the years, and running a gas station wasn't a bad way to pick up intelligence in a small town.

Reading between the lines of the terse FBI report, Brognola was certain that Bolan had made a contact with the local militia and had been able to talk his way into the organization. That was to be expected; any militia leader would want to recruit a man like Jack Vance. The question remained, though, what had gone wrong to blow his cover? And more importantly, how had he been taken prisoner?

Bolan was an old hand at the undercover business, and he should have been able to recognize when it was time for him to break his cover and get the hell out of Dodge. The fact that he obviously hadn't been able to do that meant that something sudden had happened, something he hadn't been able to prepare for.

At least Bolan had made enough of an impression on that woman at the bar that she had sounded the alarm when he went missing. But with her disappearance, too, they weren't completely back to square one, but they were damned near.

He thought about calling Dan Butterfield again and turning up the heat on him. But he already had the FBI man's feet in the fire as it was, so he would give him a little more time to produce results before adding more fuel to the flames. Nonetheless, it was always difficult to wait while others did all the fieldwork. In this case, it was doubly difficult because of his long history with Mack Bolan.

That history, though, kept him from complete despair. Bolan had been in worse trouble than this before and had been able to work his way out of it. Brognola told himself that the soldier would be able to do it again. And in the meantime, Brognola finally had something he could work on, as well. Now that he had the preliminary report from the FBI, he decided to see what Aaron Kurtzman and his Stony Man team had come up with that might fit in with it.

He knew that searching the vast tracts of mountainous national forest for a hidden camp in the Pacific Northwest was like sifting the sands at the beach for green grains of sand. But if anyone could do it, he knew that Stony Man could.

Picking up his scrambled phone, he punched in the number of the computer room at the farm.

"Kurtzman," the voice on the other end said.

"Hal. Have you been able to locate that militia camp yet?"

"I just got the initial readouts from the NRO satellite pass this morning," Kurtzman said, "and we're going over them now. But it's real dense in there, and if there's not a lot of buildings or equipment laying around, we may not be able to pick up much from the Keyhole birds. I think we're going to need a supplemental run from a TR-2 recon bird before we're done. We're going to need an infrared-mapping run to cross-check with the MAD data and the low-frequency radar."

The longer Brognola was in this business, the more difficult he was finding it to keep up with the alphabet soup and jargon of modern intelligence technology. Talking to Kurtzman sometimes was like talking to a deep-space alien for all he understood of the conversation. But then, he didn't need to understand it. That's what he had the Stony Man team for, to tell him what it meant.

"Just do what you have to," Brognola growled. "Use the Golden Trumpet authority if you need to, but get it done. He's been gone over twenty-four hours now, and I still haven't notified the President yet."

Brognola knew that giving Kurtzman permission to use the Golden Trumpet authority, the ultimate panic button, for the missions he needed flown, would alert the White House. But he wanted information before he had to tell the Man that Bolan was missing. Doing it this way would force his hand, but if that was the only way he could get the information, it couldn't be helped.

"I'm glad you're doing that instead of me," Kurtzman said.

"Right."

"I'll call you as soon as we're finished going over the data we have, and I should be able to launch the supplemental runs within two hours."

"Just keep me informed."

Brognola put the phone down and read through the FBI report again. There might have been something he had missed on the first two reads.

Boise, Idaho

BRAD GOLDBLUM WAS actually glad to be back in Boise. Dan Butterfield had ordered him out of Dilbert while Alvin Barker and his team looked for this Jack Vance, and he figured he was finished working for the FBI. "Since my job's done," Goldblum told Butterfield, "I guess I can be heading back to Seattle now. Man, I can't wait to get a good cup of latte."

"Just pour more milk in your Taster's Choice the next time around," Butterfield growled. "You're not done around here yet."

"But I did what you wanted me to," the reporter complained. "I got a list of militia guys, and I passed on the lead about Vance. Isn't that enough?"

"Not as far as I'm concerned," Butterfield answered. "I'm not sure that you've worked off that five-to-ten-year sentence behind that weapons charge against you yet."

"But that's blackmail!"

"Yep," Butterfield agreed. "It sure is. Welcome to the real world, Goldblum. Like the man said, when you do the crime, you have to do the time. But," he said, shrugging, "if you don't like this arrangement, I can always forward your case to a federal grand jury and see what they think."

Goldblum knew that he was being jacked around, but he wasn't willing to take a chance on going to court. Not for the first time, he wished that he had stayed the hell in Seattle instead of trying for the "big story." There were times when ambition wasn't a healthy thing.

"Okay," he said, "you've got me by the short and curlies and we both know it. So, what do you want me to do next?"

"I'm not sure right now," Butterfield said. "But I want you to hang around here and stay available until I get another report from Barker."

"But what do I tell my editor?"

"Anything you like." Butterfield smiled.

CHAPTER TWENTY-EIGHT

The Cascade Mountains

Ramon de Silva hadn't been to the Brotherhood's Cascade Mountain training camp before. Grey had been adamant about him staying away from it for security reasons. But he knew all about how it had come to be. He knew how a Washington State Forestry Service employee had reworked the maps to remove almost a thousand acres of forest from state control. With the other state employees thinking that the land was privately owned and the citizens thinking that it was off-limits state land, the area was a perfect place to put a camp that didn't exist.

Silva was visiting the camp now because he wasn't going to waste any more time arguing with Grey about interrogating Vance. If the man was, in fact, the one who was known as the Soldier, there was much that could be learned from him and he was anxious to get started. The Cali board would give him anything he could ever dream of if he delivered the Soldier to them, and he wasn't about to let an ignorant

Yankee stand in his way. The six men who were following him in a four-wheel-drive truck would make sure of that.

When he drove through Bender, Washington, the small town closest to the Brotherhood's camp, he stopped at the local motel and rented three double rooms. After briefing the gunmen on what he expected to take place, he got back in his car and drove on to the road leading into the camp. After being stopped at the security checkpoint, he shouldered his bag and followed the sentry into the forest, where he met the Hummer tactical vehicle that delivered him to the camp.

Commandant John Williams wasn't happy to see him and turned down his demand to talk to Vance. "I don't know how things work wherever in the hell you come from, mister," he said, "but here in the United States, a man's innocent until he's been proved guilty. Jack Vance is a Patriot, and until we've had our trial and found him guilty, you're not getting your hands on him."

Silva felt the rage build in him again. There was too much at stake for him to play stupid games with these people. Why couldn't they understand what was at stake? Not only was Vance valuable to the cartel, but he would also know what the Feds were planning to do next in Idaho and they needed that information if they were to keep from being eliminated.

Williams read the expression on the Cuban's face

and dropped his right hand to rest on the butt of his holstered pistol. "You got that, mister?"

Since he was alone, there was nothing to be gained by forcing a confrontation with Williams, so Silva backed off. Vance was safely locked in a cell, and that was good enough for now. He could afford to wait until these pretend soldiers went through their pretend trial and decided that Vance was guilty before pressing his demand to interrogate him. When that time came, though, Silva would have his own men here to back up his demand.

"I am willing to wait," he said. "Is there somewhere that I can stay until then?"

"I don't have a full complement of trainees in camp right now, so I'm sure you can find an empty bunk in their tent. It's not a hotel, but we are soldiers out here."

"I am sure it will be suitable," Silva said. "And if you don't mind, I'd like to see Vance for just a minute. I would like to take a Polaroid photo of him so I can fax it to my principals so he can be positively identified. This will be important for his trial."

Williams considered the request for a moment. "Okay," he said. "I don't see anything wrong with that. But I'm going with you."

The Cuban shrugged. "That's fine."

BOLAN LOOKED UP when he heard someone enter the building. In the dim light, he recognized Williams and saw that the commandant had Ramon de Silva with him. He instantly figured out what the Cuban was doing here when he saw the camera in his hand. A photograph of his face would go a long way to sealing his fate, but there was nothing he could do about it.

Williams stood silently while the Cuban took his prisoner's photograph. Silva checked the print and put it in his pocket. "I'll be talking to you later," he said, smiling.

Bolan didn't bother to answer.

"Here you go, buddy," the guard said as he slipped a full canteen and an Army-issue MRE field ration through the slot in the door of Bolan's makeshift cell.

Such as it was, Bolan was glad to see the food. Since he had to stay alert and be ready for any chance that came to escape, he needed the nourishment. The damp cold would sap his strength soon enough without adequate food. And while the military rations weren't gourmet eating, they were nourishing, high-calorie food. Two of them a day would keep him going.

"You wouldn't happen to have a smoke on you, would you?" Bolan asked as soon as he was done with the meal, a poor imitation of chili and beef. "I quit a long time ago, but something like this makes a man want to smoke."

"I hear you," the guard said as he fished a cigarette out of his pocket, lit it for Bolan and handed it through the slot in the door. "Here you go."

Bolan took the smoke. "Thanks."

"What's that greaser saying about me?" Bolan asked after he took a deep drag on the borrowed smoke.

"Who do you mean?"

"Silva, the Cuban."

"He's a Cuban?"

"Yeah." Bolan nodded. "It kind of makes you wonder what a Cuban is doing in the Brotherhood of Patriots. The last time I heard, that bastard Fidel Castro was still running that place down there, and democracy wasn't high on his list of favorite things."

"I didn't know that he's a Cuban," the guard said. "But I've heard what he's saying about you. For starters, he says that you're a spy, some kind of Fed secret agent."

Bolan laughed. "Do I look like James Bond to you?"

"Not now, you sure as hell don't," the guard said, chuckling. "But he also says that you're the one who turned the Feds onto the Brotherhood."

Bolan shook his head. "Why in the hell would I have done something like that?"

"Damned if I know, buddy. All I'm saying is what he's been saying about you."

"The Cuban."

"Yeah."

Bolan finished his smoke and butted the cigarette. "It's a sorry thing when a man can't even defend himself from some Cuban."

"Oh, you're going to get a chance to defend yourself," the guard said. "As soon as all the Brotherhood leaders get here, they're going to have a court-martial and you'll get your chance then."

"Who's going to testify against me? Other than the Cuban, I mean."

"I haven't heard. All I've heard is what the Cuban's been saying about you."

"Well, I guess I don't need to worry about it, then. Since I haven't done anything to any American, I shouldn't have to worry about what some Communist is saying about me."

"If I were you," the guard cautioned him, "I'd worry. The Cuban has most of them convinced that you're bad news. If you've done even half of the things that he says you have, you're working for the other side."

"It makes me wonder," Bolan said, changing the subject, "what a Communist is doing working with us anyway. It seems a little strange to me. Back when I was in the Corps, we were fighting Communists, not listening to them run off at the mouth about Americans."

"Damned if I know, mister. All I do is what they tell me to. And all I know is that this Silva guy says that you're a Fed sent to spy on us."

It was apparent to Bolan that the Cuban knew who he was, or at least had strong suspicions, and that raised the danger to him. There was a possibility that he could convince Grey and his militia buddies that this was all a mistake. There was no such hope with

Silva, however. When the Cuban got confirmation from the photo, he'd be back to kill him. That made it all the more imperative that he get out of here as soon as he could.

SAMANTHA WHITING had kept her composure during the long drive to the road leading to the militia forest camp. Having Bolton Grey storm into her house with a pistol in his hand and kidnap her had been frightening, but she wasn't ready to give up yet. Grey had told her that Jack Vance was still alive and that she was being taken to where he was. If that was the case, there was still hope to get this sorted out. Plus she wasn't about to give Grey the pleasure of seeing her panicked.

Grey had had little to say to her on the ride except to warn her that any attempt to escape would result in his shooting her dead. She hadn't seen this side of him since the Christmas when her sister had told him that she was seeing another man, and she was angry with herself for having forgotten that he could be like this. She was also angry with herself for ever having returned to Dilbert. It had seemed like a good idea at the time.

When Grey stopped at the security checkpoint and she learned that they had to go out into the forest to meet a vehicle, she started to worry. She had always thought that the Brotherhood camp would be like the militia gathering places she had seen on television, little more than an overgrown Boy Scout camp with a bunch of overweight drunks stumbling around in camouflage uniforms and guns. If this place was so far hidden in the woods that they had to use a tactical vehicle to get to it, it had to be taken seriously.

For the first time, she began to feel fear.

WHEN WILLIAMS SAW Grey step out of the Hummer with Whiting at his side, he was not happy. "Why in the hell did you bring her here, Bolton?" he snapped. "You know we don't have any facilities for women."

"She's not a woman," Grey said, keeping her covered with his pistol. "She's a traitor, too. When I took Vance into custody, she called the FBI in on us, and Dilbert's crawling with Feds right now."

"So you snatched her, left town with her in your car and gave them a lead on how to find the rest of us. That's not too smart, Bolton."

"No one followed me," Grey snapped. "And I had to get her out of there before she got a chance to blow the whistle on all of us. They were going to talk to her, and she would have told them everything she knew to save her boyfriend."

Williams shook his head. "This is going to cause trouble, Bolton, and we have enough trouble as it is right now. That damned Cuban was just here and—"

"I told him never to come here," Grey said. "What did he want?"

"He took a Polaroid picture of Vance and said that he could get a positive ID with it."

"That might be useful," Grey admitted. "But I

told him never to come here. I'll talk to him about that later. We can't have that happening again."

"What do you want me to do with her in the meantime?" Williams asked. "This is not exactly Club Med I'm running here."

"Put her in with Vance," Grey said. "They've been playing kissy-face ever since he came to town, so I know that they're in on this together."

Dilbert, Idaho

BY THAT EVENING, FBI Agent Alvin Barker was forced to report that he'd not had much luck running through the list of names of possible militia members he had gotten from the sheriff. He felt that Banner hadn't been putting him on, that the names he had put down were the genuine article. But none of the interviews from the list had produced anything useful. No one claimed to know anything about the whereabouts of Jack Vance or of any militia activities in the area. He also knew that he should have expected that. In fact he would have been instantly suspicious if any of the locals had opened up to his men.

That didn't mean that his investigation was at a standstill, however. Now he would go into the second phase, the in-depth investigation. He had already faxed Banner's list back to Butterfield in Boise, and the names were being run through every computer in the state and federal governments. Every time anyone on the list had gotten a speeding ticket, been late in their court-ordered child-support payments, had an argument with the IRS or any of a number of other petty violations, it would be printed out.

This listing of less-than-perfect behavior on the part of these local citizens would be used as a weapon when his agents went back for their second interviews. Sometimes it was useful to know a man's past sins when you were inquiring about his present ones.

The first man on the list, Bolton Grey, hadn't been interviewed, but the agents had come up with a great deal of information on him through the background checks. For one thing, Grey was the closest thing to royalty Dilbert could claim. His family had founded the town back in the late 1880s and had dominated it, both socially and financially, ever since. In fact, according to his IRS records, Grey had a finger in every pie in town that had anything left under the filling worth taking.

Barker hated to continue to report his lack of progress, but Butterfield had been adamant on that point. He was to call in three times a day even if it was only to say that he had nothing new to report. This was one time when no news wasn't good news, but he knew that his boss was forwarding his reports to that Justice Department honcho who was looking over his shoulder and breathing down the back of his neck.

If he could only find the woman who had started this whole thing, he might be able to get something from her. But his men had turned the town upside down, and there was no sign of her. It was as if she had simply stepped on the Greyhound bus and left her home town without taking anything with her. Which, as he well knew, wasn't very likely. A middle-aged woman didn't do something like that, certainly not after reporting that her boyfriend was missing.

And it was interesting that Bolton Grey was also missing the same way. But at least in his case his Cadillac was missing along with him. As that thought flashed through his mind he decided to see if there was any history between Grey and the missing woman. If that was the case, it could be that Vance had stepped on the toes of the town's big man and that Grey had simply offed his rival.

That wasn't an unknown story, particularly when an outsider drifted into a small town and picked up on a local woman. And that keyed in with the story he had picked up on about Vance having gotten into a bar fight over the woman. Whoever this Vance guy was, he sure as hell knew how to make an entrance. His exit, however, was another matter entirely.

He hated to say it, but under the circumstances, there was only the slimmest chance that Vance would be found either dead or alive. And if the man *was,* he was betting for dead. Nonetheless, he had to keep looking for him.

CHAPTER TWENTY-NINE

In the camp

"Sam!" Bolan was stunned when he saw the guard leading Samantha Whiting into his cell. "What are you doing here?"

"She's a traitor like you," the guard snapped as he unlocked the door.

"Bolton kidnapped me," she answered after the door was shut and locked behind her.

"Why did he do that?"

"I tried to get a message to the FBI about you," she said after making sure that she couldn't be overheard. "And I think that's why Bolton brought me here. He said that a bunch of Feds came looking for you, and he blamed me for it so it must have worked."

Bolan wasn't unhappy that she had tried to help him. But he knew that he couldn't sit and wait for the FBI to find him and come in with guns blazing to rescue him. And having her here now had just made his situation even more difficult. He would have to get her out as well.

She looked directly into his eyes. "You're a federal agent, aren't you? And that's why so many of them came to look for you."

"I've been working undercover for the government in Dilbert, yes," he admitted. "But I'm not a Fed."

When she looked skeptical, he tried to explain. "I suppose you could call me a free-lancer, and I've been trying to track down the foreign agents who've been bringing weapons in to arm Grey's militia. The Brotherhood of Patriots might have been a good idea at one time, but using military weapons to attack government installations can only lead to one thing. If that makes me a bad guy, then I guess I am."

"That sounds like you work for the government to me, the FBI maybe."

"I'm not with the FBI," he said emphatically. "I'm just a guy who doesn't think that any loyal American really wants to see a war break out in Idaho, or anywhere else in the country for that matter. I want to stop the Brotherhood from getting its hands on heavy weapons and starting a war with them. Violence isn't the way to effect political change in this country, and I'm just trying to keep another civil war from breaking out. I don't want to see, innocent people die in the cross fire."

Whiting could understand that. The attack on the Boise FBI office and the raid on the Grissom farm had been a little too much like war to suit her tastes.

She, too, didn't care for most of the federal government, but she didn't buy the Brotherhood's propaganda, either.

"And," Bolan continued, "I've got enough information now to get this thing shut down before it goes much further. All I have to do is get out of here and I can put a stop to this. And I'll take you with me to keep you away from Grey and his men."

"So, what do we do?" she asked.

"There's no easy way to get out of here," Bolan said, his eyes tracing the confines of their cell. "So for now we just sit tight and wait."

"But Bolton said that he's going to put both of us on trial for treason and then shoot us."

"That's what he said, yes," Bolan replied. "But it hasn't happened yet. And until it does, we still have a chance to make a break."

"But how much chance is there really?" she asked, her eyes searching his face. "There's over a dozen men here, and they're all armed."

Bolan wanted to calm her fears so as not to make the situation any worse for her, but he just couldn't. She had faced it pretty well so far, and he wouldn't start lying to her now.

"I don't know," he said honestly. "We're in a serious situation. I won't lie to you about that. But all we can do is stay loose and see if we get a chance to make a break and run for it."

"If you get a chance to run on your own," he said, locking eyes with her, "I want you to take off instantly. Don't worry about me. Keep to the woods and head south, downhill. When you reach a road, try to find a phone and call a sheriff's office or, even better, the FBI. I know you don't like the Feds, but they're our best chance right now."

She laughed grimly. "I'd kiss J. Edgar Hoover's butt in front of the White House if that's what it took to get out of this damned place."

"Good girl," he said, smiling. "And when you get through to them tell them I'm here and insist that they notify the Justice Department immediately. Then find a place to go until this thing is all over. Keep reading the papers and you'll know when it's safe to go back to Dilbert."

"What do you mean?"

"Grey doesn't know it yet, but his private army is about to find itself facing some very tough opponents. People are going to be hurt unless they decide to give it up. And they won't be given much time to make up their minds. They've been making war on the United States, and that's not a smart thing to do."

"You're talking about the Army, aren't you?"

"That won't be the first move," he replied. "But if it comes to that, yes, the President will send in the military. He won't have any other choice—no President would. He can't have a civil war going on and not do everything in his power to stop it."

Whiting frowned. "I didn't realize that it had gotten that serious."

"Believe me," he said, "it's serious, and I'm

afraid that it's going to get worse before it gets any better."

He looked out the barred door of their cell. "It's getting dark, so let's get settled down for the night and we'll deal with this again in the morning."

Seeing Jack Vance firmly take charge of the situation, such as it was, gave Whiting a new perspective on him. He was still the strong but considerate man she had known back in Dilbert, but now she knew what he had been hiding. He was more than merely a strong man; he was a leader, a man of action. And even though the situation was bad, she felt better being with him. Without him, she was afraid that she'd be in a state of complete panic.

"It's cold," she said, shivering. "Do you want to share a blanket tonight?"

"I appreciate the offer," he said sincerely, "but I think that we'd better save that for later. We don't want to do anything here that will put us at a disadvantage. We need to be ready to move out the instant we get a chance."

This would be the case, wouldn't it? she thought. This was the first time in years that she'd made a pass at a man, and look where it got her. She knew that she was getting older, but she thought that she still had what it took. Apparently not.

"That makes sense," she said reluctantly.

"You take the bunk," he said. "And I'll just make myself comfortable on the floor. I'm used to it."

"Jack?"

"Yeah?"

"Do you really think that we're going to get out of here?"

"Yeah, I do," he said firmly. "So we'd better get some sleep tonight. We need to be ready for whatever happens in the morning."

Washington, D.C.

HAL BROGNOLA HAD almost expected the FBI to report that they had made no progress in locating Bolan. Anything else would have surprised him. While he had never lived in the Pacific Northwest, he knew the prevailing mentality of the people who did. Most of them would rather go to jail than snitch on one of their neighbors, particularly snitch to a federal agent.

The government was distrusted by more and more Americans with every passing day, it seemed, but Idaho still led the nation in that statistic. The only place on the planet that could be more hostile to federal agents would have to be in a fundamentalist Islamic nation.

Nonetheless he had everything in place to pull off a rescue as soon as he had a lead as to where Bolan was being held. The Stony Man Farm teams were locked and loaded, ready to go on a moment's notice, but they had to have a target before he could launch them. Even with new recon flights, Kurtzman's Stony Man Farm team hadn't been able to pinpoint the reported militia camp. And if both they and the FBI couldn't get a lead, he didn't know who was going to.

He hadn't given up hope yet, but it looked like Bolan was completely on his own yet again.

In the camp

THE FOLLOWING MORNING, Bolan woke with the dawn. Whiting was still sleeping, and he didn't wake her. Having her here had made his situation considerably more difficult. While it might have helped for her to have alerted the FBI that he had been captured, it had backfired on her. Getting himself out of there was one thing, but he couldn't leave her behind, not with a charge of treason hanging over her head, as well. He was responsible for this threat against her, so he had to come up with a way to get the both of them out. He didn't have the slightest idea, however, how he was going to pull this one off.

"This is the day it's going to happen, isn't it?" Whiting spoke from the bunk in the corner of the room.

Bolan turned to her. "That's what they said, so we'd better get ready."

She stretched and swung her feet around to sit up. "Do they feed us around here? I'm not worth a damn until I have breakfast."

"They have so far. But it's not like eating at your place. They've been feeding me MREs."

"What are those?"

"Army field rations. They're not too bad if you're hungry."

"I'm hungry enough to eat the ass end of a pig."

"You'll love them, then."

Almost on cue, a guard showed up with two MREs and a plastic canteen of water. "Here's your breakfast," he said curtly.

It wasn't the same guard who had given Bolan a smoke the day before and he didn't look like he wanted to talk. He backed away from the door and stood silently as they ate. When they were done with their meal he came back for the MRE packaging and the empty canteen.

"I've had worse things to eat," she said as she finished her MRE cracker.

"They kind of grow on you."

"I hope this place doesn't," she replied, looking around the cell.

"I don't think we're going to be here long enough for that."

"You have a point there."

Bender, Washington

AFTER TAKING the photograph of Vance, Ramon de Silva had gone back to the motel in Bender instead of spending the night at the camp. Taking an aluminum case from the trunk of his rented car in the parking lot, he set up his laptop in the room. Engaging the built-in security scrambler, he faxed a report to the cartel's board of directors in Cali, Colombia, and followed it by faxing the Polaroid photo he had taken of Jack Vance.

The return fax from Cali early that morning was right to the point. The directors positively identified the photograph as being that of the soldier, the cartel's most-wanted man on the planet. Their orders were also to the point. The board didn't want to risk Vance being killed by the Brotherhood before he could be interrogated. They ordered Silva to take him into custody immediately and transport him to Colombia for interrogation.

After reading the fax, the Cuban handed it to his second-in-command, the man who called himself Rivera. "I told you it was the Soldier," the Colombian said. "I only saw him that one time, but it was something I have never forgotten. No two men could have those eyes."

"Get the men ready," the Cuban ordered. "We are going in there after him."

"What about the other Yankees?"

"If they get in my road," Silva stated, clenching his jaw, "they will just have to die for their revolution. The board will not accept a failure this time. We must take Vance back with us even if it means abandoning the program here."

"We have put in a lot of work here," Rivera argued. "And I hate to see it go for nothing."

"It will not be for nothing," Silva promised. "Even with the setbacks we have suffered, I think that we have put in motion something that cannot be stopped. The government is frightened of the militias, and they will continue to crack down on them.''

He smiled at his second-in-command. "Do not worry. Even if we do nothing more here, the Yankees will still destroy themselves. It has gone too far now for it to ever go back to what it was before. All of their stories about their vaunted democracy are about to be exposed for the lies that they are. There will be a war before the year is out.''

"How do you want to get Vance out of there?''

"I will go back to the camp the usual way as if nothing has changed,'' Silva said as he pointed out the checkpoint on the map. "But I want you to take the men through the woods, bypassing their checkpoint, and take up a position right outside the camp. If I can get Vance out by myself, I will. But if I call you, come running and be ready to kill. No matter what, we are not going to leave without Vance.''

In the camp

WHEN THE BROTHERHOOD came for Bolan and Whiting later that morning, the Executioner saw that they had come well prepared. There were four guards, two with AKs at the ready and two others who wore holstered pistols on their belts. This wasn't the time for resistance, so Bolan and Whiting walked calmly to the big tent that had been used as a classroom when Bolan had been in training.

The tent had been transformed into a military style courtroom. Five men sat behind one of the mess tables that had an American flag hung on the tent wall behind it. Bolan didn't know any of the men, but thought that he recognized a couple of them from the meeting about the aborted raid on the Coeur d'Alene armory.

Bolan was pleased to see that Bolton Grey wasn't sitting on the court-martial board. Apparently, as their accuser, he wouldn't also be their judge, and that would be to their advantage. He wasn't surprised to see that Silva was also present in the tent. He had figured that the Cuban would attend the proceedings, and Silva was the key to their defense. Bolan intended to expose Silva for what he was, a former Cuban intelligence agent who was manipulating the Brotherhood for his own purposes. As he had seen when he talked to the guard, the Patriots could be touchy when it came to Communists.

The guards escorted Bolan and Sam to the two chairs that had been placed in front of the table, and they were ordered to sit. The trial then opened with a short prayer and the Brotherhood's version of the Pledge of Allegiance to the United States. After that, the older, gray-haired man who seemed to be in charge took up a paper from the table in front of him.

"The Supreme Court of the Brotherhood of Patriots is now in session," he said solemnly. "Jack Vance, Samantha Whiting, stand to hear the charges that have been brought against you."

Looking over at Whiting, Bolan nodded for her to stand.

Before the gray-haired man could read the charges, Silva got to his feet. "Your Excellency," he said, "may I speak?"

CHAPTER THIRTY

The judge frowned. "I know that you're not familiar with our proceedings, Mr. Silva," he said, "so I'll tell you that this isn't the time for you to speak. You'll be allowed to tell us what you know about the accused later."

"But, Your Excellency," Silva responded respectfully, "I have important information that will have a great bearing on this trial."

After a whispered conference at the bench, the judge continued. "You may proceed, Mr. Silva. But please make it brief. We have a trial to run here today."

"I took a photograph of the man who calls himself Jack Vance," he said, "so he could be properly identified by those who know him. I faxed the photograph to my principals, and I expect to have an answer any time now. So, Your Excellency, if this tribunal can be delayed for just one more day, I am sure that I will have the confirmation I need to prove his real identity. In the meantime, I would like to ask your permission to question him about what other operations he has undertaken against your freedom fighters."

The judge didn't need to consult his bench this time. "This court isn't going to put off its deliberations to suit you, Mr. Silva," he said, "nor will you question the prisoner. You are here as an accuser in the case, that's all. If the charges you have brought are sound, we'll act on them. But beyond that, you have no other status in front of this body and will have no part in these proceedings."

Silva stood silently and let this disrespect for who he was and what he knew wash over him. He had tried to do this the easy way, but they wouldn't listen to reason. As with everything else he had tried to do with these arrogant, stubborn Yankees, they always insisted on doing it their own way regardless of the outcome. So be it. Now he would do it like he should have done from the very beginning—his way.

Rather than returning to his chair, he walked toward the exit. Safely outside of the tent, he took a small radio from his jacket pocket, brought it to his lips and pressed the transmission switch.

"Come in now!" he said in Spanish.

RIVERA AND GARCIA had brought their strike team through the woods past the Brotherhood security outpost guarding the road until they reached the clearing where the Hummer came to pick up camp visitors. From there, it had been easy for them to follow the wheel tracks through the woods to the camp.

Silva had told Rivera that the camp itself had no security, that the militiamen had no guards or check-points protecting themselves, but he was still sur-prised to see that there was none. Also the trainees in camp were out in the woods somewhere learning how to be soldiers, so there were few Americans there, and almost all of them were in the big tent where the trial was being held.

The Colombians had no trouble taking up positions right outside the tents and buildings of the camp's headquarters, and at Silva's signal, they moved in swiftly. Leaving one man outside on guard, Silva marched in with the five gunmen at his back.

"What is this?" The judge of the court came half-way out of his chair when Silva and his men entered the tent.

"I have come for Vance," the Cuban said, "and I will have him."

For all the guns in the camp, only Commandant Williams and the two guards on Bolan were armed. When one of the guards raised his AK as if to defend his prisoners, Silva shouted in Spanish, "Kill them!"

Bolan didn't wait for the command to be translated into English. This wasn't the break he had wanted, but it would have to do. Spinning out of his chair, he jerked Whiting to her feet as he dashed for the door. "Run!"

Bolan's rush took the Colombian standing in the entrance by surprise. He was still bringing his AK down to fire when Bolan slammed a forearm into his throat, crushing his larynx. He reached down for the fallen weapon, but a burst of automatic fire kept him from it, and he ran on.

Whiting had followed his instructions and was halfway to the wood line. He followed after her and almost ran into a militiaman. Bolan didn't know who he was or what he was doing, but he wasn't armed except for a bayonet in a scabbard on his field belt.

The man hesitated when he saw Bolan running toward him and was rewarded for his inaction by being smashed to the ground by a flying kick. Bolan stopped only long enough to take the man's bayonet before ducking into the woods.

INSIDE THE TENT, Williams went down fighting. Unlike his title, the Colt .45 he wore on his belt was more than a decoration. He got only two shots off before the hammer of an AK on full auto-fire cut him down, but both of his rounds hit home. One of the Colombians went down with a .45 slug through his heart. The second round wasn't too far off.

But the burst that killed him also took out one of the two armed guards. Seeing the two militiamen go down, the second guard tried to surrender, but Silva blasted him before the AK he dropped even hit the floor. Realizing that his prey had escaped, the Cuban shouted, "Garcia! Escadoro! After them! I want him alive!"

The two Colombians raced out of the tent and,

catching a glimpse of Bolan and Whiting through the trees, took off after them.

Once inside the cover of the trees, Bolan caught up with Whiting. "Follow me!" he said as he took point at a dead run. She kept right on his heels, and a quarter mile into the deepest part of the forest, he stopped.

"This is where we split up," he told her. "Head south and find a highway like we talked about."

The woman hesitated for a moment. "But what about you? Aren't you coming, too?"

"I'm going to make sure that you aren't followed. Now, go!"

Though she wanted to stay with him, she was old enough to know better.

"Watch out for Bolton," she warned him. "He'll be coming after us, and he's a good woodsman."

"So am I."

BOLAN STAYED WHERE he was and watched her disappear into the thick undergrowth. Like many women from rural America, she had been hunting often enough to know her way around in the woods. She also knew which way was south, so even if he got hung up, she would be able to make her way to safety.

The Executioner was finally in his element. He was in the woods with cold steel in his hands, and he was hunting his enemies. He had told Whiting to keep going, to head for the road on her own no matter what else happened. But for her to make good her escape, he had to deal with the two Colombians with only his borrowed bayonet. Or rather he would have to take care of one of them with the knife. After that he would have a firearm—the Colombian's.

Circling to the south, he doubled back on his own trail to wait for their pursuers, and he didn't have to wait long. The Colombians might have been good in their own element, the mountains and jungles of their homeland. But in the dense fir forest of the Pacific Northwest, they might as well have been stumbling around blindfolded.

Fortunately the two gunmen had separated so they could cover more ground. The first Colombian was making so much noise that Bolan was able to get within a few yards of him without being heard. His last step, however, snapped a hidden branch, and the Colombian spun at the sound, his AK at the ready.

Bolan stepped into his man, his left forearm batting the barrel of the assault rifle out of the way, opening up his target. Thrusting forward, he drove the bayonet to the hilt in the pit of his adversary's stomach, piercing his diaphragm.

The Colombian screamed, emptying his lungs, as Bolan savagely twisted the knife, opening the wound. The blade wasn't sharp enough to cut up through the man's ribs. So he pulled the knife halfway out and then, angling the blade slightly to the right, slammed it upward to the hilt.

The edge might not have been that sharp, but the blade was long enough to reach the man's heart. Bo-

Ian twisted the knife again and held the Colombian to him as his blood emptied out into his chest cavity.

After lowering the body to the ground, he knelt beside it and cut the straps to the man's Chinese-style chest-pack magazine carrier. Pulling it free, he tied the ends of the straps together to make a bandolier and slung it over his shoulder. Now he was ready for his other pursuer or anyone else who got in his way.

The next gunner was much easier to take out. Bolan tracked him through the trees long enough to learn which way he was heading, then slipped off to one side to set up an ambush.

When the Colombian came into view, he didn't give the man a chance. As soon as he had a clear line of fire, he zeroed in on his chest and triggered off three quick shots. The man went down with the three holes over his heart and didn't even twitch.

Bolan didn't bother to take his second victim's weapon or ammunition. He did, however, open the receiver of his AK, slip out the bolt and throw it into the brush. Now that he had taken care of their pursuers, he took off running, angling to the south to catch up with Whiting.

BEFORE THE FIRST SHOT had been fired in the tent, Bolton Grey had dived for cover and rolled over to the wall. The canvas wasn't tied down to the wooden floor, and he slipped under it. He crouched, drew his Smith & Wesson and waited. He wasn't in a position to watch the end of the tent, but he, too, caught a glimpse of Bolan and Sam Whiting when they hit the tree line.

He saw the Colombians go after them, as well, but he didn't hesitate to follow after them. He knew these Washington woods, and he knew them well. Before the Brotherhood was formed, this was where he had hunted mule deer and elk for years. He knew that he could bypass the Colombians and catch up with the two unarmed fugitives.

A quarter mile into the woods, he saw the signs where Bolan and Whiting had split up. He also heard other men coming his way and figured that it was Silva's Colombians going after Vance.

He was willing now to let the Cuban have Vance if he wanted him. If he had known that it was going to come to this, he'd have just let them have the bastard when the Cuban first came to him. But, as usual, Silva had gotten on his high horse and he had turned down his request just to deflate him. When he rebuilt the Brotherhood, there would be no contact with any more people like Silva. Foreigners had no part to play in an American organization.

But while he was willing to let them take care of Vance, Samantha Whiting was his alone to dispose of. To his hunter's eye, her tracks stood out as plainly as if they had been marked with red flags, and according to the sign, she had taken off running so he started to jog after her.

As he ran, he felt his anger building to a pitch he hadn't felt since that night so long ago when he had confronted Sam's sister, Kate, with her infidelity. He still savored the memory of the rank, musky smell of her fear overpowering her perfume. Sometimes the smell would come to him in his sleep, and he would remember it when he woke. Sam would smell the same way when he had her throat between his hands.

He didn't know if he would kill Sam quickly as he had done with Kate or take his time, as he always wished he had done with his former girlfriend. He had been so young back then, and he had allowed his temper to get away with him when she taunted him with her new lover.

A few minutes later, he heard three quick shots from the woods behind him. That would be Silva's people finally getting their hands on Vance like they had wanted. Good riddance as far as he was concerned. But Vance had had one use—he had shown him Sam's true colors.

Several hundred yards farther on, he saw that he had caught up with her and moved off to one side of her path and hurried on to get ahead of her. She would be watching over her shoulder and would run right into him.

"Jack?" she said hesitantly when she heard the noise from the brush in front of her.

"No, bitch," Grey snarled as he stepped out onto the trail. "It's me."

"Bolton!" She stumbled to a halt when she saw the pistol in his hand.

"You thought you'd get away, didn't you? But,"

he said, looking around, ''I don't see your boyfriend anywhere, so it looks like he took off and left you holding the bag. If you'd have been a little smarter, you wouldn't have turned on me, Sam. You had a good life, and it could have been even better, but you thought you were too good for me, didn't you?''

''You're a bastard, Bolton,'' Whiting spit in defiance as she faced him down. She might be about to die, but she'd be damned if she'd let the bastard see her beg. ''And you're damned right that I'm too good for you, and so was Kate.''

''And you're a filthy, treacherous bitch just like your sister was. And,'' he promised, smiling as he brought up the pistol to center of her forehead, ''now you're going to end up just like her, too.''

WHEN BOLAN BROKE OUT of the tree line on the downhill side of the ridge he had been following, he saw a flash of color on the other side of the clearing. Whiting had been caught and stood near a man he recognized as Bolton Grey. There was no way he could get there fast enough to save her, so he would have to risk a shot. Since his AK was an assault rifle, it wasn't a good long-range weapon, but it was all he had to work with. And he knew that he had time for only one shot.

Adjusting the rear sight up to the five-hundred-yard mark, he flicked the AK's selector switch to semiauto and dropped into a kneeling firing position. Shooting downhill would improve the ballistics of the short-ranged cartridge, and he took that into consideration at he took his sight picture.

When he had his aiming point, he took up the slack on the trigger, filled his lungs and let the air out slowly. When he saw Grey bring up the pistol, Bolan applied the final pressure to the AK's trigger and fired.

CHAPTER THIRTY-ONE

Whiting saw, and heard, the bullet hit Bolton Grey before she heard the report of the assault rifle. The 7.62 mm round smashed through his right shoulder, splattering her with blood. The bullet's impact, and the damage it did to Grey's shoulder, made his arm spasm, and the pistol flew from his suddenly nerveless hand.

A look of shock flashed across his face, and as he started to turn around, she sprang for the Smith & Wesson. Snatching it from where it had fallen in the ferns, she leveled it at her wounded adversary. This was no time for final words, so she squeezed the trigger.

"Kate!" he screamed. "Don't shoot me!"

She heard Grey call out her sister's name over the report of the pistol and saw the 9 mm hole appear in his chest. Not moving her point of aim, she kept pulling the trigger until the hammer clicked on an empty chamber.

By this time Grey was well dead. Of the nine rounds she had fired any one of them would have been fatal. Her only regret was that she had missed the exact moment of his death. A part of her wanted to reload the pistol, kick him alive and do it all over again.

Still stunned, she stood over his body, the pistol in her hand, shaking from the reaction.

"He's dead, Sam," Bolan said a few minutes later.

"I know," she replied, looking up. "It happened so fast."

"It usually does."

"I..." She held out the empty pistol for him to take. "I thought I was going to die."

"We're okay for right now," he said. "I took out the two Colombians who were following us, but we have to get going again. Are you up to it?"

"I'm okay," she lied.

Kneeling at Grey's side, Bolan patted down the corpse for a spare magazine for the Smith & Wesson. When he found one in a jacket pocket, he dropped the empty from the pistol's butt and reloaded. "Let's go."

"Are you going to leave him?" she asked, glancing over at Grey.

"They'll find him."

"What happens now?"

"Like I said before, once we make it to civilization and get in touch with the Feds, they'll take over. But we have to get out of here first. There's still the checkpoint by the highway, so we'll swing to the east to bypass them."

BACK IN THE CAMP, the surviving Patriots were getting the situation under control. Once they had gotten over the surprise of being ambushed in their own camp, they realized that there were more militiamen than there were Colombians. At the sound of firing, the Cadre had brought its trainees back to the camp on the run. Since they had been training on the firing range, their weapons had ammunition in them and they were ready to use it.

When the firing started anew, Silva didn't plan to stick around to shoot it out with the Americans. He had obviously failed to capture Vance as he had been ordered—the two men he had sent after him didn't answer their radios and he figured that they were dead. This was a serious mark against him, but he wasn't about to commit suicide over it. He felt that he had a good chance to redeem himself with the board and would be able to continue his militia operation in another state.

"Lay down a base of fire," he told Rivera and his remaining gunman. "And give me a chance to get clear so I can reach that vehicle. Then I'll cover you when you pull back."

When the barrage of AK fire rang out, Silva raced for the Hummer. Slipping into the driver's seat, he fired up the engine. If his two men made it out, that was fine with him. But he wasn't going to wait for them. Slamming the gear lever into first, he floored the accelerator and cranked the steering wheel all the way to the right. Dropping the clutch, he snapped the rear of the vehicle around to cover him as he ran.

WHEN BOLAN AND WHITING reached the state highway, he figured that they were about halfway between the road leading to the camp and the little town of Bender. Even though some of the people in Bender were connected with the Brotherhood, it made more sense to head there simply because he didn't know what was down the road the other way. Once he reached the town all he would have to do was make one phone call and then keep staying alive until Brognola could get someone to him.

Now that they were back in civilization, he stopped to take the bloodstained AK bandolier from his shoulder and toss it into the brush at the side of the road.

"What are you doing?" she asked.

"I don't think we need this anymore," he said, flinging the AK after it. "I don't want a state cop to drive by and see me with it. It would cause problems. I am, however, keeping the pistol just in case."

They had walked only a quarter of a mile when Bolan heard the roar of an engine approaching from the direction of the camp. "Into the woods!" he told her when he recognized the distinctive engine sound of a Hummer.

His instinct told him that Silva or one of his thugs was in the vehicle, but even if it was just some of the militiamen, they had to be stopped before they could get the word of his escape to Bender.

Waiting until the vehicle was in sight, he stepped onto the side of the road, the Smith & Wesson held in a two-handed grip. He knew that the military versions of the Hummer had reinforced glass in the windshields, but he was counting on the civilian rigs having the less-expensive regular safety glass. The 9 mm slugs in the pistol would go through it like it was paper.

When the driver recognized Bolan, he aimed the vehicle at him and sped up. Holding his AK out the driver's window with one hand, he fired short bursts, but none of the rounds even came close. When the magazine ran dry, he tossed the weapon to the road.

Bolan held his ground as the Hummer hurtled toward him. At the last possible moment, he tripped off three shots, which drilled into the Hummer's windshield in a ragged triangle.

In the flash of a second as he dived out of the vehicle's path, he recognized Silva behind the wheel. The Cuban's face was distorted in a snarl, but there was blood pouring from his throat where one of the bullets had struck him. With a dead man at the wheel, the Hummer ran off the road, over the bank and into the trees below.

The Hummer was rugged, but the old-growth Douglas fir tree it hit was even tougher. The vehicle had been traveling fast enough that when it came to a sudden stop, it had tried to wrap itself around the tree. Since the point of contact had been the driver's compartment, there was no point in checking to make sure that Silva was dead. There was no way he could have survived the impact.

"IT'S FINALLY OVER NOW, isn't it?" Whiting asked as she took Bolan's arm.

"No," Mack Bolan said as he tucked the pistol back into his belt. "In a way, it's just starting."

When she looked confused, he explained. "There's still a war going on," he said, his voice level. "And I'm going to put an end to it."

She shivered at the tone of his voice, her eyes flicking over to the wreckage of the Hummer. He sounded as if he intended to stop the war all by himself, and she had no doubts that he would.

"Let's go," he said. "I still have to make that phone call."

Under Attack!

STONY MAN™ 34

REPRISAL

In a brilliant conspiracy to restore the glory days of the CIA, a rogue agent has masterminded a plot to take out Company competition. His stolen clipper chip has effectively shut down the Farm's communications network and made sitting ducks of the field teams. With Phoenix Force ambushed and trapped in the Colombian jungle, and a cartel wet team moving in on Able Team stateside, it's up to Mack Bolan and the Stony experts to bring off the impossible.

Available in April 1998 at your favorite retail outlet.

James Axler

OUTLANDERS™

PARALLAX RED

Kane and his colleagues stumble upon an ancient colony on Mars that housed a group of genetically altered humans, retained by the Archons to do their bidding. After making the mat-trans jump to Mars, the group finds itself faced with two challenges: a doomsday device that could destroy Earth, and a race of Transhumans desperate to steal human genetic material to make moving to Earth possible.

In the Outlands, the future is an eternity of hell....

Don't miss out on the action in these titles featuring THE EXECUTIONER®, STONY MAN™ and SUPERBOLAN®!

Where there's smoke...

THE Destroyer™

#III Prophet of Doom

Created by
WARREN MURPHY
and RICHARD SAPIR

Everyone with a spare million is lining up at the gates of Ranch Ragnarok, home to Esther Clear Seer's Church of the Absolute and Incontrovertible Truth. Here an evil yellow smoke shrouds an ancient oracle that offers glimpses into the future. But when young virgins start disappearing, CURE smells something more than a scam—and Remo is slated to become a sacrificial vessel....

Look for it in April 1998 wherever Gold Eagle books are sold.

**A violent struggle for survival
in a post-holocaust world**

JAMES AXLER

DEATH LANDS®

Freedom Lost

Following up rumors of trouble on his old home ground, Ryan and his band seek shelter inside the walls of what was once the largest shopping mall in the Carolinas. The baron of the fortress gives them no choice but to join his security detail. As outside invaders step up their raids on the mall, Ryan must battle both sides for a chance to save their lives.